Leave Your Sleep

Leave Your Sleep

R.B. Russell

2012

LEAVE YOUR SLEEP & OTHER STORIES

Published 2012 by PS Publishing Ltd. by arrangement with the author.

The following stories previously appeared as noted:
'An Unconventional Exorcism', *The Sixth Black Book of Horror*, ed. Charles Black, Mortbury Press, 2010; 'The Red Rose and the Cross of Gold', *Cinnabar's Gnosis*, ed. Dan Ghetu, Ex Occidente, 2009; 'The Dress' (pseud. Elizabeth Brown), *Supernatural Tales 17*, ed. David Longhorn, 2010; 'A Woman of the Party', *Strange Tales III*, ed. Rosalie Parker, Tartarus Press, 2009; 'Mathilde', *Delicate Toxins, A Tribute to Hans Heinz Ewers*, ed. John Hirschhorn-Smith, Side Real Press, 2011; 'Gala Gladkov's Exquisite Process', *The Master in Café Morphine*, ed. Dan Ghetu, Ex Occidente, 2011; 'The Beautiful Room', Nightjar Press, 2010; all other stories are original to this collection.

ISBN
978-1-84863-325-4 (unsigned)
978-1-84863-326-1 (signed)

The author would like to thank Rosalie Parker and Jim Rockhill.

Design & layout by R.B. Russell

Printed and bound in England by MPG Book Group

PS Publishing Ltd, Grosvenor House, 1 New Road,
Hornsea, HU18 1PG, England.

e-mail: editor@pspublishing.co.uk • *Internet*: http://www.pspublishing.co.uk

Contents

An Unconventional Exorcism

My father was one of seven boys and all of them married young and went on to have large families of their own. Consequently I ended up with more uncles and aunts than I have ever been comfortable with, and the number of cousins was almost incalculable. When that generation started having children themselves I gave up any pretence of taking an interest.

My mother, though, knew not only the names of all of these relatives, but also their birthdays and wedding anniversaries. Her own family line had dwindled down to her, an only child, and she was, no doubt, relieved to be spliced onto such a fertile family tree as my father's. She revelled in all of the relatives she had acquired by marriage and loved all of the gossip, managing to keep up with news of even the most distant of them. Through her I was regularly subjected to reports of their activities. It was rare to visit her without the telephone interrupting; it would always be one of her nephews or nieces calling to keep her abreast of their news. In later years she decided to take up research of our family history at the County Archives and her grasp of the family tree then encompassed not only vast geographical areas, but also several centuries into the past.

Her one frustration was always my Aunt Imelda, a woman I had always heard referred to as morbidly religious. All that we knew was that this woman had married my Uncle Michael after his first wife had died, and had taken him and his children up to her native Knaresborough some time in the late 1970s. We knew that when they were married Aunt Imelda had only recently become the widow of a very rich importer of tropical hardwoods. Some family members were impressed that Uncle Michael had married into money and I always suspected that they hoped the wealth might be shared around.

As a child I took even less interest in my relatives than I do now, but I remember Aunt Imelda being talked about because she had apparently insisted that Michael's children were to be sent to boarding school; reason-enough, I always felt, for disliking the woman. Back in the early years of her marriage to Uncle Michael, though, she did at least write to my mother from time to time, bemoaning the standards of young people, broadcasters and politicians. Her hectoring letters never contained any personal information, though, being more likely to include some improving, religious pamphlet than a photograph.

When my Uncle Michael died in 1987 Aunt Imelda seemed to quietly slip into an almost Victorian mourning. At least, it appeared so from the distance at which she was observed. A simple, dismal card at Christmas was the only communication between her and the rest of the family, much to the chagrin of my mother. Michael's children were unknown to us, and it was said they had nothing to do with their own step-mother (although *how* we knew this was a mystery to me).

Aunt Imelda would have remained a very shadowy figure if I had not been encouraged to look her up when I moved to Skipton a few years ago. My mother hoped that I might be able to catch up on decades of lost news but I was unwilling to help; there were already too many relatives for me to have any interest in one I had never met. And anyway, I had my own, more immediate family to take up my time and energies. The last thing that I wanted to inflict on my wife and two children was a visit to a miserable great aunt who had never shown any interest in us!

Some months later, though, I received word that Aunt Imelda was very ill. I had a mental image of her living in some vast, crumbling, Gothic Revival house on the outskirts of Knaresborough. I was convinced that it would be a gloomy pile with only a little light allowed in through close-drawn blinds. There would be aspidistras, I assumed, and antimacassars on the chairs. I even imagined illuminated texts from the bible framed on the walls. I really didn't relish the thought of having to visit the miserable, decaying relative, and I told myself that if she was very ill then there was the danger of appearing to intrude. Therefore I took what I thought was the correct course and I wrote to her enquiring whether a visit would be welcome. I made a point of explaining that if it was in any way inconvenient or impractical then she should say so without compunction. I must admit that I rather hoped she would put me off.

Her reply came as a slight surprise. Aunt Imelda wrote to me in a large, clear hand, in biro, on a sheet of what looked like A4 copier paper. She extended an invitation to me to visit, although no mention was made of my wife or children. I have to admit that I was expecting a letter on dainty notepaper, in crabbed lettering, perhaps scented with lavender. Her invitation went some way towards preparing me for the demolition of the stereotype I had created.

Her house, 'The Laurels', was a white painted, 1930s, Modern Movement building in modest grounds given over to lawns. If there had ever been laurel trees in the past, they were now long gone. The house had been designed to appear sleek and streamlined, outrageously modern in its day, with bands of windows and no ornamentation. It was looking a little tired when I visited it, although not actually neglected. I decided that it really wouldn't have taken much to refresh the paintwork and make it very attractive.

Aunt Imelda's letter was in keeping with the large, hearty woman I encountered there. When I knocked at the door a voice bellowed at me from inside, telling me to let myself in. I climbed the stairs to the large, bright living room and she seemed amused by my appearance. She also looked surprisingly well, although obviously unable to move out of her chair. She was housebound she told me almost at once and reliant on help; the problem was her legs, which were bandaged and obviously gave her a great deal of discomfort.

She immediately said: 'Your nosey mother has sent you to spy on me.'

'She's concerned about you. You've never kept in touch.'

'No, well, I used to be too busy to write to her, what with Church matters. But now that I'm unable to do any of those things, and I suppose I've got the time to write . . . well . . . What is it she wants from me?'

'She only wants to fill in the gaps in our family tree. We don't even know if your step-children are married, or have children themselves.'

'You don't need to know anything about them. They've no interest in their old mother. They never visit me. They were too spoilt growing up and they're ungrateful creatures.'

'How are you coping? Do you get any help?'

'Well, I used to have a nurse come in twice a day, but now she only comes in the morning. That's all I need since Bernadette arrived.'

'Bernadette?'

'Your cousin Bernadette.'

I dredged the name up from out of the dark and neglected pool of our extended family: 'Uncle Trevor's daughter?'

'Of course Trevor's daughter.'

This seemed strange news, but it took a few seconds to remember why: 'I thought she lived in the West Country?'

'She does, or did. Then she heard that I was ill, and out of the kindness of her heart she's come to look after me.'

'That's very sweet of her.'

'I hope so.'

'What do you mean by that?'

She dismissed my question: 'She's gone out to buy some cakes, so that we can give you tea. I told her that we'd be feeding the five thousand, but it's only you. We may be eating macaroons into the middle of next week. She always buys macaroons.'

'I only have two children. Mind you, compared to the rest of my family I'm, well . . .'

'Positively abstemious?'

'Exactly.'

'I should tell you that I am an Herodian. I abhor children. I believe that sex is the root of *all* the evils in this world.'

'I respectfully disagree.'

'Well, you wouldn't be the first. Intercourse is necessary, I acknowledge that, but so is defecation.'

'I wasn't sure whether bringing along two lively children was appropriate because you were ill. I hadn't realised they'd be so unwelcome.'

'That was considerate, thank you. I suppose you thought I was on my death-bed?'

'My mother did lead me to believe you were on your way out of this world.'

'Well, I might be. Tell her I might be.' She chuckled. 'But I can't promise exactly when that'll be. I love my Maker dearly, but he's in no hurry to see me. Do you believe in God?'

'I'm an agnostic.'

'I'll take that as a no, then. Well, you've every right to choose damnation if that's what you want. I, on the other hand, will be sitting on His right hand when the time comes. And that may be quite soon. You see, the circulation in my legs has packed-up and they're talking about cutting them off completely. I get blockages in my arteries and they're worried that clots could travel up. . . . I could keel-over this afternoon . . . But then again, it might not happen until next year.'

'I'm really sorry.'

'Yes, well, my husband died over twenty years ago. And Jeffery last year. There's not much left for me here.'

'Who was Jeffery?'

'The Minister at the Church I used to attend. We became very close after Michael died. Then last year, a heart attack took him off as well.'

'I'm sorry.'

'Well, that's why Bernadette is such a comfort.'

'I'm glad. She must be company for you?'

'Well, I suppose so. But, more importantly, she talks to Michael and Jeffery for me.'

'I don't understand.'

'She's a Medium.'

'Oh?'

'And you're a sceptic, obviously.'

'I suppose I am.'

Aunt Imelda looked at me with something like pity.

'You say you're an agnostic?'

'Yes.'

'When it comes to Spiritualism are you sceptical or do you disbelieve?' she asked.

'Sceptical, I suppose. I don't know. I'm inclined to disbelieve, but I've never met a Medium. I ought to keep an open mind.'

'You've met your cousin Bernadette before, surely?'

'Not since she was ten years old, probably. How old is she now? In her twenties?'

'Early thirties. And she's good. I must say that she's brought me a great deal of comfort. A great deal.'

I nodded, hoping to suggest that I understood, or sympathised, but I did not quite know what to make of the situation.

'How does she communicate with them?' I asked warily.

'Now, that's something that I don't entirely understand. She sees them, and they talk to her, but I see nothing. It seems so unfair, when you think about it. I mean, I knew Michael and Jeffery for years, and they show themselves to her, but not to me. I'm the one who loved them, and knew them.'

'I suppose it's a gift?'

'Bernadette says that she's always had it, but couldn't use the skill properly in the past. It was only once she started going to a Spiritualist Church that she realised what she was capable of. And then she had to practice. She attends regularly, though I can't say that I approve of what they get up to. It's not what I call Christianity.'

'But you're convinced?'

'Of Bernadette's authenticity? You think she might be trying to delude an old woman?'

'No, I'm not suggesting that. I mean, I hardly know her. We haven't met in years. But I'm sure she's sincere, and if she thinks she sees your Michael, and Jeffery, then I'm sure she really believes it.'

'Your reasoning isn't at all sound!' she scoffed. 'You admit that you don't know her, but you trust her. Why on earth should you? And you say, that if she "thinks" she sees something, then she must "believe" it. You betray your disbelief.'

'I wouldn't dare to pronounce on something I don't understand.'

'It seems to me that's just what you're doing!'

At that moment there was a noise from below and a distinct pressure-change. The front door must have been opened. I could then hear someone coming up the echoing stairs.

'There she is now,' pronounced Aunt Imelda. 'You can meet your cousin, the impostor.'

'I didn't say that,' I insisted, and got up out of my chair.

Cousin Bernadette came in, still wearing her coat, and unless I had been told who she was I certainly wouldn't have recognised her. Exceedingly tall and skinny, she might have been good-looking if she did not have such an unfortunate mouth. She didn't seem to be able to close it to hide her rather large and yellowed teeth.

'You must be Nathaniel,' she asked suspiciously and I agreed that I was. She held out her hand and I shook it.

'You're a couple of years older than me?' she asked.

Aunt Imelda broke in to the introductions: 'I was telling Nathaniel how you keep me in contact with Michael and Jeffery.'

Bernadette blushed impressively and looked determinedly at her coat buttons, which she seemed to find difficult to undo.

'I don't like everyone knowing what I can do, Aunt Imelda,' she said quietly.

'Nathaniel suggested it's a gift,' the old woman said.

'It is,' Bernadette agreed, looking up at me hopefully, searching for support, or encouragement.

I smiled at her, perhaps misleadingly. I was still trying to keep an open mind, and I certainly didn't want to upset her. However, our Aunt had no such worries:

'He thinks your gift is for misleading silly old women like me!'

'I said no such thing,' I told Bernadette, who was looking between us, not sure which was sympathetic, if either.

'Aunt Imelda is making mischief,' I said.

'Am I?' the old woman asked loudly. 'But this is something to discuss over a cup of tea. Put the kettle on Bernadette. You've bought enough macaroons for the three of us, I hope?'

'I thought . . .' she replied, flustered, 'that there would be more people . . . well, never mind.'

As Bernadette shuffled out towards what I assumed would be the kitchen I turned a stern look on Aunt Imelda:

'That was very naughty of you. I didn't say she was misleading you at all.'

'You thought it, though, didn't you? Look me straight in the eye and deny it.'

'When she comes back in, you're to be nice to the poor girl.'

'Oho! So you're feeling sorry for her now? Look, if she wants to come up here and look after me it's up to her. If she thinks that she'll put in a couple of months of nursing and then get something in my Will then it's at her own risk. Maybe I'll leave something to her, maybe I won't.'

This stunned me.

'Is that why you think she's here?' I asked.

'She's hardly going to admit it, is she?'

'Do you believe she sees your husband, and this Jeffery person?'

'She gives an old woman comfort.'

I smiled at Aunt Imelda, deciding that I understood. Without thinking I said: 'You cunning old devil!'

'That's no way to talk to your aunt!' she bridled, but there was a smile underneath it.

'No,' I admitted, trying to fathom this woman. 'I wouldn't have suggested it to some frail old thing who was being taken advantage of. But perhaps you're taking advantage of Bernadette?'

She laughed now: 'You know, I always thought your family a little, how shall I put it, lacking in spirit? Wet. But it's nice to see you've got some gumption. Your mother always struck me as a little pathetic; desperate to be loved. And as for poor little Bernadette!'

'I'm sure you are capable of compassion,' I teased her, slightly uncertainly, but she took it in good part and laughed again.

'Take that up with my children!'

We could then hear Bernadette coming back down the passage towards us. Aunt Imelda raised her eyebrows, shifted her weight in her chair, folded her arms and prepared to meet her niece.

'Now, be nice,' I warned her.

'The tea's in the pot,' said Bernadette awkwardly when she returned. 'Aunt Imelda teases me, but she's in a lot of pain.'

'An awkward patient?' I asked and received a friendly smile of agreement.

'Pish!' the old woman exclaimed. 'Now, see if you can convince Nathaniel of your gift. Who else do you see here?'

'It's not a party trick, Aunt Imelda,' insisted my cousin.

'I didn't say it was. Nathaniel's a sceptic, though. Is there anyone here for him?'

She looked at her feet, shifting her weight from one to the other awkwardly.

'There is!' insisted our Aunt, pleased. 'Who is it?'

Bernadette looked up at me and said quietly, 'Your grandfather is here.'

'Really, which one?' I asked levelly.

'Your mother's father.'

'Well, do say hello to him for me.'

'He can hear you. It's just that you can't communicate with him. Well, I assume you can't?'

'No, I can't see him,' I confirmed.

'Well, he's standing over in the corner, looking out the window. He was a great countryman, wasn't he?'

'He was.'

'He wants you to know that he didn't suffer when he died. He's with his wife now.'

I nodded, unable to believe a word of what Bernadette was telling me, but feeling that I had to be polite. It seemed to encourage her, though.

'He says that you and your wife took part in an anti-foxhunting demonstration recently?'

'Yes, we did. There's a hunt local to us. We don't approve.'

'He says it's simply what they do in the countryside. It's part of the natural order of things and not at all wrong.'

'Oh,' I said simply.

As my mother would have said, Bernadette had 'over-egged her pudding'. It was likely that she would have heard through the family that my grandfather was 'a great countryman', probably direct from my mother herself. She had probably heard from the same source that my wife and I had recently protested against our local hunt. Bernadette had put two and two together but her mathematics were not sound. My grandfather abhorred fox-hunting; he would shoot foxes as vermin, but he hated to see people on horseback ineffectually tearing about the countryside and glorying in the kill. I had caught Bernadette out, but I decided that I would not say anything.

'And Michael and Jeffery?' asked Aunt Imelda.

Bernadette smiled at the old woman reassuringly: 'They're both here, and pleased to see Nathaniel. They send you their love.'

And with that she turned and left, saying that she would bring through the tea and cakes.

'Death changes people,' Aunt Imelda said simply. 'Michael was always jealous, but he seems to get on awfully well with Jeffery now that they're both on the other side.'

Her expression was one of humour and cynicism. I couldn't believe anything the old woman said.

Two years later Aunt Imelda died. The imminence of her death had become something of a private joke between my wife and me, although we wouldn't have ever let anyone else hear it. Whenever family matters were brought up, or Knaresborough mentioned, one of us would ask the other, 'Do you think Aunt Imelda has got around to dying yet?'

I know that the joke meant I didn't have to address my real concern about the arrangement that Aunt Imelda had fallen into with Cousin Bernadette. After that one visit I discussed the situation with my wife, of course, but the subject was not properly revisited until the morning of the funeral. I was going down to the crematorium on my own, putting on my best shirt and black suit. My wife was watching me go through the drawers in search of my one black tie. She commented:

'You're convinced that Bernadette was a fraud?'

'Of course. But I'm equally certain that Aunt Imelda must have seen through her.'

'And the old woman was playing along so as to have a companion?'

'I think she must have been. But Bernadette was more of a skivvy than a companion. She was ordered around all the time, and complied meekly. You know, I've always felt more sorry for her than Aunt Imelda.'

'Perhaps they deserved each other?'

'Perhaps. But I've always been worried that Bernadette might not have stayed with her just because she wanted to be remembered in the Will. She might have genuinely wanted to help.'

'Is that likely?'

'It might be. I've never known her well enough to be sure. Believe it or not, some people are naturally kind-hearted.'

'Do you think she was inventing her powers of mediumship in a silly attempt to cheer the old woman up?'

'I wouldn't put it past her. Or maybe such people really do fool themselves into believing they can see what isn't there?'

'You'd have to be pretty sad, or desperate, to do that. Is she very bright?'

'Bernadette? No, I don't think so.'

'Well, they may have been a mismatched pair, but perhaps they both got something out of the relationship?'

'I hope so.'

I did rather hope that Bernadette would have been included in the Will so that she would have earned some recompense for living with Aunt Imelda for two and a half years. As I drove to the crematorium in the rain I tried to imagine what it would have been like for Bernadette putting up with the very demanding old woman. It must have seemed like a lifetime.

At the crematorium I parked easily. There were five other cars and in a small blue hatchback sat Bernadette. I walked over and tapped on the window, making her jump. She had been staring straight ahead and hadn't seen me arrive.

'Nathaniel,' she said, once she had wound down the window. 'Get in the other side. There's still another five minutes before we have to go in.'

'I'm sure we can go inside early. There doesn't seem to be any other service going on.'

'I know. I've been in already and put out the order of service on the benches. I had it printed up with Aunt Imelda's favourite hymns. But I'd rather not go back in, not yet,' she said forlornly.

I walked quickly around and got in the passenger seat, out of the rain. Inside her cramped, stuffy little car she continued to stare straight ahead. She looked even taller and skinnier than before; gaunt even. She was wearing an oversized black shirt and her skirt was pleated and ruffled but could not hide how thin she was. Eventually she turned to me and said bluntly:

'Aunt Imelda has left me the house and all her money.'

'Good,' I said, but stopped myself from saying 'You've earned it.'

'Her son and daughter are here today.'

'How have they taken the news?'

'They don't know yet.'

'Oh.'

'Don't say anything to them?'

'Of course not.'

'I'm not sure if I can face them, not until I have to. They've already said they're not coming back to the house afterwards. Apparently they hate the place. You'll come back, though, won't you?'

'I ought to get back home after the cremation. I promised my wife.'

'Please come back with me,' she implored. 'Otherwise, well, I've got a horrible feeling it'll just be me. Or, worst still, me and the women from the church Aunt Imelda used to go to.'

I reluctantly agreed and we sat in silence until I told her that the five minutes were up. We then got out and dashed across the tarmac to what was the most miserable cremation service I've ever been unfortunate enough to attend.

Aunt Imelda's children, both of them, were sitting in the front pews. They were older than Bernadette and me, and they took no notice of anyone else. I guessed that the three other mourners who sat together had come from Aunt Imelda's old church.

'Yes,' confirmed Bernadette. 'She left because their views on morality weren't as strict as she would've liked. She caused them a lot of trouble.'

'I remember her lecturing me about sex.'

'She didn't like *any* contact between people.'

'Something must have upset her a long time ago to make her like that.'

'I suppose.'

'I can't imagine she let you bring boyfriends back to the house?'

Bernadette raised her eyebrows in horror at the idea and she grinned for the first time. She soon remembered where she was, though, and composed herself. We sat together, towards the middle of the draughty room; my cousin had refused to go any closer. On bench after bench around us there lay unmolested her badly photocopied orders of service.

We sang a very dispiriting 'Why Should Our Tears in Sorrow Flow', and then the vicar seemed to appear from nowhere and said a few words. He got Aunt Imelda's name right, and those of her children, but only by squinting at the piece of card on which Bernadette had written them. We then sang 'Winter in His Heart of Gloom' and the vicar stood once more and read some forgettable passage from the Bible that didn't seem to bear any relevance to the proceedings. Bernadette took the opportunity to open a bag of Murray Mints, which struck me as a little irreverent, but I decided that as she probably went to her church regularly she would have more of an idea of religious propriety than me.

The ordeal of the service was completed with 'In the Black Dismal Dungeon of Despair', and the coffin trundled out of sight. The words of the last hymn did get a little brighter towards the end, but I wondered if the strange humour of the deceased had prompted her to tell Bernadette that they were her favourite hymns.

We waited for the chief mourners to leave, then the three members of the Church. After a deep breath Bernadette agreed to move out as well, but then decided to collect up all of the orders of service. I helped her, and by the time we walked out to the small lobby the other mourners were driving past, out of the car park.

'I've made sandwiches,' she said quietly. 'And bought cakes. . . . Macaroons.'

'We'll have to finish them up ourselves,' I said with as much feigned jollity as I could muster. 'Now, shall I follow you back to the house?'

She nodded, and we went back out into the rain.

Bernadette drove slowly through the Knaresborough traffic and I had little trouble keeping up with her. In my car the radio was playing REM's 'Shiny Happy People' which seemed more inappropriate than even the Murray Mints had been. I turned it off and had to put up with the miserable rhythm of the windscreen wipers. I decided that by not being alive that day Aunt Imelda was not missing anything.

Back at the house I pulled up behind Bernadette's car. I waited for her to go up to the front door and open it before I got out and made a dash for cover myself. I looked up at the impressive bulk of the building; 'a machine for living in' it would have been called back then. But it wasn't quite as elegant as it might have been: a cut-price Le Corbusier. I had been prepared for a dismal gathering after the cremation, but if it had been just me and Bernadette then we might have been able to laugh at the awfulness of the situation. However, as I was about to close the front door a car drew up in the road outside and the three members of Aunt Imelda's old church were slowly decanted. I waited for them to walk sombrely up the drive and I let them inside, taking their coats. They were not particularly talkative, although they all complained to each other that they had to climb stairs to go up to the living room. I followed them, and then Bernadette told me to stay in the living room while she made some tea.

The three women in black arranged themselves on the edge of the sofa and looked down their noses at the fresh-looking flower arrangement on the varnished coffee table. I knew that the room looked impressive on a sunny day, but the light through the long windows was grey, deepening the ugly green of the carpet.

I noticed the glasses and an unopened bottle of sherry on the sideboard and offered the ladies a drink. In turn each of them declined with a slight shake of the head which suggested that the offer was inappropriate. Next to the drink I saw the sandwiches under Clingfilm and decided to try and tempt them. I went and removed the plastic covering before carrying the large plate over and putting it down on the table. I then picked up napkins and handed one to each of the unwilling guests. They did not move.

Going back to the sideboard for the third time I wondered what had made Bernadette think that a large bowl of some violently orange-coloured puffed potato or wheat snacks would be appreciated. There was also a very large vase with celery sticks poking out of it, still untrimmed of their foliage.

I stood behind the women and suggested that they help themselves to the still untouched sandwiches. They annoyed me and I was willing to provoke them, but it was then that I saw the legs.

In front of what I thought of as Aunt Imelda's chair were two prosthetic legs sheathed in blue tights, terminating in pink slippers. They were bent at the knee and the top halves were set over the edge of the seat as though the rest of Aunt Imelda should be there, sitting down. Bernadette had obviously forgotten to tidy them away. I sidled out of the room and down to the kitchen where my cousin was standing over a pot of tea.

'Aunt Imelda's legs,' I said, quietly.

'They were amputated,' she said, 'about six months ago.'

'I guessed that. Her false ones are in front of her chair.'

'No?'

'They do look a little odd.'

'But I didn't put them there. They were in the hall cupboard, downstairs.'

'Well, they're now in the living room.'

'How odd. If I make a diversion, will you take them out?'

'What kind of diversion?'

'I don't know. I can't just walk in there and simply pick them up.'

'Why not?'

'How would it look?'

'Then I'll do it,' I said, wondering why I hadn't taken the initiative before. 'You bring the tea through, and I'll tidy up the legs.'

She agreed, added cups and saucers to the tray and picked it up. I followed her down the passage and into the living room. As she walked in she screamed and dropped everything she was carrying.

It was a piercing scream followed by sobs of terror. I was thoroughly shaken and the three women were immediately hysterical themselves, jumping up and dropping napkins and sandwiches. I tried to take hold of Bernadette but she pulled herself out of my grasp and rushed over to the stairs. Without hesitating she flew down them, flung open the front door and ran out into the rain.

Bewildered, I looked around me. The women were upset and once they had brushed themselves free of crumbs they excused themselves immediately. In less than a minute I was the only one left in the house.

I looked around and decided to put the broken remains of the teapot, cups and saucers back on to the tray. The carpet was sodden and squelchy, but being such an ugly dark green I wasn't concerned about the stain. As I squatted on my haunches, picking up the bits, my eyes were drawn to the prosthetic legs across the room from me.

I was certain that Bernadette had screamed when she had seen them.

I stood up and out of the corner of my eye I could see through the large windows my unfortunate cousin down in the corner of the garden, hard up against the fence, looking distraught. I resolved to go out to her. I would try and persuade her to return to the house, but first, I decided, I would tidy away those legs. They were heavier than I expected when I picked them up, one in each hand. I carried them downstairs and put them in the cupboard. Then I pulled on my coat, took Bernadette's, and went out to her.

'I'm not going back into the house while she's there,' Bernadette insisted. She took the coat I offered her although she was already so wet it could do no good.

'Who? Aunt Imelda?'

'Of course, Aunt Imelda!'

'But don't you see dead people all the time?'

She didn't answer.

'I'll go in with you,' I said. 'Hold my hand.'

She clung tightly to me, her arm around my waist. She was shaking and uncertain, and took her time re-crossing the lawn. With great reluctance she entered the gloomy, echoing house with me, but there seemed to be some angry determination within her that willed her through the front door. A great battle was obviously raging in her skinny frame and she could not stop trembling. She clung to me tightly and made the great effort of climbing the stairs alongside me.

As the view of the living room on the first floor came into sight I looked towards Aunt Imelda's chair.

'I took the legs and threw them in the cupboard,' I said as she slowed to a halt, just four more stairs to go.

'She's still there, in the chair,' said Bernadette. 'Without her legs.'

At that moment I was clearly struck that there were only two ways of explaining what was happening. Either ghosts or spirits existed and could be seen by people like Bernadette, or the woman holding on to me was deluded and in need of medical attention.

'Can't you ask Aunt Imelda to leave?' I suggested quietly.

After a moment or two Bernadette replied:

'She won't.'

'It's not worth asking?'

'No. You see, she wants to stay and make life as awkward as possible for me.'

'Why's that?'

'I poisoned her, and she knows it.'

'How?'

'I used aluminium acetate,' she said, her voice quite calm. 'A friend told me it's good because they don't test for aluminium at a post-mortem.'

'But what made you poison her?'

'Once she'd had her legs amputated successfully she was going to live for years and years. And yet she still needed help.'

'Why are you telling me this?'

'To explain why she's here.'

'Where are Michael and Jeffery?'

'They were never here. But she is.'

'Then leave her here. Move out. Sell the house,' I suggested.

I then decided to make a joke: 'She won't follow you. She can't; she hasn't got any legs.'

It was a very poor joke, in exceedingly bad taste, but Bernadette started to giggle nervously, still clinging to me. We were till standing on the stairs.

'I never liked her, and she was rotten to me,' she said, her shaking and quivering the result not only of cold and fear, I decided, but hysteria. 'I did everything I could to make her happy. I really wanted to help her. I didn't want her horrible house or her money.'

'I know, I know,' I tried to reassure her. I believed her. 'But you can see her sitting in the chair?'

'Yes, and she's very, very angry.'

'That's not unreasonable, if you poisoned her.'

'She's more angry that I'm holding on to you. She's calling me a whore.'

'Ignore her. You said that Aunt Imelda's religious beliefs were too extreme for even her own church. She was deluded then,' I explained, and added, for comfort, 'And she's deluded now.'

It was very strange. As we stood towards the top of the stairs I could not see anyone sitting across the room in the empty chair. I was convinced that I never would see anything. Perhaps it was Bernadette's fear communicating itself to me, but it was almost as though there was a malevolent presence in the room. I could have sworn that something of Aunt Imelda's fury was there with us. And it seemed to be increasing. The room seemed to be darkening.

'She's getting angrier,' said Bernadette. 'She's calling me a prostitute and a fornicator. She's telling me to let go of you. Nathaniel, you won't let go of me, will you?'

'No, I won't let go.'

'She's calling you an adulterer. She says we're both damned. She's saying that it would be bad enough if we weren't cousins. She says she won't stay and watch such grossness.'

Bernadette looked at me, and I've never seen anyone look so frightened and yet so hopeful. She boldly and determinedly climbed the last few stairs, pulling me after her. When we were in the very middle of the room she implored: 'Please kiss me.'

I really did not know what to do. She put her arms around my neck and gave me one of the most forceful and passionate kisses I have ever received. I was about to push her away, but her kiss was so deep and so fervent and I found myself responding. I clasped her to me in return but then, just as suddenly, she broke away to look in the direction of the empty chair. She laughed, and then kissed me again. Now I tried to push her away but her arms were holding me even tighter than before and I simply gave in to her.

A few moments later she let go of me and looked to the chair again. Once more she laughed, then pushed me away from her teasingly. With deliberation she pulled her shirt up and over her head. She wasn't wearing a brassiere; her chest was so flat that she didn't really need one. She walked towards me, took my head in her hands and pulled me down to her left breast; her areolas were like two-pence pieces. I kissed her and her nipple swelled and hardened. Once again she then pulled away from me, laughing loudly, and with relief.

'It's working! She's going!' Bernadette exclaimed. 'She can't stand it.'

Bernadette came towards me once more and kissed me again, forcing her tongue inside my mouth and I was too confused to struggle. She pulled away, swung around behind me and looking over my shoulder hugged me tight, staring at the chair. She almost shouted into my ear: 'She's left us! The old devil has gone!'

I was bewildered, shocked even. I stood there stupidly as Bernadette let go of me and started to dance around the room, her big skirt billowing out as she twirled and twirled in sheer ecstasy. 'The old devil has gone!' she said, time and time again. 'The old devil has gone!'

'I think *I* had better go too,' I said, tucking my shirt back into my trousers. Bernadette gave me a grin as she twirled, and on her next revolution a childish wave of her hand. I backed out and down the stairs and she was still dancing around and around. From the front door I ran the short distance through the rain to my car and once inside I started it immediately and reversed down the drive and into the road. Before I drew away I looked back at the house; the big Modern-Movement machine for living in; the cut-price Le Corbusier. From time to time, when she approached the windows of the upstairs living room, I could see her; bare-chested, still dancing, around and around.

The Red Rose and the Cross of Gold

'I am sure that a professional gentleman such as yourself could afford to rent rooms like this as a single tenant?' The landlord smiled at Komenský ingratiatingly. 'We could come to an arrangement so that I wouldn't have to find another occupant to share with you?'

'No, thank you,' Komenský shook his head. 'I enjoy sharing. I always have done.'

'But you might end up with somebody who is, shall we say, incompatible?'

'I hope not. . . . I got on well enough with the last man.'

'Well, maybe that was luck.'

'I'm easy-going. I get on with most people.'

'So far you may have done.'

'I have to move with my work, from city to city. Sometimes I stay for six months, sometimes a couple of years. I don't have time to make friends; not proper friends. And I like to have some companionship.'

'But how long are you expecting to stay here in our city? If you are only resident for perhaps another month or so, then I suppose I could wait. After you, I could put a nice young couple in these rooms.'

'The city authorities have extended my contract.'

'They've found more sewers for you to survey?'

'This city is crumbling all around us; it is decaying. It has been poorly built, above and below ground. And there are more and more motor vehicles on the streets.'

'This building shakes when they pass!'

'By the middle of this century the streets will be infested with them, and they are getting bigger and bigger. There is the danger that all will come tumbling down.'

The landlord poured a little more Becherovka into Komenský's coffee, as he always tried to do. He came up once a month for his rent and the engineer had long-since stopped protesting that he didn't want any of the landlord's drink. The man who had previously shared the rooms had been convinced that their landlord was a dipsomaniac, but Komenský was not sure. He hoped that the bottle of Becherovka that the man carried around with him was simply a gesture of friendliness. He imagined that he offered it to all of his tenants to make the process of collecting the rent a little easier. The landlord lived in one of the two sets of rooms on the rather unsanitary ground floor, and at nine o'clock prompt on the first of every month he would begin with the old couple in the rooms opposite his own. It would often be the early afternoon before he had climbed up to the fourth floor where Komenský lived. The landlord wasn't a confident man, and needed to think of his tenants as friends. To a certain extent Komenský understood this. He thought that the man, like himself, was perhaps a little lonely.

'You've never found anyone special to live with?' the landlord asked. 'Wanted to settle down, have a family?'

'No, not really. A couple of times, perhaps . . . But my skills are specialised, and I've always had to move around to find work. I've tried to keep up long-distance relationships. . . There was one woman in the north who I would go back to . . . I would visit every weekend, for several years, but she tired of the arrangement.'

'Couldn't you get a permanent job with the authorities?'

'I specialise in sewers, vaults, crypts. . . . I have a sense for when they are becoming dangerous and liable to fail, long before it is obvious to untrained, inexperienced eyes. I've saved cities untold sums by highlighting where repairs are required before collapses have occurred.'

'And they pay well for your expertise?'

'I cannot complain.'

'Enough for you to rent these rooms on your own?'

'I am careful with my money.'

'Ah, very sensible. An early retirement? A good pension?'

'I am just careful.'

'I understand.'

He clanked his mug of Becherovka-infused coffee with Komenský's own, by way of suggesting a newly discovered comradeship.

'So, I must find another person for the second room,' said the landlord, resigned.

'I'm afraid so. And if it can be somebody congenial, I'd appreciate that. Another professional man? Of quiet habits?'

'Well, there is a gentleman who has recently asked me for a single room. He didn't want to share, and I had only the room here to offer. I told him about it, and how he would get on well with you. But I think he is looking elsewhere first. You never know, he might come back.'

'What's he like?'

'What's anybody like? I don't know. He seems nice enough. But he looks like Mephistopheles himself.'

Mephistopheles himself did not move in, but his doppelgänger did: Damian von Tripps.

'A very old family,' he insisted when Komenský asked after his impressive name, 'But very much decayed. We have a branch in Lithuania that struggles along, but I am the last of the line here.'

'Any chance of additions to your part of the family tree?' Komenský asked him. The man had only moved in a few days before but Komenský thought he understood his humour well enough to be able to ask such a question.

'No, not officially. But who's to say that there aren't a few illegitimate von Tripps scattered around the city?'

The man was preparing himself for an evening out, and Komenský had to admit that he was fascinated by the care and fastidiousness with which he went about getting ready. He had bathed for nearly an hour, then shaved and meticulously trimmed his arrangement of beard and moustache. The latter was slightly comical, being very wide and requiring wax to keep it horizontal and cantilevered out on either side of his face. He dressed in expensive clothes, quite brightly coloured, and Komenský was never sure whether the strong smell he left in his wake was after-shave or simply perfume. He really was quite the dandy.

As von Tripps was about to go out of the door he turned to where Komenský sat reading under the lamp by the fireplace. Putting his weight slightly on the ebony walking cane that was usually for show rather than support he asked:

'A delicate question, if I may?'

'Of course.'

'The landlord stressed that the arrangement here was for two single men to have tenancy of these rooms. I do not propose to move anyone else in with me, but I hope you have no objection, if I should find myself in congenial company after the play tonight . . . ?'

He must have seen that Komenský did not quite understand his meaning.

'If I was to bring a young lady back with me, I hope that you wouldn't be . . . disturbed?'

Komenský laughed and shook his head: 'No, so long as you don't wake me up.'

Komenský was not convinced that von Tripps was the man's name at all. Perhaps he really was from aristocratic stock and down on his luck, but something about him suggested that it was all an act. Komenský had not met many aristocrats, but those he had come across were not so affected as von Tripps. Presumably they were confident enough of their position in society that they did not need to prove anything. It was as if the role of dandified gentleman was being played by an over-zealous actor. However, the engineer found the man's formality amusing, and when they were both together Komenský somehow slipped into it as well. It was like a game, and Komenský was happy to play along. He was concerned, at first, that von Tripps might be offended but, on the contrary, he seemed pleased that Komenský reacted in this way. Often, in the evenings, if von Tripps was not engaged elsewhere, they opened a bottle of wine and conversed in exceedingly formal, long-winded and over-elaborate sentences, often containing convoluted sub-clauses.

Komenský thought of their conversations as an intellectual game, and von Tripps was obviously a very clever man, being well-read and knowledgeable on a wide range of subjects. He did not appear to have an occupation, or rather, he would not admit to one; he kept his personal and professional life very much to himself but still Komenský felt that he had the measure of the man. And then one morning he had cause to re-evaluate von Tripps.

Komenský was awake earlier than usual, dragged from sleep, he discovered, by the sound of von Tripps and another person moving about in the apartment. When Komenský left his room he was in time to see a woman leaving by the front door and he was struck by how young, awkward and ill-dressed she was. He also noticed the old-fashioned courtesy that von Tripps used when showing her out. When they breakfasted briefly together neither man mentioned her, although Komenský was very curious; earlier that week he had seen von Tripps, from the window, leaving the building with a different woman entirely.

However, it was the man's own business and Komenský was not going to interfere. He did feel awkward, though, that von Tripps seemed to bring his women home long after Komenský had gone to bed, and that they always left before he got up.

Komenský resolved that he would work the subject into conversation. He wanted to tell the man that he had no objection to him seeing women in the apartment at other hours of the day and, indeed, if he would ever like to be left alone with them Komenský was always happy to go out for a few hours. The day he had seen the second woman, however, they had little opportunity to discuss anything because Komenský had to be at the other side of the city by nine o'clock. He did not return until the early evening when von Tripps was leaving, dressed up as usual, and saying that he would not be back until late.

It so happened that Komenský too went out that evening, to meet up with some people to celebrate the birthday of the City's Chief Engineer. The man had just turned sixty, apparently, and he and his colleagues were drinking steadily from the early evening. By ten o'clock Komenský was tired and excused himself from the revelry. They were very scathing, drunk and belligerent, and called him a 'dirty foreigner'.

So, that was what they really thought of him, Komenský told himself.

He walked home rather than take the tram, hoping to sober up, but the cold night air only made him drowsy. As he walked through the streets to his own tenement, angry and a little sad, his thoughts turned to the buildings around him and the sewers below. He thought of all the weight of crumbling brick and powdery mortar that held everything together, his eyes going up to the dark eaves of the building he was passing. Then he looked to his feet which struck the pavement with a strangely hollow sound. Back up his eyes went and suddenly the buildings around him seemed to sway and the very pavement to move. He felt nauseous and had to grasp at some railings to steady himself. For a few seconds the buildings around him had appeared to be toppling, falling inwards towards him and if he had been able to find the breath at that moment he might have screamed.

A fainting fit, he told himself, brought about by the beer. He took several deep breaths and walked on. When he finally got back to his rooms it was as much as he could do to take off his coat and fall into an armchair. Still he could not dismiss the idea that his own tenement was moving, although he knew that it was his sense of balance that was awry.

Komenský slept in the chair until just after midnight. When he opened his eyes he did not know where he was although the lamp still illuminated the room. However, he recognised the sound of von Tripps coming in through the front door.

The man was surprised to see Komenský, and for the briefest moment he looked unsure of himself. His confidence returned, though, along with his bravado, as soon as he had appraised the situation.

'Good evening!' he said jovially. 'Or should I say good morning?'

Behind him, uncertain in the shadows, was a woman. Komenský couldn't see her properly but he knew her to be different again from the other two he had seen. This one looked a little older.

'Please forgive us,' the man implored. 'But I think we shall be retiring.' And he turned around and ushered his companion into his room.

Uncomfortable in the chair, Komenský got out of it and made himself ready for bed. When he turned-in he had to find the earplugs that he had bought when he had discovered that the last man to share the rooms snored loudly. The earplugs were good ones; the snoring that had previously reverberated through the walls would have otherwise kept Komenský awake. Now they were able to exclude the sounds of rather vigorous lovemaking from the next room.

When Komenský got up the next morning Von Tripps' companion of the night before had obviously already left. The man himself was in his dressing gown, drinking coffee at the table on the balcony and reading a newspaper. The morning was already warm and he had his slippered feet up on the wrought-ironwork. When Komenský had prepared his first coffee of the morning he joined him and von Tripps was the first to broach the subject.

'That was Iva, last night,' he said, looking Komenský straight in the eye without the slightest embarrassment. 'I've always liked Iva.'

'I had earplugs,' Komenský replied, as coolly as he was able. 'They were useful. They allowed your enjoyment to remain private.'

'My apologies. It was very rude of me. Iva can be rather too enthusiastic. I don't go to her very often. But you know how it is sometimes . . .'

'No, I don't know, not really. But that's your affair.'

He smiled: 'I simply meant that one doesn't always have the choice one would hope for. Not that she isn't worth the money.'

Komenský frowned and von Tripps smiled.

'She's a prostitute,' he said by way of explanation, and took a sip of his coffee.

'Oh,' was all Komenský could manage to say. He had hoped that his reply might have conveyed a whole range of meaning, but von Tripps seemed to take it as shock. Komenský would have liked to give the impression that he was broad-minded, a man of the world, but, if he was honest, he supposed that, yes, he was shocked.

'I frequently use prostitutes,' said von Tripps lightly.

'I hadn't realised. I mean, I knew you often had company.'

'My failing is that I enjoy sexual intercourse. I find it transcendent. I am investigating . . .'

Komenský nodded vigorously, rather hoping they could leave the subject there, but von Tripps sensed the disapproval.

'You do not wish to know. I understand.'

'It is a private matter. I don't intend to judge you.'

'I assumed that you wouldn't, but I would understand if you'd prefer me to move out, to find alternative accommodation?'

'No, not at all,' Komenský replied, a little too hastily, but honestly. Von Tripps was an odd man, but enjoyable company and despite his unorthodox behaviour he had not been any real trouble.

'I was married, twice,' von Tripps said. 'I was very young. I loved both my wives, but I craved variety. Do you understand? I get bored easily. I'm actually rather besotted with a girl right now, but I know that if I was to ask her to marry me, and promised to shun all other women, then I'd soon enough tire of her. It is a weakness of mine, I know: a flaw in my character.'

'I can see how that might happen,' Komenský said, wishing that the conversation could be at an end.

'But there is a charge of exploitation to answer,' the man admitted. 'Prostitutes are victims. It's rare that prostitution is ever a woman's first career choice. The women I go with are poor, vulnerable creatures who need protection.'

'And how do you feel about that?'

'Concerned, naturally. But I fancy that I'm not the same as all their other customers.'

'How would you be any different?'

He leant forward, slightly conspiratorially, and pulled his moustache out to it's maximum length.

'The girls all know me, and how generous I can be. We never discuss money, oh no. I'm never asked to pay, because when they leave they know I'll slip into their hand twice as many notes as they would normally have asked for. And I occasionally give them valuable gifts. Very often I'll take them to a restaurant, or get them tickets for the theatre. Some even refuse to take any money from me at all! I always make sure it's worth their while going with me.'

He sat back. Self-satisfied, but he was almost too arrogant to need to look smug.

'And they trust me,' he added. 'They all realise that I won't be rough, or ask them to do anything too strange. I won't beat them up. I have a reputation as something of a guardian angel to them. You see, a few months ago while I was down by the docks, making my choice for the evening, a couple of drunks appeared and started behaving deplorably. The girls working there were worried for their own safety so I told the two of them to leave. When they started to get violent . . .'

At this von Tripps jumped up and with a flourish he withdrew a long blade from his cane. 'Voila! My sword-stick!'

'And the girl you're in love with?'

'She calls herself "La Bella". It's a silly name, but she's never admitted to any other. She's the sweetest, prettiest girl. A rose, and not quite twenty. I'd do anything for her.'

'You love her so much that you let her go back out onto the street when you've done with her?'

He winced: 'It pains me, it does. And I do get jealous, thinking about her with other men. And I get worried about her.'

'But you do nothing to help her?'

'I see her once a week. I pay her well. But I don't have enough money to keep her as my mistress, just for myself.'

'If you lived together?'

He shook his head sadly: 'As I said, it would never work.'

The conversation was effectively at an end. Komenský was trying to understand the attitude of the man but failed to do so. He did not believe that von Tripps could be truly in love with this girl with the ludicrous name; not when he continued to act as he did.

Relations between Komenský and von Tripps became strained after that conversation. The engineer could not quite think of him in the same way because the man seemed such a hypocrite, believing himself somehow better than the other men who used prostitutes. Komenský supposed that he was indeed something of a prude, but the man's belief that he was the 'patron' of those poor women annoyed him. That evening his antipathy towards von Tripps deepened as the man dressed himself in all of his finery and took such a time about it. When Komenský went to bed he lay awake, expecting von Tripps to return at any moment with yet another woman.

And he did return, of course, with company. Even with his earplugs in Komenský could hear them, despite an earnest desire not to; he longed for sleep to overcome him too desperately for it to happen.

When the morning came around Komenský lay in bed, listening, and could hear somebody moving about in the apartment, and perhaps quiet voices from time to time. When he was finally certain that von Tripps was on his own Komenský got up, put on his dressing gown and walked out to make himself breakfast.

He had been wrong. At the table there sat a young woman sullenly eating toast.

'Good morning,' von Tripps greeted Komenský, walking in from the kitchen with a pot of coffee. 'My dear,' he said to the woman, 'this is Mr Komenský, the gentleman I was talking to you about last night. He shares these rooms with me.'

She looked over and smiled a professional smile.

'This,' he said to Komenský, 'is the lovely La Bella.'

'Good morning,' the engineer said simply, and continued on through to the kitchen. He put water on the stove and tried to repress his anger. Was von Tripps trying to provoke him? Were they both trying? She was astoundingly pretty, as he had said, and she was dressed in a most provocative manner. It was not lost on Komenský that she was wearing a garment like a bodice or basque that seemed to support her breasts at the same time as it revealed most of them.

He was not a prude, he insisted to himself, and he admired her beauty, but to be presented thus with this young woman by von Tripps had to have been a calculated act on his part. What did he want? How did he expect Komenský to react? Was the actor expecting him to avail himself of the young woman's services as well?

Von Tripps put his head around the door and bid Komenský 'Adieu,' receiving the barest acknowledgement. Komenský added sugar to his coffee and walked out into the living room as he heard the front door slam. To his surprise La Bella was still sitting at the table.

'Is he returning?' Komenský asked.

'Him? I don't think so.'

'Well, let yourself out when you're ready,' he said, and continued on to his room. He didn't like the idea of having a common prostitute left in the apartment. What was to stop her from stealing from them? Von Tripps might be in love with her but how could he trust her? And then Komenský considered again that von Tripps might have been expecting Komenský to sleep with her! He picked up his clothes and took them, with his coffee, through to the bathroom. He locked the door after him, then shaved and showered. He tried not to think about her.

It was as Komenský was dressing that he heard the front door open and he assumed that La Bella was leaving. There were raised voices and he distinctly heard the woman asking, 'Why are you back here? That wasn't the arrangement.'

The reply was indistinct, which raised Komenský's suspicions all the more. There were some unidentifiable noises and then he heard a cry from her, followed by an almighty crash. The man shouted, she screamed, there was a thud and nothing more. Komenský felt that he had no choice but to go out and see what had happened. He buttoned his shirt hastily and went out into the hall. The door to von Tripps' bedroom was open and the young woman was standing there.

La Bella was covered in blood. Komenský could see that it was not her own. She was looking in shock and disbelief at her hands, and then down at where it was splashed over her chest and stomach and ran down her legs. It was also over her face.

There was a hammering at the front door and shouts demanding an explanation.

Komenský pushed past her and went into the bedroom. He could immediately see the cause of the original crashing sound: the dressing table was overturned and everything on it was scattered; the mirror smashed. And there was blood up the wall. He looked around the side of the bed and von Tripps lay slumped in the corner. His sword-stick was protruding stupidly, and somewhat limply, from his neck. Blood had burst from the artery that must have been severed. The man's eyes stared sightlessly forward and his mouth gaped bloodily open. There was also a smell that suggested that his bowels and bladder had been evacuated.

Komenský's reaction was to kneel at the man's side. He did not want to touch him, though, to check for a pulse or any other signs of life. The lack of any movement and the glassy eyes were enough to confirm that von Tripps was beyond help.

He had never been into the man's room before and he was surprised by the incongruity of the simple gold crucifix above the bed.

Komenský stood up and immediately felt dizzy and nauseous. The whole room seemed to move around him. La Bella was standing behind him and he fell against her, steadied himself and leant against the wall. Her eyes were now fixed on him.

The demands from the other side of the front door continued.

He didn't think that he really believed what he was seeing, or fully understood it. He was scared and shocked, but had no idea how to react. He made himself ask the girl, as calmly as he could, what had happened. She, however, could only open her mouth and keep repeating 'I, I,' as though about to tell him, but unable to do so.

'It was an accident?' he asked, scarcely believing that it could be, but wanting to reassure her. 'I've got to call for the police.'

She looked at him blankly.

'The police,' he repeated. 'It's too late for an ambulance.'

Komenský walked back past her and into the hall. There was more hammering on the door and he called out that there had been an accident; he was calling the police. He watched La Bella lean back against the wall and slowly slide down it until she was sitting on her haunches. She was a pathetic sight, half-naked and covered in blood. Komenský shouted that he couldn't let anybody inside for a few moments. He would have to cover her up.

He put his hand out towards the telephone and noticed that there was blood on it. He went to wipe it on his white shirt and saw that it, too, was smeared in blood. It was already turning brown as it dried.

'Do you have to call them?' she asked quietly from where she was sitting.

'I've no choice,' he said quietly, surprised that she had spoken.

'But, I murdered him.'

'It was an accident.'

She shook her head: 'No, I murdered him.'

'There was an argument. It will've been manslaughter . . . Mitigating circumstances . . .'

'No. I thought about it. I knew he had that ridiculous sword-stick. I thought about it last night. I planned it.'

Suddenly she was shivering uncontrollably.

'But why?'

'Because I hated him so much,' she said weakly, her voice quivering. 'And because he hated me.'

'He told me he loved you.'

'Ha!' she said, but without enthusiasm, casting her eyes wildly this way and that. 'If that were true then he'd have left me alone, like I asked him to . . . like I pleaded with him to do.'

'I don't understand.'

'I had no choice but to go with him,' she said, looking up at Komenský directly, trying to control her shaking by wrapping her arms tightly around herself. 'I needed the money. But the touch of him, his horrible breath, his slimy words. I know women like me don't have much choice, that we have to put up with whatever we can. But the things he asked me to do. . . .'

'If you explain all this to the police . . .'

'But then they'll have their motive. And I did plan it. And I am glad he's dead. . . . I am a murderer.'

Komenský couldn't say anything. There was knocking at the door again, but calmer this time. He wondered if whoever was outside the door could hear their conversation.

'They'll lock me away forever,' she said. 'There's no point any more, to anything.'

She slowly and deliberately stood up and then walked into the living room. She was walking towards the glazed doors to the balcony and he initially wondered why she was going there. It was as she opened them that he realised she intended to throw herself out of them.

'Stop!' he cried, and ran across the room. She pulled the doors open and was already half-over the wrought-iron balcony before he reached her. He grabbed at her waist and with all of his weight against the ironwork he pulled her around so that she fell back towards the room. As he did so the balcony moved as something snapped but didn't quite give way. He made a grab at the frame of the door and at the edge of his vision he saw La Bella's head hit the stone sill with a sickening crack. Then the wrought iron moved again and Komenský leapt back inside, over La Bella's unmoving body.

When he turned he saw the whole structure of the balcony swing away from the building, with La Bella on it. He grabbed at the young woman and was able to pull her back inside in one rough movement.

He was still holding her, watching as the blood pulsed from the gash on her head, ran over his own feet and pooled on the parquet floor. He bent down close, looking for signs of life, but her eyes were closed and when he put his hand on her chest she wasn't breathing. He had no idea of how to administer first aid. He didn't even know whether she was still alive.

He hardly noticed the next sound, that of the front door being forced open. Two neighbours rushed in and stopped when they saw him. He could imagine how it would all look to them. Could he explain what had happened? Would anyone believe him? He could hear that another neighbour had already discovered the body of von Tripps.

This was the point from which Komenský later decided he could not trust his memory. He was in a state of shock; he accepted that. He was upset and afraid, and what then happened took place so quietly and efficiently that he became an observer rather than an active participant.

Two tall men of aristocratic bearing wearing expensive suits came in and, without showing any identification to the neighbours, persuaded them all to leave the apartment. One man walked over to where Komenský sat with the bloody body of La Bella and said simply, 'A Red Rose.'

A minute later the other walked in to join his companion, presumably having seen the body of von Tripps in his room. He said: 'So much blood.'

'And so much noise,' replied the first man. 'And too much anger, and hatred. There should have been more love: I am concerned.'

'The surfaces can all be washed down,' said the second contemplatively. 'But the air in here is too full of violence.'

Komenský laid La Bella down and was helped to stand up.

'I do so hope that you are not hurt?' asked one of the men.

'No,' he replied simply, and the man took his arm and walked with him to the bathroom.

'She's dead?' Komenský asked.

'You'll need to shower,' he replied with patience and compassion.

'And my friend?'

'The process has begun,' he said solemly. 'You wash, and I'll find you some fresh clothes from your room.'

Komenský did as he was told, his mind refusing to consider what he had just witnessed. He stripped off and showered, the water at his feet first red, becoming pink, and then running clear. He dried himself mechanically and put on a dressing gown. When he felt able to open the door, one of the men, he wasn't sure which of them, was waiting outside with a set of clean clothes.

Komenský dressed in the bathroom, and when he walked out the man was waiting for him. Komenský was ready to submit himself to the authorities, and their calmness reassured him.

'You'll be late for work,' the man smiled. 'But it will be all right; we will take you there. It will soon be as if nothing has happened.'

And his day *did* pass as if nothing had happened. He arrived on site where he was greeted by members of the city engineering team and was expected to get straight to work. He numbly acquiesced. Not surprisingly he was distracted, at times distressed even. He was surprised that his colleagues made allowances for him without asking any questions. The Chief Engineer even deigned to make an appearance at the end of the day, as though Komenský was an employee of such importance that he felt honour-bound to discuss the progress of their work with him. When it was time to leave a junior member of the team was told to drive him home.

They travelled back across the city without any words and he was able to contain his nerves only because of his confusion. When the car pulled up outside Komenský's building the young chauffeur asked if he was all right going inside on his own.

Komenský took a deep breath, nodded, and got out of the car. The street looked exactly as it had done when he'd returned home the previous evening, before anything had happened. How could everything be going on just as before?

He climbed the stairs slowly, with leaden legs, and took several moments when outside his own door before he could find the courage to fit the key in the lock. The door had been forced open that morning but now it looked absolutely fine. There was no damage to be seen; it looked to be a new door and frame.

Komenský turned the key and it unlocked the door.

The lights were already on inside. Komenský did not cross the threshold. Von Tripps walked into the hallway from the living room with a sad smile. He tapped his nose conspiratorially: 'Let us not speak of this morning, my dear fellow. It will be as though nothing untoward ever occurred. Come in,' he said, holding out his hand.

'But you . . . how? And La Bella . . . ?'

'My lovely rose is no more. The price we pay for perfection.'

Leave Your Sleep

A few months ago I mentioned to my mother and father how, as a child, I had lived with my grandparents for a year. My mother frowned, and so I explained:

'When our house in Lewes was being rebuilt.'

'Oh no,' she laughed. 'You only lived with them in Brighton for two or three weeks at most.'

'But I was made to go to another school while I stayed there!'

'You were, but only to keep you out from under your grandmother's feet.'

'It was certainly for less than a term,' my father agreed. '. . . three or four weeks at most. I expect it felt like an eternity because you were away from home and all your friends. And it might've seemed as if we were rebuilding that house, but it was mostly superficial. The roof was re-tiled and the external walls re-rendered.'

'It needed a lot of interior redecoration as well,' my mother reminded him.

'But I've so many memories of staying with my grandparents,' I said. 'And they're so clear; the house was on Upperton Crescent, wasn't it?'

'Yes, but they moved to Church Road not long afterwards.'

'I remember that tapestry in the hall, and the stuffed white owl. My grandfather never seemed to complete a huge jigsaw puzzle that was all over the dining room table.'

'I'm sure it would be the house at Church Road you remember,' insisted my mother. 'We used to visit every couple of weeks. We'd go there when your father went to the football.'

'But I remember the living room at the back of the house, with big windows looking out over the garden. And I can still picture my bedroom very clearly. I'd never slept in a double bed before, and there was a paisley-patterned eiderdown.'

'Oh, well, that probably would've been at Upperton Crescent; you're right.'

'And, at some time in the past, the house had been linked to the one next to it; there were locked doors between the two.'

'I don't think so,' said my mother, but my father remembered the details:

'Yes, it was originally a big old place owned by some industrialist, but it'd been divided into two houses. There was a curtain over the doorways between them. My mother used to say you could hear the neighbours through the doors, singing hymns of an evening; they were terribly religious. They belonged to some Christian sect that didn't believe in procreation. They thought it wrong to bring yet more sinners into the world.'

'Oh, they had children,' I told him. 'I remember playing with them.'

'Really? I always thought it must've been so dull for you there without any friends. That's one of the reasons we made you go to school.'

And then, recently, my parents were tidying out their attic room when I dropped in on them. Amongst all the rubbish they were throwing out was a box containing some of my old toys and school exercise books.

'I'm not quite sure why we kept them,' my father said, 'but if you don't want them they're going to the dump.'

I wasn't certain that I remembered the battered matchbox cars, playing cards and broken microscope set. I was surprised, though, to recognise the exercise books that we had been made to cover at home to protect them, and I remembered the paper I had used. The work inside didn't look at all familiar, though. The last book I looked at was uncovered and obviously from a much earlier date. It was tatty and had the word 'English', written in pencil in the top corner, only just legible against the dark blue cover.

'I had a flick through a couple of them,' said my mother, 'and they're not too awful. You got good marks, on the whole.'

I looked inside the blue exercise book, and I wouldn't have recognised the childish handwriting as my own if I hadn't written my name, and 'January 1976' on the first page. In my mind I was immediately transported back nearly forty years to a large classroom that smelt of polish, glue and disinfectant. It had an atmosphere that seemed absolutely unique to me at the time because there were both boys and girls in it, and I was used to attending an all-boys school. I could also see before me a teacher called Miss Hanratty who was very tall and friendly.

In the exercise book, in the opening sentence, I explained simply that I was staying with my grandparents while my mother and father were building a new house.

'I'm sure,' I told my mother and father, 'that I didn't have to do some project that all the other children had already started. I was told to write something like a diary in this book instead, and I remember working really hard on it.'

'I saw that,' said my mother, looking over my shoulder for a moment. 'You wrote a great deal, but I couldn't make much sense of it. Your handwriting and spelling weren't very good.'

'He'd only've been ten at the time,' my father excused me.

'I noticed, though,' said my mother, 'that you mentioned friends called Jason and Sarah. And I think you were right; they must've lived next to your grandparents.'

The exercise book, as a physical object, had dredged up fragmentary suggestions of the past, offering a glimpse of a colourful and slightly frightening inner-city classroom. But the names 'Jason' and 'Sarah', mentioned together and in connection with my stay at my grandparents', brought to the surface memories that almost had the power to make me gasp. Like the fleeting after-images of a powerful dream, the whole atmosphere of that time was almost overwhelming, and just as inexplicable. And then I began to recall the games in the street, I saw Jason and his strange eye, and I remembered that I had made him very angry, but I had never understood why. After more than thirty years the sense of unfairness came back to me absolutely undiluted.

I took the exercise book into the living room while my parents went back upstairs to finish tidying their attic. What I read was simply and artlessly told, and the detail I have added to the story is based on those memories that resurfaced while I read it. The following reminiscence was written later that same evening, while the specifics and the whole atmosphere of the time were still clear in my mind:

I enjoyed staying with my grandparents because they spoilt me, although their house seemed quite austere. My grandmother smoked, but always at an open window, and it smelt of ash and bleach, and rarely felt really warm. My fondest memories were of the evenings when, unlike at home, we ate our meals in the living room in front of the television. Not only was my grandmother a good and generous cook, but she was content for me to choose the programs we watched. It is probably unfair, but they always seemed to have more time for my childish games and ideas than my parents did. My only complaint about staying with them was the injustice of being made to go to bed unreasonably early every night. Even now I can recall what seemed like endless hours lying awake in bed, with my curtains closed against a world that was still awake and going about its business. It was especially frustrating because I could hear other children continuing to play out in the street. I was forbidden to read or play with any toys and I didn't want to get caught, so I simply lay in bed, bored. I recall distinctly the paisley-patterned eiderdown in red and gold, and I remember how, from the top left corner, I was sure I had once found a way through the pattern, as through a maze, to the top right corner, but I could never do it again.

One evening I became especially frustrated, angry even, at the sound of children playing in the street when I was expected to be asleep. I found the courage to get up, knowing that my grandparents were downstairs at the back of the house and wouldn't hear any creaking floorboards. I went to the window and saw a half a dozen children outside, playing in the middle of the road. There was a clear sky and nearly a full moon and I could see them very distinctly in the silver light. I wondered that they didn't get told off, but there didn't seem to be any adults about, and there was no passing traffic. The lack of cars made me think that it was probably later than I realised, although that made it all the more strange that they were allowed to be outside.

I watched the children for a while, unable to understand what game it was they were playing; there were two different groups and at some shouted command that I couldn't hear clearly, an individual would run from one group to another. Very occasionally two would run at the same time and if they were from opposing groups there would be laughter. The game was overseen by a tall, thin boy standing at the edge of their game.

I left the window and went back to bed feeling a little left out. I envied them their freedom, and for some reason I decided that they wouldn't want to play with me anyway. The following night, however, I changed my estimation of them. I had heard them out in the street again, and once more I went to watch them from the window. This time I was spotted by a girl, and I was about to back away when I realised that she was waving and smiling. She pointed me out to the tall, thin boy and he waved too. He beckoned me to come down but, of course, I couldn't. I shrugged, mouthed the word sorry, and went back to bed.

When I left the house for school the next day I looked out for the children in vain. In the playground at break time I wandered about, but didn't recognise anyone from the street. Of course, Brighton has many schools and with the special arrangements my parents had made, I wasn't certain that I was going to the one nearest to my grandparents' house. The friends I made at school certainly didn't live at all close to me.

That night I was listening out for the children in the street from the moment I went to bed, but for a long time I couldn't hear them. Several times I got up and looked out of the window but they were not there. Cars passed infrequently, the moon was obviously behind clouds, and I was disappointed not to see them. Although I was envious of the children, I decided that I preferred them to be playing out there without me rather than not there at all. I lay in bed feeling a little lonely and homesick, wishing that I could meet up again with all my friends from my old school, and resenting having to go to a new one. My thoughts were quite miserable, but then I heard a shout and I jumped out of bed. The moon was now showing in the sky and everything was lit almost as bright as day. The children saw me and rushed over to the edge of the small front garden. They started to call for me to come down and this worried me so much that I nearly went straight back into bed; I was sure that my grandparents would realise what was happening outside, and why. I stood away from the window, worried, but still they called. I realised that I had to do something, and so opened the window.

'Come out and play,' called the tall, thin boy who seemed to be in charge.

'I can't,' I said, vainly trying to get my whisper to carry all the way down to them. They seemed to understand and there was a quick conference. The boy turned back to me:

'Then we'll come up to you! Go to the door on the landing, between your house and ours.' It took me a moment to understand what he meant, but when they all seemed to be running into the front garden of the house next door I realised the implications and was even more afraid. Unwillingly, I crept out of my room and into the passageway. I went down to where the door between the two houses was hidden behind the heavy curtain and pulled it back. I was relieved to see that it was bolted on my side.

I had seen the door before and it had been explained to me by my grandmother. I had not noticed, though, that there was a large keyhole. I looked through it and could see a dark passageway that was like ours, and a light came on at the far end. And then I could hear, distantly, what sounded like many, muffled feet running up stairs. Lights came on in the passageway itself and a whole gang of children appeared running towards the door. I instinctively took my eye away from the keyhole and moved back just before the children crashed into the door, making everything shake.

I was afraid that my grandparents would have heard them and so I put the curtain back. There was no sound from downstairs, though, apart from the distant sound of the television set. From behind the curtain I could hear the sound of bolts being moved back and I was horrified to think that the children had some way of opening the door from their side. I didn't dare go near it as I heard the doorknob moved to and fro and then rattled in frustration. When I was sure that they couldn't get through, I went back behind the curtain and realised that there must be bolts on both sides.

'Can you open the door?' came a voice through the keyhole.

'No,' I lied, my mouth against the gap between the door and the frame. As I looked I could see the light seeping between the two.

'My name's Jason,' said the voice, 'Like with the Argonauts.'

I told him my name and he asked if I wanted to come out to play with him and his friends. I was too ashamed to admit that I was meant to be in bed at that early hour; I guessed that the boy was probably three or four years older than me.

I bent down and looked through the keyhole. It was dark at first, then whoever was probably trying to look through it at me moved back and I could see the boy's face.

'These are all my friends,' Jason said, and he told me their names. He seemed to be trying to point them out to me, but most were beyond my restricted view through the keyhole. The only face I saw and could put a name to was a girl called Sarah who was sitting next to him. We talked for a while but then I became worried that I'd be discovered and said that I had to go. I had also started to get very cold in just my pyjamas. Jason made me agree to return to the door at the same time the next night.

I stood up from my crouching position at the keyhole and carefully emerged from behind the curtain. On the other side of the door I heard the rushing, tumbling feet as the children ran away from the door.

I went back to my bed, excited by my adventure, but also worried by it. I was pleased I hadn't been caught by my grandparents, and decided that I'd been clever not to tell the children that there were bolts on my side of the door that I could have opened if I'd wanted to. I was frustrated, though, that I didn't know what the time was and wouldn't know when to go to talk to them the next evening. I resolved that as soon as my grandparents had said goodnight to me and had gone downstairs I would make my bed look as if I was sleeping in it by putting pillows under the covers. I'd then be able to go out in the passageway and hide behind the curtain until the children came.

I followed my plan and was waiting behind the curtain very early that next night. Once again I almost despaired of them appearing. I was cold, although I had remembered to put on my slippers and dressing gown, and I found myself nearly nodding-off from time to time. And then, without warning, I heard a voice through the door. Jason was there with Sarah and they took turns in sitting back and letting me look at them through the keyhole. I tried to do the same but they couldn't see me properly in the dark behind the curtain.

They decided to sit back and talk loudly while I looked through. Jason said that he was fourteen, and Sarah was thirteen. I was thrilled that these older children seemed to want to be my friends. I lied and said that I was twelve, and immediately regretted it; I was sure that they'd find me out at some point, but they didn't seem at all concerned about our ages. I explained that I was staying with my grandparents and they said that they weren't living with their parents either. They seemed a little confused about quite who they were living with and I wondered if the house was a children's home, like a friend from my old school lived in. If that was the case I decided not to pry.

It was hard to make them out properly through the keyhole because the light was behind them and their faces were in shadow. I had noticed, though, that there was something wrong with Jason's left eye. It disconcerted me that it was so much darker than his other eye. It actually looked black, and I found myself staring at it, trying to make it out. I could see that he blinked normally, but it was as if the eyeball itself was covered in something which seemed to reflect the light. From my vantage point I found myself staring at it in a way that I'd have been too embarrassed to do normally.

They asked me about myself, my parents and grandparents, and exactly why I was living there. They asked about my new and old schools, and my teachers, and they seemed to find this fascinating, although I thought it all quite boring. I explained that I was used to going to an all-boys school, but was now going to one with girls as well.

'So your old school only had boys in it?' Sarah asked, concerned. When I said yes she asked what happened to the girls.

'I suppose there must be some all-girls schools as well,' said Jason, and I confirmed this.

'But why shouldn't girls and boys be together?' she asked.

'I don't know,' I admitted.

'Which school do you prefer?' asked Jason and though I wasn't sure that I believed it, I said that the mixed-sex school was better. He nodded and they both said they agreed with me, and I was pleased to have said the right thing as far as they were concerned. I really wanted them to like me, and I was flattered that they wanted to know all about me. I could see through the keyhole that they were genuinely interested when I explained what books I liked, and what television programs I watched.

Two other children joined them as we talked, and when one of them left another three came and sat and listened. And then I remembered the danger of being caught not only out of bed, but out of my room, and nervously I said I had to go. I asked what school they went to, wondering if I would see them at mine the next day but Jason said with a smile, 'Oh, we don't go to school.'

The following night only Jason was on the other side of the door when we started talking. He was very relaxed and friendly and managed to persuade me to open the door. I could only just reach the top bolt on tip-toe to push it back, and the lower one was slightly rusty and took several attempts. I was worried about opening the door, but Jason seemed very happy to talk quietly and sit on his side, and for me to sit on mine. I appreciated the warmth that came from his house.

'You'll be wondering about my eye,' said Jason matter-of-factly, almost as soon as we were both able to see each other properly. The passageway on his side of the house was warmly lit but his face was still in shadow. He moved so I could look at his eye properly and I could see that it was very dark but flecked with yellow stuff.

'Something happened to it before I can ever remember,' he said. 'I think it got poked with something very sharp and it got infected. I can see through it, though, in a way.'

'Oh,' I said. 'Does it hurt?' I was trying to appear matter-of-fact and as though it was quite an everyday thing to see.

'No, it doesn't hurt at all. It seems quite normal to me . . .'

At that moment we both heard somebody coming up the stairs behind him. Sarah appeared and she seemed pleased to find us there. She came and sat down next to Jason.

'I was explaining about my eye,' he said.

'Take a proper look into it,' said Sarah. 'It seems to go down and down forever.'

So that there was full light on his face he turned back to his house and I moved slightly inside it as well. I looked down into his eye and Sarah was right. The strange flecks were actually golden in the light, and the blackness was mottled and gave an odd suggestion of depth.

'So, what can you see through it?' I asked.

'When I look through both eyes at once I can see through and around things. But if I just look through my funny eye,' he said, closing his good one, 'I can see amazing things. I can see great battles, and monsters, and castles and huge ships on stormy seas.'

'That's rubbish,' I protested.

'You don't have to believe me.'

'Prove it,' I found myself taunting him.

'How can I? You can't see through my eye. And you wouldn't want me to poke yours so that it turns the same as mine.'

'I believe him,' said Sarah. 'Because he tells me what he sees, and he doesn't describe normal things, not like they'd be in real life; it's all magical and bright and gorgeous.'

She seemed proud of him, and I didn't want to argue so I said I'd believe him too if he told me what he could see.

Jason seemed a little annoyed that I doubted him, but he obviously relished the opportunity to tell us a story. He closed his good eye and said:

'I can see a country that's rocky and barren and nobody appears to live there except lizards, and scorpions. And then, one day a beautiful river appears and it slowly carves out the land to create mountains, hills and valleys. It breaks up the rocks and seeps into the dust and creates soil that allows grasses to grow. And then there are flowers, and slowly trees appear and whole forests. The soil becomes dark and rich, and the land is so lush that animals move in to it, and birds live there. Then men and women arrive and build huts and grow food, and keep the animals. But the river has even greater ambitions. It flows over and through the rock in the most intricate and cunning ways, and it creates beautiful buildings with great halls and tapered towers. It makes roads and pathways like mazes between the buildings, and a whole wonderful city is created. Other men and women are then able to come to the city and they make wonderful things in exchange for the food that others grow. Some work with metals and make horseshoes and nails while others make clocks and watches. Those that make cloth either produce sacks or fine clothes, and the people who work with glass make bottles for beer or perfume. Everyone is busy and useful and happy. The river is tired from all of its exertions and slowly and lazily flows in a course through a land that does not change for years on end.

'And then, over a period of time, the sun seems to glow stronger in the sky, and brighter, and almost unbearable. The crops dry and wither and the river flows low in its bed. But it isn't the sun that is causing the drought; without warning a golden, flame-breathing dragon suddenly swoops down out of the sky and seeks to destroy everything with flame. The people cry out in terror and are amazed to see the river rush up from its course to help them.

'A battle commences between the dragon and the river, but all the people can see of the great fight are vast swathes of mist that churn and swirl all around them. There is a deafening roaring and the noise of water rushing and hissing, that goes on all day, and at night the sky and surrounding countryside is lit-up by glowing lights that move and dance slowly all around; now to the north, then to the south, then east, then west . . .

'And then suddenly all goes quiet and the people are at a loss to know exactly who had won—the dragon or the river. It takes days for the mists to clear, and the people fear the worst. Finally the mists thin and they can see that the dragon has disappeared. The river, though is only a fraction the size that it had once been. It has won, but at a great cost to itself.'

Jason's story was finished, and I realised that there were now another five or six children in the passageway with us. We all clapped Jason and insisted on another story, but he said that the next story would have to be on another night. He explained, as though he understood my situation, that I had to go back into my grandparents' house. The other children ran off and I said good-night to Sarah and Jason. I closed the door after them and then slid back the bolts on my side; I didn't want my grandparents to discover that I'd opened the door. I listened, but couldn't hear Jason and Sarah do the same with the bolts on their side of the door.

The next night the children were waiting for me, and I opened the door without thinking about it. Straightaway Jason closed his good eye and told us another story. As he talked I found myself staring at his strange eye. It was very hard making myself look at something else in case I appeared rude.

'This time I can see a very old lady who is living in a very old house with a thatched roof that hides most of the upstairs windows, as though the place was in need of a haircut. It is a big house, and as the old woman doesn't want to live there on her own she looks after children who don't have any parents. They are all living together very happily when, one day, a large man in expensive clothes comes and knocks loudly and rudely at their door. He tells them that he's bought the land that their house is built on and that they will have to leave.

'The poor old woman tells the man that she has nowhere to go. The big man, though, says that he doesn't care. He says that their house is old and ugly and falling apart, and that he plans to knock it down and build something ugly and new in its place. And then he will find people to live there who'll pay him much more rent than the old woman could ever afford. He says that they have to leave the very next morning.

'Well, the old woman and the children don't know what to do. They go to bed and cry themselves to sleep. The house, though, is not sleeping. It never really sleeps; it just dozes year after year. It breathes in once at night, and out in the morning, which is when the people inside hear its timbers creaking.

'The old house waits until everyone inside is in their deepest sleep, and then it gets up. It lifts its walls at the edges like a girl might lift a dress that she doesn't want to drag along the ground. The night is at its darkest and the house walks as carefully as it can, as far as it is able, so as to be off the land that the horrible man has bought. When it feels that it is safe the house lets down its walls and sits back down again. As it does so the creaking of its timbers are especially loud and the old woman wakes up. She looks out of the window and there is just a little light appearing in the east. As the sun makes its way up to the horizon she can see that the view from her window has changed and she rubs her eyes in disbelief. By the time the sun creeps over the edge of the earth she knows what had happened.'

Once again I was enthralled by Jason's story, but as soon as he had finished my nerve began to desert me and I insisted I had to go back.

'No. Come with us,' Jason said. 'We'll go downstairs and out into the street. We'll play games and I might tell another story.'

I shook my head and he turned to the others:

'You go on out. I'll see you all in the street.'

Once they had gone he turned to me:

'I'm going to tell another story that I can see through my funny eye.' He closed his good eye again. 'It's going to be about flying on the back of a giant dragonfly, and going down to a garden and discovering that either the flowers and the grasses are as tall as trees, or . . .'

'But I can't come and play,' I said. 'It's late and I'll get into so much trouble if I'm caught out of bed.'

Sarah was still in the passageway, waiting for Jason, and had been listening.

'But tomorrow,' she said, 'You will have to come down and play with us outside.'

'I can't,' I replied. 'But it would be great if you'd come up here again.'

'No,' said Jason. 'Tomorrow we're having a party. You'll have to come down.'

'What time will it be?'

'After you've gone to bed, I expect,' he said, and there was a mocking tone in his voice.

'It will be a proper party,' Sarah said. 'You'll be formally invited.'

'Well, that's different,' I replied. 'If it's a proper party then I'm sure I'll be allowed to come. As long as it's not too late.'

I closed the door after them and slid back the bolts. Once again I listened but Jason and Sarah did not lock the door on their side. In my room I hung my dressing gown up on the back of the door and took off my slippers before getting into bed. As I lay there, feeling sleep approach, my great fear was that the party would be starting too late and my grandparents would forbid me to go. As I lay there worrying I could hear the other children out in the street again and I didn't dare look out of the window at them.

When the morning came the first thing I thought of was the party. I got myself washed and dressed and downstairs in time for the post to arrive, but there was nothing addressed to me. When I came home from school that afternoon there had been nothing in the second post either, and I told myself that the invitation would probably be delivered by hand. It was a shame that it would not give my grandparents much time to make any arrangements, but I would only be going next door, after all. We had dinner, and soon it was time for me to go up to bed. My grandparents could tell that I was upset about something, but I didn't feel able to explain what the problem was. I couldn't tell them that the children next door were inviting me to a party because I would have had to explain how I'd met them, and that would have resulted in trouble for me. I was upset with my new friends because they seemed to have forgotten all about inviting me.

I had been in bed for a few minutes, feeling sad and angry, when I heard them in the street again. At first I refused to get up and look out of the window; I hid under my bedclothes, but I couldn't stop imagining them out there without me. I wondered if there was actually a party, or whether they were simply playing as before. Perhaps, I thought, it had been cancelled. I made myself get up and look, knowing that either way I would still feel thoroughly wretched.

I was distraught. They *were* having a party. The children were all dressed up in outlandish costumes and were playing games and dancing. There were many coloured lights, like little lanterns, and there was bunting and streamers, and some of the children had sparklers. It seemed amazing that they were actually having a proper, organised party out in the road!

It occurred to me to check the door between my grandparents house and theirs. I put on my dressing gown and slippers and, once I was sure that there was nobody about, I crept out into the passage. Behind the curtain I was surprised to see that the door was wide open. I didn't have time to wonder how it had been opened from my side, because in the light from their passageway I could see an envelope on the floor.

I picked it up and felt the thick textured paper it was made from. The envelope was the colour of cream and I noticed that it was addressed to me in very flowing, violet handwriting. I opened it as carefully as I could, not wanting to tear it too much, but eager to get inside.

The invitation was written in the same script and as I ran my finger over it I could feel that it was raised, like the company name on my father's business cards. It looked as though they had actually gone to the trouble of printing my name on it! And I wasn't just invited to any old party; it was a 'Special Fancy Dress Party'. I was overjoyed, and looked up to see Jason in the passageway before me, with Sarah standing just behind him. He was dressed as a kind of clown, but in black and white. Today I'd probably recognise him as a Pierrot, but then he just looked very odd. He also had a patch over his good eye which seemed, somehow, to even up his odd eyes. Sarah was dressed as a princess, wearing a large gauzy dress and a tiara in her hair. She had an animal on the end of a lead, but I couldn't tell if it was a dog or a cat.

'So you're coming down?' asked Jason, as though he was worried I might not agree to do so.

It was the invitation in my hand that persuaded me it would be all right. I was about to walk forward when I thought, 'But I don't have a costume!'

'Come in your pyjamas and dressing gown,' said Jason with a laugh. 'There are already half a dozen princesses, and three cowboys, but nobody has thought to come as though they're dressed for bed!'

We went down the passageway of panelled, polished wood which reflected the lights from the chandelier on the landing. When we were under it, at the head of the stairs, I could see that lights were blazing through the open doors of all the bedrooms. Inside them I saw more polished wood, patterned wallpapers and heavy, coloured materials. It was such a beautiful house that I wanted to explore it all, but Jason and Sarah were already bounding down the stairs and calling me after them.

I followed them down the richly-patterned stair carpet that flowed to the hall where there was another chandelier, but this time all the lights in it were different colours. A grandfather clock was chiming the hour in a slow, even, mellow tone, and I was surprised to be able to count all the way up to ten. I hadn't realised what time it was, but I decided that it was now too late to return.

I walked with the children into a kitchen where there was a table laden with sweet-looking party food. The room was lit by numerous little candles that reflected and danced off copper pans that hung from the ceiling, and from real crystal glasses that were presumably set out for us to use. An open fire burnt in a grate and I wondered that anyone would have such a thing in a kitchen today. It seemed so old fashioned, though comfortably so.

We went out the door and though there was a small garden, the party had been organised, as I had seen, out on the street itself. The children looked around and saw me and there was a cheer that made me feel quite important. A couple of them lit roman candles and sparks cascaded out and onto the road where they bounced away. I was worried that my grandparents would hear them, and come and investigate, but I had an invitation in my hand that actually had my name printed on it.

I joined in the game they were playing, although I wasn't sure I understood what it was and I was pleased to see that it was coming to some kind of an end. Then a new one was started and Jason explained it; we all stood in two long parallel rows with a partner opposite. Between us we held a long willow stick and the couple at one end lifted theirs high and ran down the outside of the rows holding the stick above our heads. The taller children had to duck to let them past and there was a lot of laughter. The first two joined on the end and we all moved forward until it was our turn to do the same. When the smaller children ran back with their willow stick over everyone else's heads we all had to duck and there was yet more laughing. And then there was more than one pair running back down the outside as we moved forward, and it all sped up until we were all running forwards and backwards, under and over, in one great ecstatic movement. When, eventually and inevitably, somebody tripped over, the whole thing fell apart and we collapsed on top of each other, screaming with delight. The fact that we were all rolling about in the middle of the road did not seem to be a problem at all.

There were street lights at even intervals, but the party was really lit by a moon that I was sure was now absolutely full, and seemed to get bigger and bigger as the party progressed. The next game was one I knew; musical statues. Then word went around that we would be eating the party food after a game of Blind Man's Buff. I was pleased that I thought I knew that game as well, but theirs was different from the version I had played before. In theirs, we played within a large oval that was drawn on the street in chalk by Jason. We were all told that we must not cross the chalk line or we would be out of the game. A child was blindfolded and ran around trying to catch the rest of us, just as I expected. However, when they had caught someone, that child had to stand still while the blindfolded one kissed them on the lips and had to identify who they had kissed. If they were right they went and chose a prize from a table laden with brightly coloured parcels and could leave the game. If they were wrong everyone chanted 'Blind eyes, blind lips, never again will you be kissed', and they left the oval but didn't get a prize. Whatever the result, they had to pass the blindfold over to the person they'd caught and it started again.

I started to play the game quite light-heartedly and then realised that I only knew Jason and Sara, and that if I was caught and blindfolded and managed to catch anyone it was unlikely that I'd be able to correctly identify them. This worried me, as did the possibility of catching a boy and having to kiss them, which hadn't happened yet but filled me with dread. I imagined there would be some horrible chant attendant upon that outcome.

I must not have appeared to be enjoying myself as much as the others, because I was grimly determined not to be caught. I played the game well and the numbers of participants decreased, but each time another chalk line was drawn within the ones before the oval became smaller and smaller. Whenever the blindfolded person was close to going over the line they were pushed back inside by those who were out, accompanied by the bizarre shout 'Indigo!'

Inevitably I was caught, despite my best efforts. I was glad that at least the person in the blindfold was a girl. She was tall and pretty and though embarrassed, I didn't mind her kissing me. She guessed my name incorrectly and left the oval sadly. I was now very worried, and I decided that my only hope was not to catch anyone . . . I stumbled around ineptly. I swept my hands out before me slowly enough, I hoped, to let anyone close get away. Twice I nearly left the oval and was pushed back in with cries of 'Indigo!' And then I managed to catch another child.

I was sure it was a girl; my hands had touched the generous material of a dress. As the others had done before me I felt for her face, we drew closer and I kissed her lips. I remembered long afterwards that they were soft and that she smelt of honey. I only knew Sarah's name and so I said it out loud, and there was a cheer. I removed the blindfold and I was so relieved to see that she was standing there before me. My heart leapt and I passed her the blindfold. I ran happily over to the table and chose a gift; a large one wrapped in red paper.

I was about to open the present, as all the other winners had obviously been doing, when I looked back and saw Jason deliberately allow Sarah to catch him. It was quite obvious, and I thought it very strange until I realised that all of the catching, despite appearances, was probably arranged; all of the children, apart from myself, had allowed themselves to be caught by a friend they liked (or, perhaps, objected to least.) It worried me that I hadn't understood any of this, but I was pleased that somehow I had got through it.

Back in the oval Sarah kissed Jason and shouted out my name. There was a great deal of laughter from the other children, along with the chant 'Blind eyes, blind lips, never again will you be kissed!' Now I was very confused; how could she have forgotten that I was already out? I mean, I was the one who had caught her!

Sarah walked out of the oval, apparently quite happy, leaving Jason standing there looking angry.

Sara came up to the table and I wondered if she had misunderstood the game and was hoping to take a present as well. I was about to explain the rules to her but she said with a determined smile: 'You must leave now.'

'Why?'

'Because Jason will want revenge. This is his party.'

'I don't understand.'

'No, and don't ask me to explain because I can't. Jason's the only one who knows everything. *It's his party*.'

I turned and looked up at my bedroom window, which was dark. There were no lights in any of the windows of my grandparents' house.

'You need to go,' she said. 'Now. Come into the house; we'll go back through the door and you'll have to lock it afterwards from your side.'

She led me away by the hand and I noticed that the game of Blind Man's Buff had restarted, and already Jason had caught someone. Sara's fear was infectious, though.

'We'll tell Jason we're sorry,' I suggested as I ran with her. 'He'll have to forgive us.'

'He'll know. His eye will show him exactly what we've done, and what we were going to do. You can't escape his eye.'

We ran around the house and into the kitchen where the lights of the little candles still danced around in the reflective surfaces of glass and copper. I looked at the party food longingly as we passed, and I slowed down. I dearly wanted to stay, but Sarah pulled me into the hallway and once again, as we entered, the grandfather clock chimed slowly, as if trying to detain me. I didn't have time to count, but the dial showed that somehow three hours had passed. I was pulled around to the bottom of the stairs and we started to climb up to the brightly-lit landing. I was aware that, though Sarah was a little older and bigger than me, I could probably free myself if I wanted to, and go back down to Jason and try and make friends with him.

There was a sudden loud shout from down below and fear coursed through me. I allowed Sarah to pull me again down the passageway at the end of which was the open doorway to my grandparents' dark house. As we ran towards it I could hear Jason leaping up the stairs behind us. He was no longer shouting and that worried me all the more.

Sarah pushed me through the door and slammed it shut behind me. She implored me to push back the bolts on my side. I reached up to close the top one but the door was wrenched open again and I nearly fell into their passageway. Jason was standing there trying to control his emotions.

Sarah tried to close the door but he wouldn't let her. Nevertheless, he didn't cross over the threshold into my grandparents' house. I could do nothing but tremble and hope that he might calm down.

'I'm sorry,' I said, 'For whatever I've done wrong. I don't know what it is. I want to be friends.'

'You're no friend of mine,' he said with a deep-seated rage. The mottled flecks in his bad eye seemed to be moving around, and the darkness within it pulsated. I couldn't help but look at it and be horrified. It appeared to be independent of Jason, struggling to escape, but trapped within him.

I was shaking, wondering what would happen next, when Sarah hit Jason in the chest and shouted, 'You're a beast! I hate you. I hate your games, and your party, and your house.'

He looked down at her and smiled horribly.

'Go with him, then,' he said, nodding towards me with an expression of disdain.

Her reaction was to burst into tears and run back off down the corridor.

Jason turned his head and watched Sarah go. When she was out of sight he turned to me and appeared to tap his strange eye with his finger. He then used that finger to point at me, and without saying anything else he shut the door. The warm, coloured light disappeared and I was in the darkness and the cold. I heard the bolts shoot back into position on the other side of the door, and then nothing else at all.

I hastily put the bolts back on my side of the door and went to bed. I lay in dread of any sound, not from my grandparents (to whom I longed to explain and apologise and confide), but from out in the street. The full moon was still shining, illuminating my room, and I seemed to lie there for hours, waiting.

I could only think of Jason and his eye, and how he said that he could see through and around things. I knew that a bolted door and a curtain were no barrier to him seeing me.

And then I remembered that someone must have unbolted the door between the two houses only that evening.

When sleep finally claimed me I dreamed of Jason, and of his eye. In dreams afterwards I would never meet Sarah, or their other friends. I would always be running from Jason and his eye down passageways which became progressively darker and colder. And at some point flight would give way the sensation of falling; falling ever downwards into something even darker, and colder, and more terrible.

The Restaurant San Martín

The Restaurant San Martín in Mendoza did not appear to have changed at all in its ninety-five year history. It was still richly decorated and plushly upholstered in a hopelessly antique style, and Ernesto Galman revered it. He liked anything old and unaltered that suggested stability and quality, and the restaurant exemplified all of these virtues. He was amazed that it was so well preserved, but it was dark inside, which hid some of the tattiness. He enjoyed the fact that the staff had unfashionable pinafores and deferential manners. The cutlery and crockery were tired and past their best, but they were reassuringly heavy.

On the first Monday of every month Ernesto Galman would take the early bus into Mendoza and visit his various clients. He would snatch lunch without much thought, depending on where he was in the city, but before going to catch the bus back to San Juan he would always visit the Restaurant San Martín. He would arrive there at any time between two-thirty and five o'clock, but would always sit at the same table. The position was, he had long ago decided, the best in the establishment. Others would probably disagree for only two people could sit at the table comfortably and there was no sight of the outside world through the impressive etched glass windows. It was dark there and commanded a very restricted view of the interior of the restaurant, which was why, he realised, it was usually free. But that was how he liked it; the modern world did not intrude.

Ernesto Galman was a man of habit and not only was his choice of table always the same, but so was his selection of refreshment. He would order one of San Martín's home-made white chocolate *alfajors* (which were so much better than those you might buy at a kiosk in a foil or wax-paper wrapper). It would be served with a thick yellow cream. If his wife had been aware of this indulgence she would not have particularly minded, but he kept the visits to the restaurant a secret from her and from everyone else. He was not ashamed of going there, but the fact that nobody else knew anything about it gave an especial savour not only to the *alfajor*, but also to the glass of *esperidina* that he would always drink with it. The half hour that he would spend at the Restaurant San Martín would be entirely for himself; he would have no thought of his family, the business, or any other concerns or cares. His real self-indulgence was to step off the streets of the busy city and lose himself in a comfortable and perhaps unreal world, and he had been doing so since he first discovered the place in the late 'sixties.

And the particulars of each visit were almost identical, right up until one Monday in the later 'nineties. On that afternoon he entered the restaurant as usual, started to walk towards his table, but then saw that somebody was already sitting there; a woman. It was rare, but not unknown, for another customer to have taken the table and his reaction was to quietly leave and return later. The staff were always quick to respond to new customers, sometimes opening the door to them as they were about to walk in and if he had to leave he normally did so with some embarrassment, play-acting an excuse for his retreat. This time a waitress he didn't recognise had seen him and was walking towards him with a welcoming smile. He patted his pockets in the hope that he would appear to have left something in a shop or on a bus. He was able to go back outside with some of his dignity intact.

Galman decided to head up towards the Cerro de la Gloria. He didn't know how far he would get, but after twenty minutes, he resolved, he would stop and turn back. The woman sitting at his table would have had time to finish the glass set before her, and Ernesto reasoned that his *alfajor* and accompanying *esperidina* would taste all the sweeter for the wait. It was still early, and he could catch a later bus back to San Juan.

Ernesto Galman had first visited the Restaurant San Martín when, aged twenty, he had been given the position of representative for the Galman Conserve Company. In an attempt to find his first sale of jams and pickles he had ventured tentatively inside the restaurant and was shown down to the kitchens in the basement. There he found a very elegant blonde woman arguing with a stout, bald and wrinkled old man. Galman was received with disdain by the man, although the woman seemed relieved that he had arrived. The tension between this odd couple was palpable. Galman had offered to return another day, but they both insisted he stay and state his business. He could soon see that he was being used as a pawn in some power struggle between them; the toad-like old fellow, with great solemnity, asked to try each of the samples on small slices of crustless white bread. The man considered each with profound concentration and insisted on comparing them to the brands that they were currently serving and cooking with. The woman watched disdainfully and after much deliberation the man agreed that Galman's was a superior product. He gave his name as Ocampo and walked away, telling Galman that Señora Goyeneche would arrange the details of their order.

The young representative was relieved to be able to depart, and not simply because the atmosphere in the kitchen had been so unpleasantly charged. He had previously been very uncertain about his position in the company; he had felt some pressure because he was not simply a new employee; he was the grandson of Jorge Galman who had founded the business many decades ago. For young Ernesto to be given the Mendoza Province was preferential treatment, and he wanted to live up to the expectations his family had for him.

Thirty years later he remembered that meeting with Señor Ocampo and Señora Goyeneche clearly. They had both made an odd impression on him, and in Galman's eyes they gained a certain mystery because he had only ever seen them again once or twice over the intervening years, and never together. Galman did the mental arithmetic and decided that he had revisited the restaurant something like three hundred and sixty times. That meant three hundred and sixty *alfajors* and three hundred and sixty glasses of *esperidina*. It wasn't until he had to stop for breath on the way up to the Cerro de la Gloria that he realised that his calculations had to be incorrect. When he had first been given the position of representative for the Mendoza Province he may have visited the restaurant more than once a month. And he had somehow managed to forget the three years when he had worked in Buenos Aires, employed in the more significant position of representative for the capital. Then he had been given a small office and had lived in the city, and had no reason to visit Mendoza at all. Over his whole time with Galman's Conserves, though, he decided once a month would be a reasonable average. He liked order, and three hundred and sixty seemed to him to be an orderly number.

But then, he considered, there had been those years of change and upheaval. In 1980 Jorge Galman died and his son Roberto (Ernesto's father) had taken over the Galman Conserve Company. Sadly, within that year, Roberto had also passed away. Aged only thirty-two Ernesto had inherited the family business and moved back to San Juan where the preserves were made.

These memories occupied him all the way back to the restaurant. As he had turned around with the views of the city from the Cerro de la Gloria not quite attained, he had thought for a brief instant of the woman at his table, and had wondered briefly what he would do if she was still there. He dismissed the idea in a moment, for although some people did often wait, taking their time over food or drink, most seemed to come and go quite quickly. There never seemed to be many, like him, who were inclined to linger in the Restaurant San Martín.

It seemed even dimmer inside the restaurant when he returned. Automatically he walked towards his table and was annoyed to see that it was still taken. It appeared to be the same woman sitting there. In the gloom he found himself a little confused.

He would have been content to leave again, to return once more a little later, but ill-luck meant that he was greeted by the same waitress he had seen earlier.

'Señor Galman,' she said, although he was sure she had not been working there on any of his previous visits. 'So good to see you. Your white chocolate *alfajor* and a glass of *esperidina*?'

'Yes, thank you.'

Was he such a regular that a new waitress would have been told who to expect, what he would like and exactly what his order would be? He was suddenly aware, perhaps for the first time, that visiting the restaurant as regularly as he did was not so much a habit as an eccentricity. Had he been able to leave once more he would have done so and would never have considered it at all odd. But being suddenly confronted by his eccentricity he realised that he required it for the sake of his soul and he could not explain why. This was the first serious threat to it in thirty years and he did not know how to react. He felt hot and uncomfortable in his suit, and his tie seemed to be choking him. He wondered if he was unwell.

He was still standing, panicking, when he noticed that the waitress had already set his food and drink down at his table. The woman was sitting opposite his accustomed place.

'Please join me, Señor Galman,' the woman said simply. It was then that he realised who she was: Señora Goyeneche. Her wonderfully deep, velvet-like voice went right through him.

Ernesto wondered how long he had been standing there, not noticing the passing of time. He felt terribly self-conscious, as though not only the woman but the whole restaurant was watching him. There was no way that he could leave now, not if he wanted to return next month, or the month after that.

'Thank you,' he said, and he did as she had asked him.

'You came in earlier and then left.'

So, he had been seen.

'Yes, I realised I'd forgotten something.'

'I didn't take it personally. I've been waiting here for you. It's nice to have company.'

'I always sit at this table.'

'I know. It's the most private. That's why I sit here as well.'

'But I've never seen you in the dining area of the restaurant before?'

She shrugged.

'You are Señora Goyeneche?' he asked. 'We first met in the kitchens, thirty years ago.'

'Is it really that long?' she replied, with a lift of an immaculate eyebrow. She smiled, and he realised that it had been an ungallant remark because it inferred that he knew something of her age. He inevitably attempted the calculation, knowing that when they had met she had to have been at least five or ten years older than him. Even in the poor light he could see that she was still very beautiful, but was she fifty like him, or sixty even?

He picked up his drink to cover his embarrassment. Normally he would savour the aroma of orange, taking small sips, but now he gulped some back and turned immediately to his cake. He felt very uncomfortable and decided to finish his refreshment as quickly as he could and leave. He picked up the small spoon with which he always ate his *alfajor* and made a start on it.

'You appear hungry,' said the woman.

He looked up, startled, and saw that she was looking at him with a smile of amusement.

'I'm, sorry,' he stammered. 'I hope you don't mind me sitting here. The waitress assumed . . .'

'No, it's not a problem. As I said, I've been waiting for you.'

'For me?'

'You are Ernesto Galman.'

'Yes.'

'You own and run the Galman Conserve Company,' she added.

'I do.'

'I like your jams,' she replied very evenly, giving nothing away. 'And your pickles.'

'We only use local fruit,' he said earnestly. 'We make it in San Juan. The melt water comes down and helps us grow some of the best fruit in the whole of South America. This is why Galman's Preserves are so good; they could not be made anywhere else in the world.'

'I'm sure,' she replied indulgently.

He regretted his little sales pitch. It was beside the point. She had sought his company for a reason.

'And once a month you come to Mendoza, and eat in this restaurant,' she said.

'Exactly so!'

'It is fate that has brought us together, you know.'

'Fate?'

'I think so.'

'But why?'

'Consider every little thing that has shaped your life, the smallest decisions that you have or haven't taken. At this moment you might have been anywhere in the world, doing anything. And it's the same for me. But we've come together here, right now, at this time, and in this place.'

'But you have something to do with this restaurant. And me, I visit once a month. It's not surprising that we meet, especially if you have been waiting for me.'

Her face seemed to fall slightly, and he could see that he had said the wrong thing again. He attempted to make up for it:

'Perhaps we were always meant to meet, but for some reason we've been kept apart by circumstances.'

'Until today.'

'Exactly.'

She nodded thoughtfully: 'I think you may be right. Perhaps fate has kept us apart until today. You think there is some design? Some intelligence moving us around like pieces on a chessboard?'

'Perhaps,' he said, not believing it for one moment. He took the opportunity to eat a mouthful more of *alfajor*.

'Will you join me in a glass of champagne?' she asked.

'I don't know if I should. It's very kind of you to ask, but I've a long bus journey, and there's a chance I might fall asleep.'

'Is that a bad thing?'

'Yes, because I find travelling very stressful.'

'Even after thirty years?'

'It's worse now than ever!'

'You may not know it, but we have had a relationship for thirty years. I think we should celebrate it with champagne.'

'I don't understand.'

'You said that I have something to do with this restaurant. In fact it is mine; I own it,' she said, and with the smallest of movements was able to call forward a waitress. She ordered two glasses of Tattinger champagne.

'Oh. What about Señor Ocampo?'

'When we have tasted our wine I will explain.'

It arrived in long-stemmed glasses and she proposed a toast to their friendship, to which he agreed uncertainly.

'I first met Bernard Ocampo over forty years ago,' she explained. 'I was seventeen and ambitious and everybody told me that I was beautiful. I took a job as waitress in this very restaurant, but Mercedes Goyeneche was meant to be the name of an actress, not a waitress! Now, Bernard was a successful businessman and politician here. He was expanding his empire into Buenos Aires and intended to make movies. He had all the contacts, and he was rich. He discovered me, and Mercedes Goyeneche was going to be his first star. But he had enemies and his business and political rivals combined to ruin him; he lost everything. At the last minute he transferred ownership of the restaurant and this building to me, and kept it out of their hands.'

'He wasn't able to build his business back up?'

'Yes, slowly. He has some power again, but he is not the man he was.'

'And you kept the restaurant?'

'Yes. I would have transferred it back to him but he did something to hurt me so badly that I refused to. He's never forgiven me. And he has an attachment to this place.'

Galman wasn't certain that in the dim light she hadn't shuddered as she had used the word 'attachment'.

'I wouldn't normally discuss such matters with a stranger,' she pointed out.

'Well, I have been coming here for thirty years . . . But I wasn't quite sure who I had to thank for the continued orders, and the refreshment. But now I see that it is you.'

The champagne had relaxed him. He licked his finger and picked up the crumbs of his cake from his plate. As he transferred them to his mouth he realised how uncultured he must appear.

'Señor Ocampo does still have a minority share in this place. You have him to thank for the fact it hasn't changed in all these years.'

'I'm glad of that. I'm wary of change. When I took over my family business I was afraid of changing anything for fear of it leading to failure. I allowed myself to be counselled by older and wiser heads. For nearly a decade the company stood still and in business that's not always so good. Competitors gained advantages over us and I was at a loss to know what to do. But then people started to value how old-fashioned we were. We stressed that we had been using the same recipe for years, and only selected the best local fruit. Now we are appreciated precisely because we never changed.'

He was worried that again he had said too much about his business. However, that was not the reason why she was shaking her head; 'I'm not sure if keeping everything the same is good for the restaurant.'

'But it is. I love it! Although I'm old-fashioned, I suppose.'

'Nothing has changed here because Señor Ocampo and I will never agree on how to change it. We are sworn enemies,' she said, her gaze penetrating his own eyes. He looked down, embarrassed, and saw that she had put her hand very close to his on the table. He took up his glass and sipped the champagne.

'The world around us changes,' she said.

'It does.'

'It does not get better. It does not get worse. It just changes.'

'The secret is to hold on to the good things, and to embrace changes that are worthwhile. The secret is in being able to identify what is of value, and not simply expedient in the short term.'

'Yours is a philosophy, but my position is not so dignified.'

'I am told that I am too conservative; too unwilling to embrace change.'

'But some things do not need to change . . .'

'I'd like to think so, but perhaps it is inevitable. I'll retire in a few years and pass the company on to my son, Gato. He'll change things. Maybe he'll ruin Galman's Conserves, or maybe it'll expand and he'll export our jams and pickles worldwide. He's already talking about franchising our name.'

'Señor Galman,' she said, not interested in his business. 'I wish to talk to you in private. It is a personal matter.'

'Oh?'

'Will you come to my apartments upstairs? Like the restaurant, they has changed very little in all these years. You might be interested to see them. And the matter I wish to discuss is a rather delicate and personal one.'

He felt uneasy. Being asked upstairs by a woman he didn't know worried him. He had to tell himself that he was an unlikely target for a *femme fatale*. Thirty or forty years ago he was indeed quite a handsome fellow, but he had put on weight, and he knew that he was now a little stooped. This elegant woman had suggested it was a personal matter, but that didn't necessarily mean anything untoward.

'Elegant' was the precise word he decided, following her across the restaurant. Three steps behind he marvelled at her figure and still could not guess at her age. They passed through the door through which the waitresses came and went, and there was a small lobby with a dumb-waiter and stairs leading down to the kitchens. There was also another door which she opened and he was invited into a surprisingly narrow and dilapidated hallway with a rickety staircase. A further door to the busy street was slightly open and she walked over to close it, obviously annoyed.

In the moment that she stood in the thin shaft of glaring sunlight, looking outside suspiciously, he was able to get a better idea of how old she really was. The bright light did not flatter her; he realised that she had to be at least sixty. She slammed it shut and turned to him, forcing a smile. Galman knew from his wife's efforts before the mirror every morning that the judicious application of cosmetics could hide a decade of aging, and Señora Goyeneche had excelled herself in the art. However, in that instant of revealing light the deeper wrinkles had not been hidden and the tone of her skin had been too matt and even. Even with the street door closed, now in semi-darkness, he could see that her eyes and lips were heavily made-up and he knew that much could be masked by that.

He followed Señora Goyeneche as she climbed the stairs, her shoes loud on the uncarpeted treads. She waited at the half-landing for him to catch up and then they climbed to a door on the next floor. She unlocked it and he unwillingly followed her into a very large, dark room that was very comfortably and probably expensively furnished. The heavy damask or brocade curtains were drawn across the windows and swept over the dimly patterned deep-pile carpet. The furniture was ponderous and upholstered in similar fabrics, and even the flock wallpaper seemed to be of a great weight.

She explained:

'As with the restaurant, nothing in here has been changed for many, many years. Señor Ocampo lavished money on this place in the hope that I would become his mistress.'

Galman found himself wanting to know if that had come to pass.

The woman turned on a lamp at a table and from everywhere came hints and reflections of dull gold from gilt mouldings, fittings and decorative features.

She wanted him to look at a photograph in a frame that was standing on the table. It was an old-fashioned studio shot that must have dated to the very early sixties.

Señora Goyeneche appeared to be about twenty in the photograph and she looked stunning. He turned to her and she was smiling at him. She was still the good-looking woman of the photograph, with the same fine bone structure, but he remembered that he had recently seen her in the unforgiving sunlight.

'I am a very uninteresting, vain and shallow woman, Señor Galman.'

He replied that she had to be wrong.

'No, that is what I am. When I was seventeen I was effortlessly slim and beautiful. I was so beautiful that a man I did not know gave me this whole building! I didn't deserve it. I never earned it.

'He couldn't get me into the movies, so I lived a life of idleness. I didn't worry about anything. After his business collapsed he was always worried, afraid of his enemies. He was annoyed that I would not be his mistress; resentful that I had the restaurant and the building. I just lived up here, lazy, indulgent, spending the profits earned downstairs. I never once lifted a finger.'

She walked over to a table on which stood a decanter and glasses. Pouring them both a glass of wine she continued:

'I still wanted to act; to make a name for myself, but I never got a part. I auditioned, but Bernard told me that his enemies were to blame. I think, though, he was trying to be kind. I looked the part, but I just hadn't the talent. It took a long time to accept that. And then I took a lover. . . .'

She looked wistful and Galman wondered if, or when, she would resume her explanation. He could not understand why she wished to share these confidences, or what she wanted him to do. He enjoyed being in her company, though, and found her voice mesmerising. Eventually she continued.

'I became pregnant and Bernard was enraged. I still do not know what happened to my lover, what Bernard did to him.'

'Did Señor Ocampo threaten him?'

She looked Galman straight in the eye: 'Bernard Ocampo isn't the kind of man who threatens anyone. If my lover was lucky then Ocampo will have simply have had him beaten up and driven out of the city. If he was unlucky he will have killed him.'

'Surely not?'

'I know what the man is capable of. He married another woman even younger than me and on his wedding day he had me beaten up as a punishment. I think he hoped I would miscarry my child, but my lovely daughter *was* born alive. I was in the hospital for months and my child was there for many more years. She has grown to be the most beautiful young woman but she is very disabled; incapable of doing anything for herself. She lives as a reminder of my folly and Ocampo's hatred. She mocks me by her beauty and by her youth. She looks just like I did at her age, but her looks are wasted.'

'I am very sorry.'

'Ocampo has designs on her. I have to protect her from him. He no longer desires me because of my age, but she is beautiful and helpless.'

'That is very cruel.'

'After her birth, and my beating, I came home and looked in the mirror. I was not only scarred by what he had done to me, but I had lines around my eyes and my mouth. I had aged. I was horrified and knew I had to do something about it. It was then that I realised there might be some purpose to my wasted life. I decided to dedicate myself to looking young. It became a full-time concern. And today that is all I do. My one and only interest in life is my appearance. I diet meticulously, I exercise, I have a regime of beauty treatment that would tire a Hollywood actress.'

'You have succeeded,' Galman said automatically. He swirled the wine around in his glass but did not want to drink it. He didn't really want to be discussing any of this.

'I still manage to attract younger men,' she said. 'I have a lover at the moment who is so young that he could be your son. In fact, he looks a lot like you!'

'And Señor Ocampo?'

'He suspects. He is insanely jealous. In fact, I am expecting him here at any time. I arranged for word to get to him that my lover is up here with me at the moment.'

'But why? There is only me up here!'

'He will assume that you are my lover.'

'That is ludicrous!'

'Of course it is. My lover is his own son!'

Galman tried to take all of this in. 'But what will he do when he discovers me?'

'He has a gun that he always carries with him.'

'A gun?'

'Yes, he will try to shoot you. And me as well, possibly. But don't worry. Here . . .'

And from a drawer she brought out a silver handgun which she tried to pass to him. He refused to take it.

'There!' she announced. 'I heard the door open downstairs! He will haul himself up here and hope to catch me in your arms.'

'I don't understand why you are doing this.'

'Señor Ocampo will try to kill you,' she said levelly. 'Though not before he has delivered an interminable monologue. It will be kill or be killed.'

Galman had not heard the door open downstairs as Señora Goyeneche had done, but he heard the heavy tread of a man outside of the apartment door. It crashed open a few moments later. In walked Ocampo, elderly and very overweight, sweating profusely and holding before him a black, ugly gun.

'Mercedes!' he bellowed. 'Now I have caught you!'

He looked at Ernesto with pure hatred in his eyes.

'You!' He spat. 'You! You will die.'

He aimed the gun at Ernesto who looked to the woman for help. In a moment her gun was in his hand and he aimed at Ocampo who was letting forth a string of insults but still not pulling the trigger. Ernesto did not know what to do. Was the man really going to shoot him? Should he shoot the man first?

'I will kill you both!' Ocampo was saying, now moving the gun from Galman to the woman and back again. And then the gun was trained on one position in the room because Señora Goyeneche had moved behind Galman and was pressing herself against him. Her hand reached along his arm to his hand as it held out the pistol. He closed his eyes and felt the pressure of her hand over his as Ocampo continued with his threats and insults.

There was a sudden roar as the gun jumped violently in Galman's hand, making him drop it. He opened his eyes only a moment later but already the great bulk of Ocampo lay lifeless on the carpet.

'My God! What shall we do?' he asked helplessly.

The woman was by his side, apparently quite calm.

'I will say he was killed by an intruder.'

'Who? Me?'

She walked over to Ocampo and picked up his fallen gun.

'You are the obvious candidate, I'm afraid. I suppose I will be forced now to shoot you in self defence.'

She lifted the gun, and in a reflex action he stooped and picked up the one he had dropped. He aimed it unsteadily at her.

She smiled:

'But I know that you don't have the strength to pull the trigger. I am so sorry. You are obviously such a nice man.'

He thought that she was probably right and he felt an infinite sadness come over him. He closed his eyes, waiting for her to fire, but like Ocampo she was still talking. Being unable to see her he found it quite easy to put pressure on the trigger. He increased it slowly, unwillingly, and suddenly it went off, jarring his hand again and causing him to drop the weapon for the second time. He waited for the sound to stop echoing around the walls. He waited for her to take a turn at shooting him as if in some old-fashioned duel, but nothing happened. Reluctantly he opened his eyes, expecting her knowing smile to be the last thing he would see but she had fallen back on top of the body of Ocampo.

Galman moved towards her, then backed away. Both of them appeared to be dead but he could not bring himself to touch either of them to feel for a pulse. Besides, the side of the man's head seemed to have been shattered and she had a wound in the centre of her chest. He looked around in vain for a telephone and then realised that he did not want to be found there, to be in any way associated with what had happened. He made himself walk around the bodies before running to the door to the stairs and then bounding down the rickety stairs three steps at a time. The street door would not immediately open but after some desperate scrabbling at the catch he was able to run out into the bright street and kept on running. Later he realised that he must have looked a wild sight, and he wondered how he had found the strength to run all the way up to the Cerro de la Gloria. At the monument dedicated to the Army of the Andes he plunged off into the trees and buried himself in the undergrowth. He hid his face in his hands and hummed loudly as a child might do so as not to confront what had happened.

Much later that night he made his way wearily down to the bus station. He felt weak and was beyond caring about himself. As he waited for an early morning bus to take him back to San Juan he remembered that his fingerprints would be on the gun that had shot Ocampo and his mistress and it seemed inevitable that he would be found by detectives. The prints would be on the glass that she had given him, he realised, but he decided not to dwell on that. He looked around him, wondering from which direction the police would approach to apprehend him.

He remembered that the waitress had seen him with the woman. So, they would have a witness. He looked down at his hands and knew that the police could do tests which would show that he had recently fired a gun.

Still the police did not come for him, and finally the bus arrived and he pulled himself up the steps and found a seat.

Señora Galman called a doctor to her husband the following day when he refused to get out of bed, but the doctor could find nothing wrong with him. Galman was tempted to explain that he was simply waiting for the authorities to knock at his door, but a feeble desire for self-preservation prevented him.

The following day Galman did get up, although he refused to go into work. He decided that he would retain some dignity by presenting a decent appearance to the police when they inevitably appeared. Señora Galman was pleased to see him shaved, bathed and dressed, but her patience was already at an end and she berated him for his apparent laziness.

On the third day he went in to work to escape his wife's questions and complaints. The police might as well find him there, he reasoned, as anywhere else. And so he found himself very half-heartedly back in his old routine, killing time.

As more days passed he hardly dared think that he might have got away with it, but after a couple of weeks he awoke one morning and decided that he might possibly be able to get on with his old life for a while. And after a few more days he found himself savouring every moment that he was a free man because it seemed inevitable that they would come for him in time. Still the days passed as though nothing had ever happened, and still he waited.

In almost every waking moment he replayed the events in the woman's apartment in his mind, trying to make sense of them and after a while they became almost unreal. He was reminded of when he had taken a school examination and had wanted to write the simple word 'extranjero'; the more that he looked at it the more unlikely, bizarre and meaningless it had become. As the weeks now passed he did not once forget what had happened, but he could not quite believe that it had been real; that it had happened to him. It seemed too outrageous and unbelievable.

After the first couple of nights he did manage to sleep his full eight hours, but invariably awoke recalling odd details of dreams relating to what had happened in Mendoza. Strangely, they seemed mainly to be of the staircase he had climbed to Señora Goyeneche's apartment. In his dreams he was ascending or descending at random, in the dark, fearful of what he was about to encounter on the next floor.

At the end of the month it was assumed by everybody that Ernesto Galman would be travelling once again to Mendoza but he knew that it would be impossible. To forestall any questions he waited until the day before travelling there to announce his decision. He suggested that his son, Gato, go into the city on his behalf.

Galman took the day off work and went for a drive in the countryside with his wife. He talked to her about retirement and his hopes that their son would soon be able to take over the business. He explained that he wanted a smooth transtion so that young Gato would not find the responsibility suddenly dropped onto his desk as he had himself. His wife was pleased because, whatever had been wrong with Ernesto the previous month had taken its toll. He looked older than before, more haggard, and if he had lost some weight she wasn't sure that it was necessarily a good thing.

It was three months later that Ernesto Galman overheard his son mentioning the Restaurant San Martín to a man in their sales department. It took a considerable effort to ask, as casually as he could, what the reason was.

'I noticed they'd stopped ordering from us,' Gato said. 'So I visited them last week.'

'Is it still there?'

'Yes. And a horrible old place it is too. I had to go and talk to some old fellow deep in the bowels of their kitchens.'

'In the kitchens?'

His son shrugged: 'Some joyless old fellow called Ocampo, although he laughed when I said who I was. He said he remembered you and laughed unpleasantly. I didn't like him at all.'

Galman could hardly breathe. The room spun around him and he had to sit down. His son brought him a glass of water and then helped him back into his office. Galman stared at his telephone for a long time before looking in his contacts book and picking up the receiver.

'Señor Ocampo, please,' he asked when it was answered. His mouth was dry and he was shaking. As soon as he heard the man's voice he was going to put the phone down.

'He can't come to the phone,' the voice said. 'Can I take a message?'

'No, no message, but . . .'

'Yes?'

'Can I speak to the owner, please. Señora . . .'

'Señora Goyeneche?'

'Yes,' he said shaking so much that he could not keep it out of his voice, and feeling so weak he could hardly keep his grip on the telephone.

'You need another number,' said the voice, and read it out to him slowly, insisting he read it back so that he had it correctly. It was such an effort to keep in control that when he put down the receiver he slumped onto his desk and only after several minutes managed to master himself and his emotions.

The following phone call took even more courage than the first had done. He recognised Señora Goyeneche's wonderfully sultry voice immediately and replaced the receiver with alacrity, without saying anything.

Ernesto Galman did not know what to think. He was stunned. He was also relieved that for a half hour nobody came into his office. He allowed himself to feel a growing certainty that apparently Señora Goyeneche and Señor Ocampo were both alive after all, but his relief was tempered by a confusion over what he had seen happen. He rejoiced that he could not now be charged with murder, but how were they still alive? Somebody must have investigated after he had left and they must have received medical treatment. Why had he not called for the ambulance himself?

When he was checked upon by his son, Galman sent him away. He was thinking the situation through and trying to understand. If both of them were alive, why had they not reported him to the police? None of it made sense, and as the day wore on he became angrier with them, especially Señora Goyeneche who had undoubtedly set him up.

Galman could not concentrate on work, and when he did not eat dinner that evening his wife became concerned for him once more. He went to bed early but was obviously not sleeping. She guessed that his mood was related to his recent illness, but could not account for the relapse. She would have called out the doctor once more, but after a couple of days her husband seemed to have reached an uneasy equilibrium. He did, though, have a tendency to be uncharacteristically short-tempered one minute, and then surprisingly affectionate the next. She was at a loss to understand him because he would not discuss his problems with her.

He knew that there was only one possible way to face his torment, and that was to return to Mendoza and the Restaurant San Martín. He could not quite find the courage to simply take the bus into the city and, besides, if he said he was going there for anything other than work then his wife would want to go with him to do some shopping. And so Galman announced that he wished to make one more trip, for work, at the beginning of the month.

There were storms the night before Ernesto Galman left for the city and he did not sleep well. The next morning dawned overcast and cold but remained dry. The bus journey seemed interminable, but his old customers greeted him warmly, pleased to see him once again. From time to time over the years they had realised it was a little strange that the owner of the company himself visited them, but they all appreciated the personal touch. They were especially saddened to learn that this visit would be his last. He asked after their families and they asked after his; many had already been visited by his son, Gato. Their discussions moved on to politics and sport, they confirmed their orders and he went on his way. At one small café he was persuaded to have a meal as they showed off the talents of their new chef, and he drank a second glass of beer that he had not been meaning to accept. Another old and valued customer refused to let him go on his way without a glass of wine, and it was in good spirits that he decided to walk back towards the bus station. It was, perhaps, too hot to go all that way on foot, he decided, and the drink made him feel a little uncomfortable. Without thinking, he was approaching the Restaurant San Martín. It was only a hundred yards ahead of him on his side of the pavement.

He slowed his steps and looked behind. Visiting the restaurant was the reason he was meant to be in the city, but he had allowed himself to forget this. He wondered, now, whether he shouldn't just return to San Juan and try and forget about it altogether.

To go back and around the whole city block would not add a great deal to his walk, but he wondered if a taxi was a better idea. He moved to the edge of the pavement but in neither direction did there appear to be any. Automatically he was still walking towards the restaurant and so he stopped himself. Another pedestrian bumped into him and called him a fool, which he resented. He felt angry, and then turned the emotion towards the restaurant. He questioned why he was having to change the habits of thirty years to such an extent that he could not even walk down this particular street? He was the one, he reasoned, who had been badly abused in the whole affair. He walked on, though without any great resolution, and just a few feet before the façade of the restaurant he stopped.

It was no longer there. Or, rather, it had changed completely. There seemed to simply be two huge sheets of plate glass behind which was the antiseptic interior of a modern bar. He walked slowly up to it, incredulous. Everything had been ripped out, and the walls, floor and even the ceiling was covered in something like textured stainless steel. It was one big open space, busy with young people. There were flashing screens showing rock musicians posing with guitars and the thud, thud, thud of music that made the huge windows vibrate.

Ernesto Galman looked around to see if he was on the right street. There could be no doubt that the Restaurant San Martín had been gutted and modernised. He stood back and looked at the garish sign that now proclaimed it to be the 'Bar San Martín'.

Before he could register who's arm was through his own, a young woman was pulling him back across the pavement to the door, laughing, and calling him 'Silly Señor Galman' and 'Funny Señor Ernesto'. He had to watch his footing as he was dragged into the bar because he nearly fell over. The music was loud and insistent and the woman had to shout at him.

'We owe all this to you!' she was saying, pulling him towards the bar.

'Señora Goyeneche?' he asked, but knew he was wrong. In the bright interior he could see that this woman was young, her skin almost flawless and obviously free of cosmetics. He remembered that Señora Goyeneche had a daughter but he was sure that there was meant to have been something wrong with her. This lithe young woman was not in the least disabled. He didn't know what to say to her. From behind the bar two champagne flutes were produced and filled.

'This is what we always drink together, isn't it! Drink!' she ordered, and he found himself doing as he was told.

'But who are you?' he managed to shout over the music.

'Silly Señor Galman,' she laughed. 'I am Mercedes! And look, here is my love, Bernard!'

The man approaching them was young and good looking and had a distinct resemblance to Bernard Ocampo. It was as if the years and the excess flesh had fallen off the man. Ernesto found himself awkwardly embraced.

'More wine for Señor Galman!' he bellowed to the young woman, too close to Ernesto's ear.

'But what has happened?' he asked. 'What happened to Mercedes Goyeneche and Bernard Ocampo?'

They both looked amused, raising their eyebrows at one another.

'Not so loud!' said the man, embarrassed. 'There is a secret between us, no?'

Ernesto nodded vigorously. He had forgotten himself. He had somehow hoped that these two might be the couple he had shot. For a moment he had allowed himself to think that the memories had been false, a fiction, or at least misremembered.

As if the man had read his mind he put his arm around Galman and said 'We must talk, upstairs. Bring your drink.'

Galman was escorted by the young man to the door at the back of the bar. Like the restaurant, the hallway had been modernised. The old staircase had been ripped out and replaced by one engineered in steel with disconcerting glass treads. It all seemed lighter and not nearly as narrow as before. He prepared himself for the changes wrought upon the apartment on the first floor, but then asked himself why had he returned at all? And why was he allowing them to lead him up the stairs? He realised that he was shaking, sweating and far too hot.

The apartment, as he guessed, had also been modernised. It was light and airy with just a few items of contemporary and uncomfortable-looking furniture isolated on an expanse of highly-polished light wood-flooring.

'I'm so pleased you came back,' said the man.

'*We're* so pleased,' the woman corrected him.

Ernesto took a mouthful of wine so that he didn't have to say anything, and as he looked around the room the woman refilled his glass with the bottle she had brought up with her.

'You would like an explanation,' she said gravely, and he was able to croak his agreement.

The young man sat down in a chair of steel and leather:

'Ernesto Galman,' the man said, and then frowned. 'Do you not like what we've done to the building?'

'Well,' he started to say, but couldn't think of words that wouldn't be impolite.

'Of course he doesn't,' said the woman, 'but it can never again be how he would like it.'

She walked up to him and pressed her hands over his eyes. She exerted pressure and it was all he could do not to fall backwards. Then she gently let go and they were back in the room as he remembered it from before. Standing in front of him was the original of Mercedes Goyeneche, and sitting down was the Bernard Ocampo that he recognised.

'But how?' he asked frowning so profoundly that the woman laughed at him.

'Señor Galman,' she said. 'You are living right here, right now, are you not?'

She waited for him to nod in agreement before continuing.

'You are on a planet so perfectly balanced in the solar system that it produces not only life on earth, not only human life, but you, personally.'

'How amazing is that?' Ocampo asked him seriously.

Galman nodded, unwillingly because he did not know where this was leading or how it came to explain what had happened.

'In all the millennia that the universe has existed,' she continued, 'and will exist, it happens to be exactly the moment, right now, when you happen to be alive. What are the odds, eh? They're too remote to bother calculating. So, how do we explain this?'

Galman shook his head dumbly.

'All this is an illusion,' she explained, and put her hands back over his eyes as before. He allowed her to do so, bracing himself against the pressure once more. When she removed her hands he was again looking upon the younger woman and man.

'The passing of time is an illusion,' the young woman smiled. 'Life and death are illusions. I am Mercedes Goyeneche and this is Bernard Ocampo. We allowed ourselves to get old because we knew no better. I didn't want to, of course.'

'What about your disabled daughter?' Galman blurted out.

'We are, or were, a part of one another.'

'You've taken over her body? Her youth?'

'No, no,' she insisted. 'We were aspects of the same person. There is something of me, and her, and her daughter, and my mother, all here in me now.'

'We have found our way backstage,' Ocampo said. 'We have discovered how the Master Magician tricks us into believing in the world of decay and death—of passing time. We know how the illusion is created and we are no longer bound by it.'

'Oh.'

'To cheat the fanciful notions of life and death we had to go through that charade with you. I am so sorry, but we needed our fate to be bound together with a stranger who would remain alive and aging. Now, the least we can do is the same for you. Would you like to find your way backstage?'

'I, I don't know,' he stammered, looking from the woman to the man and back again.

'It's easily done,' Ocampo said, and jumped up from his chair. He walked casually over to a desk and pulled something out. As he then walked over to Galman he seemed to be excited; to be about to offer a gift. What he was holding was a gun.

'Oh, Gato,' Madam Galman cried, waking him the folowing morning. 'It is you father. He is dead!'

The young man rubbed his eyes and took a few moments to work out where he was. He tried to find the sense in what the woman had been saying to him before she had collapsed into helpless sobbing.

'My father dead? How?' he asked sitting up in the narrow bed and reaching out to console her. 'Where?'

Everything seemed familiar but wrong. The woman managed to control herself and explained, 'He didn't come back from San Juan last night. The police arrived a few minutes ago. They told me he was shot.'

The young man did not know what to say. He felt the stubble on his face and looked down at hands that were almost familiar. They were not his, but he knew that he would get used to them. He was sure that he was the one who had been shot in San Juan the previous day. He was scared, but excited. He felt full of youth and vitality.

He saw the look of horror on Madam Galman's face and it took a few moments to understand that it was because he was laughing. Ernesto Galman was dead and he was laughing.

Leave Your Sleep

Another Perspective

She was an odd-looking, insubstantial little thing; ill at ease in their company, sipping determinedly at a sparkling water that didn't seem to get any lower in her glass. Her attention was firmly fixed upon it.

'And what do you do?' Scott asked.

Her sister, Hattie, replied for her:

'Kate's not working at the moment. She's been ill.'

'Oh, I'm sorry to hear that,' he replied. 'On the mend, I hope?'

It wasn't meant to be at all interrogative, but that's obviously how Hattie took his comment.

'It's none of your business.'

'No, of course not,' he apologised. Hattie glared at him, and he tried to cover his apparent *faux pas* by picking up and drinking from his empty wine glass. He knew that his cheeks had flushed red; they did it all too easily. He wanted to add 'I was just trying to make conversation, trying to include Kate,' but the moment had passed.

He was intrigued by Hattie's sister, though. She looked like a ghost, in an old-fashioned dress that didn't seem to fit, her hair long and loose, her face unmade-up. They had been in the restaurant for a half hour that Saturday lunchtime and she had said hardly a word beyond 'yes' or 'no' when asked whether she wanted to sit on a certain chair, was she comfortable, and if she wanted a drink.

A short while later though she spoke unprompted:

'I have to go out for a cigarette,' she said quietly, and got up from the table.

'Don't be too long,' Hattie told her. 'It's chilly out there.' And then Hattie continued to tell Terrance about something that had happened at work.

Scott looked around, hoping to catch somebody else's eye, but they were all listening to Hattie's story. Nobody else seemed to have noticed what had happened. He wasn't surprised that Kate had felt the need to ask her sister's permission to leave for a cigarette, but what was amazing was that Hattie had said yes, and without any comment. She was continually railing against the habit when others admitted to the addiction, which was one of the reasons he had recently given up himself. He had been trying to ingratiate himself with Hattie at the time and he was now pleased that he hadn't succeeded. He had come to realise that she was a bully. He could see that any relationship he had hoped for would have been doomed to failure.

'He's a complete idiot,' Hattie was saying of one of her colleagues.

'That's a little harsh,' Terrance said. Scott knew who she was talking about. He had met the man once and agreed with her; he was just glad that he didn't have to work alongside either the idiot *or* Hattie.

When Kate returned, clutching a bag so small that it could only have contained her cigarettes and a lighter, Scott made himself ask if it was raining outside and she simply nodded and looked down at her first course, which had just arrived. All that he could fall back on was amateur psychology; timid little Kate was the sister of opinionated Hattie, who was holding court for old friends. Who wouldn't be intimidated under the shadow of such a sister? Hattie had charisma and the habit of verbally terrorising people. He hadn't noticed this at first, of course. He had only seen the good-looking, professional woman whose knowledge and understanding of current affairs and politics were impressive. Her sister would not be able to compete.

The main courses arrived and Scott devoted himself to his unappetising vegetarian lasagne with determination. He hadn't eaten breakfast and he was happy to work his way through the uninspired plateful while Terrance supplied Hattie with questions that she answered amusingly and eruditely for the enjoyment of all six of them. He noticed that Kate barely touched her salad, but Hattie ate her seafood with an alarming efficiency considering how much she was talking.

Something changed for Scott that evening. Any desire that he had once felt for Hattie disappeared. She annoyed him, perhaps unreasonably, and he delighted in finding fault with her. Perhaps it was simply the result of the brush-off she had given him a couple of weeks before, but it had been coming for a while. He was slightly uncomfortable that his complete disillusionment coincided with his interest in her quiet sister, who once again got up from the table when everyone had finished. She said quietly that she needed another cigarette.

'I'm so glad you gave up that filthy habit,' Hattie smiled at Scott.

Just to annoy her he found himself replying:

'It's unreasonable to make assumptions about me.'

'You've not lapsed?'

'I'm afraid so,' he lied, and stood up. 'I might have to go and ask your sister for a cigarette.'

'Don't you dare!' was Hattie's immediate response.

Standing there he could see everyone looking from him to her. He could feel his face and neck becoming red again, knowing that this minor medical condition made him look odd; guilty even. He also knew that he had to assert himself for once.

'You're not my mother,' he replied as patronisingly as he could, and then walked out, listening for the conversation to resume at the table. It did, after a few moments, but for once he could not hear Hattie's voice. His remark had been carefully calculated; he knew how sensitive she was that she was seven or eight years older than all of her friends.

Scott found Kate by the front door. Spring had officially turned to summer but the temperature was well below average and she was shivering in the cold, a newly-lit cigarette already in her hand.

'I told Hattie I was coming out for one of those,' he explained, and she held out her packet. 'But I'm not sure that I want one after all. I'm meant to have given up.'

She said nothing, and he continued: 'Hattie told me not to come out, but I don't much like being ordered around.'

It was Kate's cue to agree that her sister was a little too bossy, but still she did not speak.

'Hattie is almost enough to make me take smoking up again,' he continued, desperately wondering if it was possible to provoke Kate into talking.

Eventually she said, quietly: 'Wanting to upset somebody isn't a very good reason to start smoking.'

'No,' he agreed.

'Do you live locally?' he tried again. 'Hattie said you used to be somewhere down south, but you moved up here a few weeks ago.'

She nodded and said: 'It's more convenient for Hattie.'

'Oh, I see.'

She frowned, then added: 'Not in any selfish way. I don't suppose it really matters where I am.'

'Okay. You're able to be flexible . . . ?'

'It just isn't important.'

'Alright.' He was attempting to suggest that he understood. As Hattie had said, it was none of his business. By the time he and Kate returned to the table together he had decided that she was too much like hard work.

'So you've cracked, then?' asked Terrance. 'You're back on the old cigarettes?'

Scott ignored the glare from Hattie:

'No, Kate persuaded me that it was a silly thing to do.'

'Good on you, Kate,' Terrance said boisterously, and she smiled, embarrassed, without looking up.

At that moment the waitress appeared with a board upon which a selection of desserts were chalked up and they ordered in turn. When the woman had gone Scott was able to tell a story about an old friend known to everybody except Hattie and Kate. He finished just as the desserts were served, and he started his while Terrance began to tell a further story about the same friend. Hattie carefully asked an innocuous and pertinent question. Before Terrance could pick the story back up she adroitly moved the conversation in a direction that suited her. Scott did not allow his dislike of the woman to obscure his admiration for the clever conversational manoeuvre. Once she had resumed talking he stopped listening. Scott could not stop himself from turning his attention back to Kate. He had idly considered earlier that she might be anorexic. However, she was eating her large piece of chocolate cake with obvious relish.

By the end of the meal Scott was resolved to forget about both women. When the party broke up he walked back towards his office with Terrance while the others went in the direction of the town centre.

'Kate was quiet,' said Terrance.

'Have you ever met her before?'

'No. I realised there was a sibling, somewhere down near Lincoln. But this is the first time Hattie's produced her for our inspection. Quite the opposite to her, eh? Not much conversation. . . . but with Hattie as a sister. . . .'

'Exactly.'

It was almost a week later, a Friday, that Scott saw Kate again. It was his lunch hour and he had a few errands to run before returning to the office. As he was leaving the ironmongers on King Street he could see her on the other side of the road coming out of the newsagents with another, older woman. Without thinking he crossed the road to say hello. She didn't see him until he was a few feet away.

'Hi, Kate,' he greeted her, and the young woman's immediate reaction appeared to be fear. She looked to her friend for support and he instinctively backed away. Nevertheless he said:

'Do you remember me from the restaurant last weekend? I'm Scott.'

'Oh yes,' she said timidly. 'You thought you might want to start smoking again, but you didn't.'

'That's right.'

She looked up at her friend and explained, very seriously: 'He was going to smoke just to annoy my sister.'

'I can understand that,' the friend replied with a laugh, and then smiled at Scott. 'I've met Kate's sister too. She's a little . . . forceful.'

'You get used to her,' he answered, not knowing exactly why he was defending her.

'It was a nice meal, wasn't it?' he added lamely, and then remembered his indifferent lasagne. 'The dessert was especially good. You had chocolate cake.'

'Kate likes sweet things,' said her friend, and Kate pulled a large bar of Fruit and Nut from out of her coat pocket.

'I come out for cigarettes and sweets,' she said.

'She can buy them in the hospital,' her friend explained. 'But it's best that she comes out and gets some fresh air. Otherwise you'd just be stuck on the ward every day, wouldn't you? Watching telly and reading old magazines? You should come and visit Kate. Otherwise she only sees her sister and the other patients.'

'If I do visit, I assume that chocolates are a better idea than flowers?'

'Definitely,' she said simply.

'And cigarettes are probably frowned on?'

'There's a room where we can smoke,' said Kate, and again she shot a worried glance up at her friend.

'There's a no smoking policy in the hospital and the grounds,' the woman said. 'But, yes, there's a room available. . . .'

'That sounds very irregular,' Scott said.

'It is,' she. 'Officially it doesn't exist.'

'Oh, you don't have an illegal gambling den as well?' he joked, and saw immediately that he was wrong to do so. Kate simply looked confused, while her friend frowned.

'Come and see,' said Kate.

'Yes, do,' agreed her friend. 'Visitors are welcome. Ward Fourteen; follow the signs. Any time, but not between ten and twelve in the morning. That's protected time for the patients.'

'Okay,' he agreed, wondering quite how the arrangement had come about.

'When?' asked Kate.

'I don't know.'

'When's convenient for you?' asked her friend.

'Um, would half-five tomorrow afternoon be okay?'

'Yes,' said the older woman, 'Consider yourself booked in.'

Scott didn't feel that he had any choice but to go along the following day to visit Kate; he had been invited, after all, but he still did not know how he had managed to find himself under the obligation. He assumed that he wouldn't be sitting at Kate's bedside; he didn't know what was wrong with her, but she seemed to be able to leave the hospital. He assumed she must spend time there because she was on dialysis, or needed some other regular, specialist care. He was convinced that her friend was a nurse rather than another patient, but he hadn't considered for one moment that he would find Ward Fourteen to be a psychiatric ward.

It said so above the door. When he arrived, as arranged, he stood outside, debating whether or not he should go in after all. It suddenly seemed horribly intrusive when he didn't even know Kate properly. At length he decided that he had made a promise and had no choice, but when he tried to open the door it appeared to be locked. He looked around and saw an intercom and a discreet message saying that he should press the button to gain admittance. While he was reading it a doctor appeared behind him

'Have you buzzed-through?' she asked.

'I was about to.' He could feel the blood suddenly unnecessarily hot in his cheeks.

'Who're you visiting?'

'Kate,' he replied. Hoping she had the same surname as Hattie he added: 'Wilkins.'

'Come with me and we'll find her.'

The doctor opened the double doors with a swipe card and Scott followed her through. They were in an anodyne, pastel-coloured corridor with bright prints of flowers framed on the walls. Twenty yards away was a reception desk where two further corridors branched off left and right, but there were no obvious beds or anything that looked like medical equipment. Scott was asked to sign his name in a folder and to write down whom he was visiting, and the time he had arrived.

'Wait here,' said the doctor, and she walked off to where Scott could hear the sound of a loud television from a room at the end of the corridor on the right. A minute or so later Kate appeared in the distance, smiled faintly when she recognised him, and started to walk in his direction.

He didn't know if he should wait for her to reach him or to go down the corridor and meet her half way. If he attempted the latter he knew he would have walked well over half the distance, intrusively deep into the ward, because she was moving so slowly. He decided that he ought to stay where he was, by the reception desk.

'Hello,' she said when she was finally just a few feet away. 'It's Scott, isn't it?'

'It is. I've some cigarettes for you, the kind you were smoking before. And a bar of dairy milk chocolate.'

She took the gifts without thanking him and said they should go and talk in her room. He started to follow her down the other corridor, but after only a few feet a nurse appeared and called out:

'No visitors in your room Kate. And if you're going to smoke . . .'

Kate turned around: 'Silly me,' she said, and started to walk back down towards the television room. Scott obediently followed, and noticed, as they passed the television room, that a couple of people appeared to be watching *The Dam Busters*. He and Kate continued on to the last room of all, the smoking room. It reeked of stale tobacco and was cold. One old man was sitting there with the remains of a roll-up between his yellowed fingers.

'The nurses keep coming in and opening the windows,' she said, 'which is why it's so chilly. The room's not meant to be here,' she added, 'so don't tell anyone.'

Scott agreed to keep it a secret and they sat in comfortable but rather tatty-looking chairs facing each other under the window.

'How are you?' he asked her.

'I don't know,' she said, taking a half-opened packet of cigarettes out of her small bag and lighting up. She put the packet back into her bag and was just able to force in the new one as well. Only then did she think to offer him a cigarette, which he declined.

Scott had found the rank smell in the room unpleasant when they had entered it. Suddenly, however, the smell of fresh smoke from her cigarette pulled at him almost physically. It was as much as he could do not to succumb, but she had zipped up her little bag.

After a couple of further pulls on her cigarette she said:

'I've been worse, I know. But if I was well, then I suppose that I wouldn't be here.'

'That sounds reasonable.'

'Is it? I don't think any of it's reasonable. Me being here at all isn't reasonable. I'm sick of this place already and I've only been in this hospital a few weeks.'

'I'm sure they're doing their best to get you better, and to get you out as soon as possible.'

'I don't know about that. Well, maybe they are, but it doesn't always feel like it.'

She pulled in more smoke greedily and looked him straight in the eye: 'I'm sick and tired of the ward, but I'm allowed out if I'm with someone who's considered "responsible".'

'Like your sister last weekend?'

'They'll let me go out any time, but it has to be arranged in advance. Perhaps I could go out with you one day?'

'Where would we go?'

'I don't know; just walking up and down the High Street would be better than staying in here. We'll go tomorrow,' she decided. 'I'll arrange it now.'

Kate got up and left. There was not much to look at in the room so he stared out the window at the car park. He wished he'd suggested to Kate that later next week would be a better time to go out of the hospital with her, but at least they would be off the ward. The place unnerved him because it didn't seem like a hospital ward, although it was obviously institutional. It was almost too normal.

After five minutes he thought about going to look for Kate but decided to wait. The old man got up and left and a young, very nervous man with acne came in and lit up. Scott wondered if Kate was ever coming back, whether she'd forgotten he was still there, when a nurse came in.

'Hello, you're Scott? And you're a friend of Kate's?'

'Yes, well, a friend of her sister, really.'

'Kate says you're happy to take her out for an hour tomorrow? You're just going up and down the High Street, doing a little shopping?'

'Yes, well, if that's what she wants?'

'If you come at, say, half past two, she'll have had her lunch.'

'Okay, but is there anything I should know, or do?'

'No,' she frowned, not understanding what he was alluding to. 'There won't be much open on a Sunday, but you can always go for coffee in the supermarket café? Just try not to be late getting here. A trip out like this means a lot to Kate.'

'Is she coming back now?'

'I don't think so. She said you had to leave. She's gone back to her room.'

Scott asked himself how he had got into such a situation. He had already made other plans for the Sunday afternoon that had to be cancelled. He didn't want to cause trouble or upset Kate, but he supposed that his other plans were really rather unimportant. The alternative was hardly onerous, and he didn't really mind seeing Kate again. The idea of walking up and down the High Street just sounded a little dull. He tried to be positive; he was genuinely curious about her, and anyway, she was expecting him. No doubt agreements had been made with medical staff and it would have been rude to do anything else.

He arrived outside the ward five minutes early and pressed the buzzer. A disembodied voice asked who he was and he gave his name and said he was there for Kate. The door clicked open and he went inside.

To his immediate horror he could see Hattie standing at the reception desk. The moment he saw her he thought of her as a looming presence; even from a distance she was channelling anger in his direction. It was a long walk down the short corridor and he felt the unaccustomed sensation of the colour draining from his face.

'What the hell do you think you're doing?' she demanded while he was still some distance away.

'Miss Wilkins,' the doctor admonished Hattie calmly but authoritatively. 'We'll discuss this in a private room, please.'

'If there's a problem I can just leave,' he offered, his pace having slowed to a stop still several feet away from the group. He suddenly noticed Kate standing behind Hattie.

'We'll talk in a moment,' the doctor said patiently and professionally, and showed them all into a large room with far too many armchairs for their immediate purposes.

'Kate doesn't even know this man,' insisted Hattie. 'I've no idea what he thinks he's doing coming to see her, try to take her off the ward, taking advantage. . . .'

'Now,' said the doctor, silencing Hattie, and turning her attention to Scott. 'Can I ask, how well do you know Kate? You see, she's quite a vulnerable young woman and we have a duty of care.'

'I don't know Kate particularly well,' he admitted, and suddenly his cheeks and neck felt exceptionally hot and he knew how foolish he must appear to them. Nevertheless, he explained, as calmly as he could, how and why he came to be there that afternoon. 'But if there's any problem at all then I'll forget it,' he said.

He then saw that his words were a little tactless; Kate had been listening to him, looking a little confused, but now she appeared upset and annoyed. However, her anger was directed at Hattie:

'I'm not allowed any friends of my own!' she said. 'You brought me up here to this hospital where I don't know anyone just because it's convenient for you. And now I've got a friend you're frightening him away.'

'Kate,' said the doctor, 'Now it's your turn to calm down. Hattie is just concerned, as we all are, that anyone who takes you off the ward is responsible and suitable.'

Scott wanted to ask 'And I'm not?' but he could see it from the doctor's point of view. He had asked the nurse if he needed any aspects of Kate's illness explained to him before they went out and she had said no. But the doctor obviously out-ranked the nurse. Kate seemed pretty much okay, but he did not know exactly how he would have to be 'responsible' for her. He didn't even know what was wrong with her!

'There are things I have to tell Scott,' said Kate determinedly.

'Perhaps,' suggested the doctor, 'you could tell him those things here, on the ward?'

'I'd rather he wasn't here at all,' said Hattie determinedly, and Scott had a presentiment of what she might be about to say. He had done nothing wrong and had nothing to hide, but she was about to make him out to be very a very unsuitable friend for Kate. He had come to know how her mind worked.

'A few weeks ago,' Hattie said slowly, confirming his fears, 'Scott expressed some strong feelings for me, but I had to let him down. I'm sorry, but he's not my type. It's natural for me to be worried that he's subsequently taken an interest in my sister.'

She hadn't needed to say anything else. The words were calculated to imply so much.

'Thanks Hattie,' he said and stood up. 'It was very silly of me to have said anything to you, to have felt anything for you, but I know you so much better now.'

To the doctor he said, 'I won't take up any more of your time,' and then to Kate he simply said, quite formally, 'I'm very sorry. It would've been nice to go out and maybe get a coffee, but it obviously isn't appropriate.'

'Don't go,' she pleaded, but neither Hattie nor the doctor tried to stop him.

Scott was furious with Hattie, but he was also annoyed at himself for getting into such a stupid position. He had been humiliated by the woman, but could not imagine what else he could have done. He also felt very guilty, although he didn't know what for; he had never considered that he might have wanted to somehow take advantage of Kate. If anything, he felt that he had inadvertently been taken advantage of himself. He tried to think positively and be pleased that he was no longer under any obligations.

He tried to put it all out of his mind, and might have been able to think of it all as some horrible mistake if Hattie hadn't told a mutual friend about the incident. She had carefully chosen the one person who would delight in spreading the story. When he saw Hattie a few weeks later at Terrance's he asked to talk to her privately. It took unusual courage on his part but he knew what he had to do. He realised that she mustn't be allowed to continue to have an advantage over him. He was red in the face before he had even closed the kitchen door behind them:

'You told Colin that I'd been hitting on your sister,' he accused her.

'I wouldn't have used that exact phrase, but the meaning is exactly what I was trying to convey.'

'I did no such thing!' he protested. 'And you've no right to go around saying I did.'

'I am simply stating the truth; you were trying to take advantage of a very vulnerable young woman.'

'The only thing you're stating is your own misunderstanding of events. All you're showing is your ignorance.'

'I disagree, you were going to . . .'

'Shut up for once,' he shouted, uncharacteristically. 'You've never bothered to listen to the other side of the story, have you? And telling people I was on the rebound from you is a pretty low thing to do.'

'Not at all,' she said airily. 'I was trying to explain your odd behaviour when other people seemed confused as to your motives.'

'I don't know why you're so happy to think the worst of me?'

'I'm trying not to despise you,' she replied with a smile. 'I'm trying to understand what your problem is.'

'I don't have one; you do. In fact, you have several, and the worst is probably that you don't seem to care what your sister might want. Her opinion doesn't seem to count with you . . . '

'Don't you dare tell me how I feel about my sister!' she finally rounded on him. She had seemed amused before, but her anger now was very real. 'You know nothing about us and what we've been through.'

'I'm horrified at what a nasty, suspicious mind you've got.'

'Kate's well-being is my only concern.'

'She told me you'd brought her up here, away from her friends, just for your convenience.'

'Listen, you stupid little man. That may be how it looks to you from the outside, but she's been very ill. Kate can't get a proper perspective on it herself, although she's a lot better than she was. We're trying to get her to spend more and more time out of hospital because at some point they're going to release her. If she's up here I can spend time with her and eventually she can move in with me rather than going out to some awful hostel or Council bed-sit. If she was still down in Lincolnshire she wouldn't get to go off the ward so often, and then, one day, they'd have simply thrown her out, without any support from anyone, to look after herself, unprepared.'

'All I ever intended to do was walk up and down the High Street with her, perhaps have a cup of coffee somewhere, and return her the ward.'

'So you say!'

He knew there was no point in arguing. He added lamely: 'She said she had some things to say to me.'

'As I said, she's a lot better than she was, but she still has delusions. She'd have wanted to tell you about the voices in her head; to warn you to keep away from children in school uniforms because they're mini-policemen. Can't you see,' Hattie asked, finally losing patience with Scott and almost shouting, 'My sister's a fucking loony!'

He was unable to answer, and was pleased afterwards that he had said nothing. Letting Hattie have the last word was for once the right thing to do. He left her in the kitchen, said goodbye to Terrance and refused to let him talk him into staying.

Scott walked out into an afternoon that was a strange lemon-yellow in the early evening sun. It wasn't far back to his own house but he walked to the old Catholic Church first and from the steps looked down on the town. At the far side were the flat roofs of the hospital; the scene of his real humiliation. It was hard not to dwell on what had happened, and how Hattie had reported it to everybody. He felt singularly friendless and looked forward to the coming week so that he could lose himself in work.

Scott soon discovered that Terrance was a good ally, remaining in contact with him and refusing to agree with Hattie's attempts to assassinate his character. It put a strain on their friendship, though, and Scott was aware that a number of their other friends found it difficult because Hattie and he refused to meet in the same company. He could tell that social occasions all through the summer and early autumn had required some tact, diplomacy and even subterfuge so as to keep them both apart.

It was Terrance who suggested that Hattie was putting in as much effort to shun Scott as he was to avoid her. He suggested that Scott should simply resume his old social life because she would do her best to keep away from him anyway, and it appeared to work.

Scott didn't mention Kate to anyone, and her name was not brought up in Scott's company, although Terrance later told him that he had heard news of her relapse. This saddened Scott, but he was trying to forget all about both sisters.

Six months passed and in many ways Scott's life was back to normal. Hattie kept her distance, although she let it be known through mutual friends that she blamed Scott for Kate becoming ill again. However, those few that mentioned this said that it was one accusation too far, and nobody claimed to believe it.

And then, one evening in early December when he was leaving his office, there was Kate walking towards him on the pavement, on her own. He couldn't avoid her, and he could see she recognised him.

'Scott!' she said. 'You stopped visiting me.'

'I was warned off by your sister.'

She raised her eyebrows and said: 'You don't want to listen to anything she says.'

'I try not to. . . . So, how are you?'

'Much better. I'm meant to be coming out of hospital very soon.'

'That's great news.'

'But not to stay with Hattie.'

'Oh?'

'She's upset, but I want to be somewhere on my own. There's a flat I can have, from the Council, not far from the hospital.

There're people who'll come around and see me, to make sure everything's okay.'

'That sounds like a good arrangement.'

'As long as I can persuade them I'm making progress.'

'Surely it's not a case of persuasion? They'd be able to see? Even I can tell you're so much better than when I saw you last.'

'Will you walk with me back to the ward? I'm allowed out on my own, but only if I promise to be no more than a half hour.'

He agreed and they wandered slowly in the direction of the hospital.

'I don't know how much Hattie told you,' she said, trying to be matter of fact, but obviously rather embarrassed. 'But when I'm ill I can get a bit confused and upset.'

'Nobody's ever said exactly what was wrong.'

'Good,' she said, and some moments later she added, 'I want to choose who I tell, and what I tell them.'

They spoke little as he walked her to the hospital on the edge of the town. He reflected that they had not had time to build up any friendship, let alone any intimacy. What had happened between them seemed to make it unlikely they would ever do so. A part of him, he knew, wanted to prove Hattie wrong by being uninterested in Kate. He didn't attempt to initiate any conversation, not that this appeared to bother Kate.

At the main doors she told him she would go the rest of the way on her own, and she said she hoped to see him again.

'As you won't visit me, I ought to come and visit you!' she said with a smile.

'I'd like that,' he said automatically, but they parted without him telling her where he lived.

Scott did not see Kate again until after Christmas. He had almost forgotten about her. A promotion at work gave him extra duties and responsibilities, and moving to another office in the same building meant that he now had a desk alongside a woman called Emma. He had not really been aware of her before, but every evening after work for the first week they found themselves together in the King's Arms for a drink. They just talked at the time, enjoying each other's company. It was Emma who suggested that if they continued in their new routine then they would soon become alcoholics, and he invited her back to his house for a meal. In reality it was she who made all the first moves, although she carefully didn't let him realise how she had orchestrated the start of their relationship.

They had been going out together properly for two weeks when Kate appeared in the street one evening when they were both leaving the office together.

'Hi Scott!' she said. 'Guess what? I've just moved into my new flat.'

'Kate, that's great news. Congratulations.'

'It's a bit of a dump,' she admitted. 'But it's my own. I can shut the door and choose who I see and who I don't.'

He introduced Emma, and Kate said hello very politely. It was clear though that she would rather Scott had been on his own. She offered him a scrap of paper.

'This is my new address. Come and see me in the mornings, or evenings,' she said. 'I'd like to talk to you.'

'Okay, I'll do that,' he agreed.

'Who's she?' asked Emma. 'An old girlfriend?'

'No, she's Hattie's unfortunate sister. I told you about her.'

'Oh yes, Hattie thought you had designs on her.'

'That's her.'

'Are you going to go and see her?'

'I don't know. I feel a little awkward after what happened.'

'She said she had something to tell you.'

'I know, but it all still feels a little strange.'

'You're still afraid of Hattie, aren't you?'

'Yes, I am!'

It was Emma's suggestion that Scott take a pot plant as a flat-warming gift when he visited Kate a couple of days later. He felt rather conspicuous carrying it through town, but it was dark, cold and snowing and he didn't see anybody he recognised. He found his way to the block of flats on the estate by the railway station and felt even more self-conscious carrying the gift past a group of youths standing at the foot of the stairwell; they peered out at him from their hooded tops and in the sodium glare of the streetlamp he couldn't see their expressions. He climbed up to the second floor and found Kate's flat to be the very first on that walkway.

'You've brought me a plant,' she said, frowning, when she opened the door.

'It's to help brighten up your new home.'

'Oh, okay, come in,' she agreed, and watched with amusement as he stamped on her mat to remove the snow from his shoes. She asked: 'Would you like a cup of tea? I don't have anything else at the moment.'

'Tea would be great,' Scott said and followed her through to the tiny kitchen off the living room. He put the plant down in the middle of the small table where he decided it looked a little gaudy; the leaves were so shiny that they could well have been plastic and the flower itself, whatever it might be, was a little too bright. Already the snow on it was melting.

He took his coat off and looked around him. The flat was very minimally furnished with the kinds of items he had sometimes seen in the local Salvation Army charity shop. The magnolia walls were bare and the floor covering was utilitarian, but there were a few personal touches; a wind chime of colourful metal tubes at the window and three battered stuffed toys looking down from a shelf. There were a couple of wine bottles with candles stuck in them, and a small sewing basket was open on the worktop. Kate appeared to have been embroidering a lampshade, probably to conceal the bare bulb hanging down from the ceiling.

Not knowing how else to start the conversation he asked how she was feeling.

'Does everyone get asked that, or am I paranoid?' She was filling the kettle. 'The community psychiatric nurse was here earlier and she asked me that exact question. A couple of days ago I saw my doctor and he always asks the same thing. . . . My sister does it . . .'

'Well, it's a polite thing to say to anyone; ill or not.'

'If you say so. But anyway, I'm not too bad at the moment, thank you.'

'They must be convinced you're fairly well or they wouldn't have let you out of hospital?'

'Perhaps I've just got better at playing the game.'

'How do you mean?'

She switched on the kettle and turned to Scott, giving him her full attention.

'The exact question my doctors always asks is "How are your thoughts?" I assume that when I'm really unwell I tell them and so they keep me in hospital and give me more pills. When I'm feeling better, though, I realise that keeping quiet, or saying what they want to hear, does me more good. So if they ask me if I'm hearing voices or believe I can walk through walls, or whether the government are out to get me, then I say no.'

'You mean, you still believe those things, but you know they're unreasonable?'

She gave a wry smile: 'When I'm more in control I know that other people will think certain beliefs are unreasonable so I shut up about them. It's like being followed; I've realised it's not worth mentioning.'

'And when you're completely well do you think those things?'

Turning away to drop teabags into the empty pot, she then looked at the blank, black window and said 'I don't know if I've ever been, or ever will be, completely well. When I'm more in control I just know what to say to the doctors.'

'I understand.'

'Do you?'

Kate tidied up the work surface while the water boiled and Scott tried not to watch her. He felt uncomfortable and wondered how soon he could leave without appearing rude. Kate appeared to enjoy bustling about her kitchen and they fell naturally into small-talk. He asked her where she did her shopping, and she talked proudly about some meals she had cooked for herself. She was pleased when he admitted she was more inventive than he was. She enthused about a herbal supplies shop she had discovered and talked about some long walks she had taken out through the park and into the countryside. She was obviously relishing her freedom.

When the tea was ready she turned on the radio and sat down opposite him at the table. She looked serious and said quietly:

'I wanted to talk to you because I think you might understand what I have to say.'

'I can't promise to, but I will listen.'

She stared intently into his eyes and he had to look down at his mug.

'I turned the radio on because, well . . . I'm worried about telling you this . . . I'm told my beliefs are a symptom of my illness . . . but I'm sure they're trying to listen to us.'

'Who?'

She appeared to be uncomfortable, and shrugged: 'I don't know. I think it might be the government.'

'What makes you think they'd do that?' he asked, feeling uncomfortable.

'This will sound even worse. . . . I've been told it.'

'Who by?'

'I don't know. People who are trying to help me, I think. Only, I'm not sure where they are. The doctors say they're only in here . . .' she tapped her head. 'And they're not real. I know that they're meant to be a symptom of my illness too. But, wherever they come from, they seem to make sense.'

'Why would the government be listening?'

'This is really hard for me to explain, to admit to, but over the last few years, at different times, I've been sure that I've been able to do things that'll probably sound quite absurd.' She took a deep breath before continuing. 'I've been sure that I can fly, and I think there've been times when I've been able to walk through walls.'

'Do you remember actually doing those things?'

'I'm not sure. I have problems remembering what's happened, and when. It's because of the medication. The pills dull my senses, my perceptions . . . and also my abilities. I'm told that I've done those things . . .'

'By the voices?'

'Wherever they're coming from, yes. It's hard to know what to believe, especially when I'm not on much medication, like now. It's when I seem to be getting better and the doctors lower the dosage that my abilities seem to return, but I can tell that they're watching me. I mean, just think of the implications if somebody could actually fly, or walk through walls! I'm sure that I'm being followed again; everywhere I go there're people watching, spying on me. I'm convinced that they want to catch me doing those things. So, of course, I make sure that I don't do them. If they caught me they'd take me away and try to work out how I do it. Mad eh?'

'I don't know.'

'I think that maybe it gets out of hand sometimes; I mean, my illness gets out of control. I see their spies everywhere, not only in policemen, but traffic wardens, school children; anyone in uniform. . . . I know, it's silly. As I say, at times I've been convinced of things that must be absurd, but I think the pills have done that to me. I kind of lose track of time, of how long I've been in hospital, and how often. . . . I can't remember where I was, or how I was, when I believed different things. . . . It doesn't help that some of the things I've believed can't've ever been true.'

'Like what?'

'I don't want to tell you. They really have been the beliefs of somebody who's psychotic; I know that. They would undermine the things I've told you. You see, I'm not a reliable judge of any of this.'

Kate put her hands over her face.

'I don't know what to say,' considered Scott. 'I've no experience of anything like this. What you've been through, well, it's completely alien to me.'

'I'm glad,' she replied, composing herself. 'Really, I am, for your sake. I hope you never have to know what it's like not to trust your own mind.'

'Have you tried doing those things, the things you believe you can do, when you're completely off the medication?'

She nodded.

'And . . . ?'

'I think that I could do them, if I'm not on much medication, but I'm worried they're watching me, waiting to see how it's done. So I don't usually try.'

'It would be lovely,' he said, hesitatingly. 'You know . . . to fly.'

She nodded and laughed nervously.

'I wish that I could convince just one person. Then I wouldn't mind everyone else telling me it was a delusion. I'd go along with it. I'd take my pills like a good girl and not resent them all calling me mad. You know what my sister calls me?'

Although he remembered Hattie's outburst he shook his head.

'A loony. I'm an embarrassment to her.'

Scott put his hand out over the table to hers and squeezed it. She stared down at him and he released her.

At that awkward moment there was a knock at the door and Kate frowned.

'I'll see who it is,' she said and got up from the table. Scott sat back in his chair and wondered if the new visitor might not be the cue for him to leave. He heard the door open and was horrified to hear Hattie's rather booming voice.

He then heard Kate say very precisely: 'Could you come back another time?'

'Why? Is there somebody with you? Who is it?'

'A friend.'

'Who? You don't have any friends.'

'You can't come in. This is my flat.'

'I still need to keep an eye on you, for your own good.'

'Hattie, no!' protested Kate, but Hattie was obviously through the door, into the hall and then Scott saw her enter the sitting room. When she saw him she looked appalled.

'You again!'

He stood up, 'Hattie, listen . . .'

'Get out!'

'Hattie!' protested Kate. 'I'm well-enough to be out of hospital and have my own friends. You can't stop me, and nor can anybody else.'

'I certainly can!' she announced, and then pointed at Scott: 'You, out, now!'

'No!' insisted Kate. 'I'm talking to Scott, explaining things.'

'What? Are you telling him that you're schizophrenic? That you hear voices? That the schoolchildren are following you?' she asked. 'And is he saying that's okay? It's not a problem? Have you told him those embarrassing things you've done, like walking around naked because you thought you were invisible?'

Hattie then turned on Scott:

'And are you so desperate for a girlfriend that you'd sleep with a girl who I once found smearing herself in her own excrement?'

'I never did!' said Kate. 'You're just being horrible.'

'Oh yes you did. He needs to be told what a loony you are; a nutcase, a freak!'

'Stop this now,' insisted Scott. 'What you're saying is wrong.'

'And what would you know about it? Okay, let's talk about this sensibly.'

Hattie took off her coat and sat down in a rickety armchair.

'Sit down,' she ordered Kate, who did so nervously, perching on the edge of the sofa. Scott unwillingly brought through the kitchen chair and sat down a calculated and careful distance from both women.

'Now,' Hattie said, presumably trying to keep the patronising tone out of her voice, but failing. 'Kate believes she can walk through walls, and that she can fly. Did you know that Scott?'

'She told me, yes.'

'And do you believe her?'

'Kate believes it.'

'That's not what I asked. Do you believe her?'

'I think it's highly unlikely . . .'

'Nicely put.'

"But I see no problem with discussing it with her.'

'Why? It's a waste of time. You know and I know that it's utter rubbish. And if Kate believes it, then it's proof that she's a nutter.'

'If she has an unreasonable belief . . .'

'Yes?'

'A belief that doesn't get in the way of her functioning in everyday life, then what's the problem?'

'You're not being serious?'

'I am. Look, why is Kate's belief any more silly than, say, a belief in God? From my perspective as an atheist the whole concept of God seems just as unlikely. But we're meant to respect those who have a religious faith.'

'That, Scott, is rather different.'

'No it's not.'

'Why isn't it?'

'Believing that some bloke two thousand years ago was the son of God, was crucified and then came back to life . . . it sounds like nonsense to me. But if people want to believe it, then the best of luck to them. Why should I care?'

'What you don't appreciate is that they have a religious faith. What Kate has is a chemical imbalance in her brain. Her beliefs are potentially dangerous whereas religious ones aren't.'

'Religious beliefs aren't dangerous? What about all the wars in history?'

'That's hardly helping your argument . . .'

'Stop it, both of you,' shouted Kate, standing up. 'At this moment I don't know if I can fly, but sometimes I just want to let myself go up into the air, and go up and up and continue up and up and leave this whole horrible world behind me.'

'I think I understand,' Scott said.

'And what do you think you'd find up there?' asked Hattie.

'I don't know. Angels?'

'Angels?' her sister raised her eyebrows and looked at Scott with pantomime incredulity.

'I don't know,' Kate replied. 'It sounds better than passenger jets or weather balloons.'

'See, she's mad,' said Hattie simply.

'You believe me,' Kate turned to Scott. 'Say you do. You're the one person I want to believe me.'

'I don't know what to think. But does it matter?'

'Of course it bloody matters,' said Hattie.

'Why?'

'I thought it mattered,' said Kate. "I thought that I wanted Scott to believe me. I thought, for some reason, that he might, but I don't suppose it does matter.'

'What you need to realise . . .' Hattie started to say.

'No, wait,' said Kate with quiet determination. 'Scott, would you think any the better or worse of me if I actually could or couldn't fly?'

'I don't think it would make any difference. It would be marvellous if you could, but . . .'

'Okay,' she held up her hand to stop him. 'Hattie what is it you want from me?'

Her sister frowned, and then looked uncomfortable.

'I want you to be well, to be normal.'

'Not a loony, not a freak?'

'Look, why are we even having this conversation? This whole business can be simply cleared up. All you have to do is fly, or walk through that wall into your neighbour's flat. If you succeed, then *I* will apologise and agree that you're not ill, but amazingly gifted. If you fail then *you* ought to agree to stop believing these things are possible.'

'Okay,' agreed Kate and stood up.

Scott saw the psychiatrist after he had been give the all-clear from the fracture to his skull, although the complications from his broken collar-bone would persist for another six months.

'I know what I ought to say,' Scott told him, and the psychiatrist smiled. 'I know what the appropriate response should be, and if that's what you want then I suppose I'll have to give it.'

'But it wouldn't be what you really believe?'

Scott didn't reply.

'It's entirely reasonable to have a false memory of what happened after Kate walked out of her front door that evening.'

'I know, and it's been explained to me that I probably don't actually have any real memory because of the injuries I sustained.'

'Your mind will have tried to make up for the lacunae, to imagine the events in an effort to explain them. Those thoughts are what you're remembering; not the actual event.'

'But all you've got against my word is that of the young men who'd been hanging around outside her block of flats?'

'We've rather more evidence than that, I'm afraid.'

'Hattie can't contradict me.'

'Her sister? No, apparently not. She'd remained sitting in the living room until she heard your screams. But the boys saw Kate climb over the railings two storeys above them. They saw you trying to stop her but you couldn't quite grab hold of her properly. You did what you could. . . .'

'I'm sure I remember that I nearly had a hold of her, but she slipped away from me; she was too insubstantial to get a grip on . . . . I have it my mind that she just flew away from me, into the night, out among the great big flakes of sodium-coloured snow.'

'I know that's what you want to believe happened, but it wasn't what the witnesses saw. They saw her fall, and then you lose your balance and fall after her. She hit the ground first.'

'They said that?'

'They said she simply fell without a sound, the snow doing nothing to cushion her fall on the frozen ground. She died instantly; she wouldn't have been in any pain.'

'How come she died but I survived? After all, I landed on my head!'

'It was a fluke. You apparently flailed around as you fell, shouting, before landing awkwardly, but luckily.'

'Luck? I suppose so.'

'It was a miracle you didn't break your neck at the very least.'

'I was told that Kate's legs crumpled up beneath her. Her pelvis was shattered and her spine broken.'

'As I said, she died immediately; she wouldn't have been in any pain.'

'I'm glad of that. But . . .'

'But?'

'None of that is how I remember it,' Scott said quietly. 'She slipped through my fingers but she was flying away from me; up, not down. Why are you trying to convince me otherwise?'

The psychiatrist shook his head: 'It's my job to. From where I am sitting yours is an unreasonable belief, but I don't know. . . . So what? I'm wondering whether it will make you a happier, better person if you accept my version of the facts? Is society really in danger if you believe that Kate Wilkins flew? I think not.

'Scott,' the psychiatrist said, 'I'm sorry for your loss, and for your injuries. But I don't think you need my services.'

The Dress

I awoke this morning in what appeared to be a strange house and I lay between unfamiliar sheets trying to remember exactly where I might be. I was not especially worried at first. I was wondering whether I had been put to bed drunk after a party, but I did not feel particularly jaded. I was tired, but then who isn't, first thing in the morning? And it did seem to be early morning; the bright sun, only just above the horizon, came in through the large bay window and lit the room with precision. This was silly, I thought, and I decided to get up, asking myself who my host or hostess might be.

I walked, slightly shakily, across the carpet in my bare feet and looked out of the window. I appeared to be in an elegant arts and crafts house with a short drive and a well-tended garden. There was a pleasant view out over what I thought might be the Lake District.

When I turned back to the room I was not sure that it was entirely unknown to me after all. I looked up at the ceiling and there was an old cracked patch in the plaster moulding around the light fitting. I knew it; I was sure that I did. But why did this knowledge reveal nothing to me? This was just one of a number of important questions that I needed to have answered, but my attention was taken by a photograph on the chest of drawers. In a thin silver frame, it was a studio portrait of a very elegant young woman with heavy eye makeup. She was wearing an angel dress from the 1960s, but who she was I could not imagine.

And then I noticed a copy of *Pride and Prejudice* on the window-seat. I picked it up and turned it over in my hands and felt as though I had been reunited with an old friend. The blue cloth was worn and soft, and the coffee-ring on the front suggested to me that I had seen it before. I opened the book and noted the name, 'Cecilia', written on the flyleaf with a bold 'C'. But who was Cecilia? Was it me? And if the book was mine, what was it doing here, in this strange room?

I put it back down and picked up a Moorcroft vase, causing something to clank inside it. I did not need to look to know that there was an old, rusty key in it that would not come out; I knew that it had found its way inside the vase during some dim, far-off childhood, and that for some logic-defying reason it would not now come out.

I looked down at myself, in a plain white nightdress, and that, too, was familiar. I realised, of course, that something was fundamentally wrong. I walked over to the full-length mirror by the door and the moment before I saw my reflection I was afraid that I might not recognise the person that would be staring back at me. For a whole second, perhaps, the reflection was a surprise.

I had shoulder-length dark hair, reasonable features, not too lined for my age, and I was quite slim. And as I considered my reflection I decided that perhaps the way that I looked was not completely alien. But I could not have said that the reflection was really mine with any confidence.

So who did I think I might be? If the book on the window-seat was mine, and that was my vase, then yes, I even had a vague memory of the mirror I was staring into.

I opened up one of the cupboard doors and the clothes inside dismayed me. Even if I thought I had known them before, they could not possibly have been mine. There were dresses, possibly hundreds of them; they were beautiful, of the best possible quality, but they were old and belonged to another time. From their styles and colours they dated from the late fifties and early sixties.

They seemed to suggest that this was *not* my house after all. And surely I ought to know my own home? My own bedroom? I looked down at my hands, and I felt the same way about them as I did the objects around me; they might well be mine, logic suggested that they were, but I was only just able to recognise them, and it took a while to do so.

Panic and tiredness engulphed me in a combined wave; I felt nauseous and my limbs were suddenly heavy. I had to sit on the edge of the bed, not wanting to give in to the weariness because I had to make sense of what I was experiencing. It seemed to me that the first time I looked at anything I believed it to be new to me, but then I doubted that first impression. However, given a little time, I would then accept that whatever I was looking at did belong to me after all. But I did not like the fact that I believed these things to be mine without any understanding of them. I was worried that I was deluding myself; that my mind was trying to assure me that everything was fine, when deep down I knew that it was not.

What really thwarted my attempt to feel at home in that room were the dresses in the cupboard; however hard I tried I could not appropriate them for myself. I was becoming scared, and looked around to see if there was anything else that could explain my situation.

On a chair by the door was a pile of papers, and with a tremendous effort I made myself get back off the bed and walk over to them. When I picked up the documents, mainly letters, I was sure that I hadn't seen them before; they all related to a patient at Lancaster Hospital called Sylvia Smith and her address was

Hilltop Cottage. I sat down in the chair to look through them properly.

Among the items, towards the bottom, were a passport and a driving licence. These both had photographs on them and to my relief they showed the woman I had seen in the mirror. All of the papers related to each other, referred to me, and seemed to make some kind of sense. It all explained who I was and where I lived, but it was all at one remove. Looking at the photographs again I decided that I must have lost a lot of weight since they had been taken.

And then the tiredness made me feel sick again. Some of the panic had subsided, though, and I felt able to sit back and close my eyes.

I slept. And when I awoke I knew that there had been a significant change. I was still in the same room, but this time I remembered it, albeit only from when I had last been awake. The papers had dropped on to the floor, but I did not bother to retrieve them. I stood up, with some resolve, and walked over to the door. It opened softly and beyond it stretched a long, bright, white-painted passage with stairs at the far end. I walked with one arm out at my side, the tips of my fingers against the wall to help me balance. I could hear a distant voice, and as I got to the stairs I discerned movement from the hall below. Someone was approaching; I could see it was a man and I tried to decide whether I knew him or not. He looked up, surprised, and he quietly said, 'Hello?'

'Hello,' I replied.

'Do you not know me?' he asked, in a very reasonable voice. 'I'm your husband.'

We had inherited the house from my Aunt Cecilia and had moved into it in April with great excitement. After our terraced house in Manchester it seemed idyllic; so vast and beautiful that we did not feel worthy of it. And we inherited all of her furniture, which was a godsend because we did not have enough ourselves to furnish the place. Those first few days in the house were like an adventure and I recollected them fondly. But then something had gone wrong. I had started to worry about so many things; small problems grew to vast proportions, and by May I was seriously ill. For almost a month I had been in hospital; not that I recalled anything about that time.

'You've been home for a week,' my husband told me as he sat on the edge of my bed. 'Every day you've woken up and asked where you are. You've wandered around for a while and then gone back to bed. But every time you've woken back up we've had to start the process all over again. This time you seem better.'

I told him that I had managed to get out of bed earlier, only to doze off in the chair. When I had woken up again, though, I was aware of what had happened before.

'That's progress,' he said with a smile that was kind and reassuring, and which I was so glad that I recognised. It was only now, looking back on my temporary memory loss, that I found it really frightening.

'Why have I been sleeping in here, rather than our bedroom?' I asked him.

'We've been sleeping apart since you were first ill. You were very troubled in your sleep, and then you stopped sleeping at all. . . . And I thought you'd be reassured waking up in this room you said you'd loved as a child?'

'When I used to stay in this house, with my Aunt Cecilia, I thought it magical to have such a large room to myself. And a window-seat, and windows on three sides . . . The light in here is marvellous in the mornings.'

'When we first moved into this place you didn't want any of your Aunt's things changed.'

'I remember. I think I was a little unreasonable. I think that was a part of my illness?'

'Well, I might have been unreasonable too; when you were away in hospital I moved a lot of her furniture out to the garage and brought ours inside.' He then added hastily: 'But I've not thrown anything away.'

'It's hard for me to be quite sure of what happened, once I was becoming ill, but I do remember us arguing about what to keep and what to get rid of.'

He nodded: 'It wasn't easy to work out what was going on, for either of us. But we can take our time and start again. When you're up to it you tell me which things of hers you might want to keep, and what we can get rid of.'

'You left her photo on the chest of drawers.'

'When you were ill you accused me of trying to eradicate all traces of her, but that was never my intention.'

I held him tight. Some of that time was coming back to me and it was frightening; I found it hard to believe that they were my memories. I had been very afraid of something, but I couldn't recall what it had been.

Two days later my husband decided that I was well enough for him to be able to go back into work for a few hours and to leave me alone in the house. To be honest, I found this rather daunting, but I didn't say anything. The doctor had visited a couple of times and pronounced me well on the way to recovery. Already my strength was returning, but the doctor seemed to me to be too positive and cheerful. I wasn't convinced that we knew exactly why I had become ill in the first place, and I was therefore worried that it might happen again. I was simply told to take my medication and to rest. The patronising old man had even told me 'not to worry my pretty little head over such things' and I came close to telling him to get out of my house.

But at least I now knew that it was my house. I had always loved it and always found it reassuring. The white-painted woodwork indoors and the stone surrounds to the windows suggested a timelessness that comforted me. The outside world did not need to ever intrude on the fantasy we created within.

Now that I was recovering I tried not to think about what had happened to me. I did try to rest, but felt better when I had tasks to distract me, and so I set about completing the process of moving in. We had made a start together, and then my husband had made the decisions alone; some pieces of my Aunt's old furniture had been kept, and some of our own had been introduced. On the whole I agreed with what he had done, although there were one or two of her garish prints from the nineteen-fifties that I decided I could not live with. These I took down and hid at the back of the garage.

I had emptied out my Aunt's chest of drawers when we first moved in, but I had not started on the cupboards. The room where I was still sleeping on my own had been used by her as a dressing room.

'I did think about turning out all of the rest of her clothes,' said my husband. 'But you told me some of the dresses were very expensive, and I wouldn't know what to keep and what to get rid of.'

'She used to let me dress up in some of them when I was little, but others were too precious for me to be allowed to try on.'

'I'm not sure if antique clothes have any real value?'

'If some of them have come back into fashion they might,' I said, but I was not optimistic from what I had seen. I wasn't sure that any of them had anything other than a kitsch value to offer.

On that first morning alone I decided to go through them, assuming that most of them could be assigned to charity shops. I took up a number of bin bags for those that I was going to throw away. I was wondering if there were really going to be any hard decisions to be made, but as I walked down that corridor to Aunt Cecilia's dressing room a memory came back to me; there had always been boxes of her most precious dresses carefully put away on the floor of the far wardrobe, at the back. I had been allowed to look at them, supervised, but I had never been allowed to wear them.

Where I had expected them to be, I found a half-dozen colourful cardboard boxes carefully stored, and I thought that I might have made a discovery. One had printing on it suggesting that it was by André Courrèges and another was by Yves Saint-Laurent. Inside the boxes the dresses were wrapped in tissue paper and when I took them out they were obviously of the finest quality. The labels were authentic as far as I knew. There was no reason for them not to have been.

I laid them out on the bed and realised that I would need a specialist to come and tell me if they still had any value. The box that excited me the most, though, contained a dress that I was sure had to be by Paco Rabanne. If so then I knew it had to be worth several hundred pounds, if not thousands. There was no printing on the box, and it did not have a label, but it was characteristic of his space-age dresses; it was made of small petal-shaped metal tiles held together by delicate chains. I searched through the box to see if there was a receipt or anything else to give it provenance, but there was nothing.

I picked up the dress and it was surprisingly light. It could have been an imitation of his work, of course, but it was once again the quality that convinced me of its authenticity. Guiltily, I asked myself if I might try it on?

My Aunt Cecilia had been a petite woman, and I had only been able to get into her clothes when I was a child and a teenager. They should not have fit me now, but I had lost so much weight during my illness that I thought I might just be the right size after all. I resolved that at the first sign of this dress being too tight I would take it off because I did not want to damage it.

I was not expecting anybody to come to the house that morning. I took off all of my clothes, including my underwear and stood before the mirror. This was not necessarily the best thing to have done because I have never felt very good about my body. I have always thought that my hips were too wide, my thighs too fat, and my breasts too small. As I stood there with the dress lifted up, ready to be dropped down over my head, I asked myself what on earth I thought I was doing? Why would I possibly think that an expensive, classic, designer dress like this one would look good on me?

I looked up, though, to make sure that I knew where my arms were going through the dress and I dropped it down over my head. I had a momentary fear that it would get stuck and I would be standing there stupidly with my arms trapped in the air, but it slid down my body and the cold metal from which it was made sent a thrill through me. I looked in the mirror and was astounded by what I saw.

The dress fitted me perfectly. Suddenly I looked amazing and yet my shape had not changed. I had never worn anything before that was so flattering. And physically it felt astounding. I ran my hands over myself, gently so as not to snag my fingers on the many little plates, and it felt almost as though each piece of metal sent a little electric current into my skin. I had never experienced such a delight in the way that my own body both looked and felt.

I don't know how long I stood there, unashamedly taking pleasure in wearing the dress, but from downstairs I heard a knocking at the front door. I walked to the bay window and looked nervously around the side of the curtain, not wanting to be seen by my visitor.

The first thing that I noticed was the car; very old but immaculately presented. And then I saw the man as he stood there with his back to me, looking out over the garden.

I then looked down at myself and felt like a child who was in danger of being caught doing something very naughty indeed. I wasn't sure that I trusted myself to take off the dress in haste without damaging it, so I simply stood there, watching, hoping that he would go away.

The man knocked again, and after waiting for another minute, during which time I hardly dared breathe, he tried the handle and opened the front door.

My heart raced. I was too scared to try and take the dress off, up over my head, so I pulled my trousers on over the dress which was tight around my hips. I then put on my shirt, trying to do up the buttons too quickly and fumbling with each one.

'Hello?' came a tentative voice from downstairs in the hall as I put the last button in place. I went out onto the landing with a boldness that surprised me. I walked to the head of the stairs.

'Who are you?' I asked.

The man walked into sight and looked up.

'Cecilia?' he asked, uncertain, confused.

'No, I'm Sylvia. Her niece,' I said, standing my ground.

He continued to frown, baffled.

'I'm afraid that my Aunt died recently,' I explained.

His confusion appeared to deepen.

'So you're not Cecilia?' he asked.

'No.'

'No . . . now that I look at you . . . you are very different. But you say she's dead?'

I nodded. And then he visibly sagged. He reminded me of a cartoon character who only falls into a chasm once they have finally noticed that there is no solid ground beneath their feet.

'I'm so sorry,' he said quietly, 'My condolences.'

The words were said automatically and without real meaning; his thoughts were obviously elsewhere. He appeared deeply affected by the news.

'It was a shock,' I admitted. 'A heart attack, but she died in her sleep; it was peaceful.'

'But I only saw her, I don't know, a few months ago?' he said, almost to himself. Then he looked up. 'I've been away.'

'Did you know her well?'

'Yes, I did, for several years.'

His grief moved me, and I walked carefully down the stairs to where he stood. He watched me descend without really registering my presence.

It was as I was two steps from the bottom that I thought, if he had known my Aunt so well, and for so many years, how had he ever confused the two of us?

I walked past him and showed him through to the front room, and he followed, distracted. As he did not really appear to notice me I took the opportunity to look at him, wondering how old he was? It was very hard to tell, but I decided that, like me, he had to be in his late thirties. He sat down without being asked and I was about to take the seat opposite him when I thought that I might not actually be able to sit while wearing the dress!

And so I stood, and he stared up at me.

'My name is Weaver,' he said.

'Oh,' I replied, wondering why he answered so formally. 'I'm Sylvia, Sylvia Smith.'

He looked about him: 'You've changed things.'

'We've been here a few months.'

'Just driving up to the house I could tell that it was different. But you . . .' He looked at me and shook his head as though he found me to be a poor substitute for the woman he had been seeking.

He was acting very oddly, but I did not distrust him. I think that I was at ease with him because I felt as though I might have seen him before. It was an experience similar to those when I had woken from my illness a few days before; when I had looked at my hands, or that copy of *Pride and Prejudice*. Did I know him? Was an explanation about to present itself? One that would make me laugh at the idea that he was a complete stranger?

'Have we met before?' I asked bluntly. 'I've been ill. My memory isn't what it was.'

'I don't think we can have done?'

I was disappointed at this. Disconcertingly, I considered that if he had been presented to me two days before as my husband I might well have accepted him in the role.

'What do you do for a living?' I asked, dismissing the thought.

'Me? Well . . .' and he frowned again. 'Oh, I don't know how to best describe myself. I'm something in the City.'

He had looked around the room nervously, as if for clues.

'I, I . . .' he started to say, but lost confidence, and then offered the information: 'Your Aunt and I were lovers.'

'Oh, I didn't know that.'

'When her husband was alive we had an affair. And when he died we carried on as though there was still someone to hide from . . .' and he trailed off.

'I'm sorry,' he said, standing up. 'I'm imposing. I'm taking up your time.'

'No, sit down, do. Can I get you a drink or something?'

'I'm fine, thanks. It's just, sitting there, with you standing . . .'

I laughed. 'Actually, I'm not sure that I can sit down at the moment.'

'Why's that?' he asked. He then apologised again; 'I'm sorry, that might be personal. You don't have to answer. I'm not doing very well am I? I just walked in. I should go.'

'You're fine,' I assured him. I was not certain that I trusted his dissembling; perhaps he could tell what I was wearing under my trousers and shirt? The dress felt so strange against my skin, which had become hyper-sensitive. I found myself pressing my hands to my hips to feel the dress against me, not certain whether the sensation was pleasurable or not.

'It's just that I've done something very silly.'

I didn't know why I was going to tell him what I had done, but for some reason I wanted him to know what had happened.

'I've put on one of my Aunt's dresses,' I explained. 'It's wonderful, and I look great in it, but I'm afraid that I might damage it. It's under this,' I pointed to my shirt and trousers. 'If I sit down I think it might rip, or tear . . .'

'Which dress?'

'A rather nice one, and possibly a rather expensive one.'

'She did have some magnificent clothes, and looked marvellous in them.' He nodded and smiled in confirmation of the memory. Then he looked at me and remembered himself: 'As I expect you do, too.'

'That's very sweet of you to say so,' I dismissed his afterthought.

'But, which of them is it?'

'Which dress? I'd rather not say.'

He appeared to relax for perhaps the first time.

'It's the Guy de Welch dress, isn't it?'

'I don't know. It didn't have a label.'

'It looks like a Paco Rabanne? It's not a copy. It was made as a private commission for Cecilia by a man who worked with Rabanne.'

I looked down at myself, embarrassed, but not entirely uncomfortable. I have to admit that I felt quite excited. I knew what was going to happen. I knew that I was going to show him the dress.

He lowered his gaze and with a movement of his hands dismissed the idea: 'I shouldn't have mentioned it. Really, I'm sorry. It's just that I remember Cecilia wearing it. It's unique.'

'Would you like to see it?' I asked.

'Of course I would, but I'd understand if you'd rather not show me.'

Was I after the approval, the admiration even, of a complete stranger? I don't believe that I would have done such an audacious thing if I didn't feel that I could trust the man. And for some reason I did trust him, although I could not explain him.

'Look away,' I said, and he nodded and walked over to the window and stared out of it.

I very carefully took off my shirt, and then undid my trousers, lowering them along with the short length of the dress hoping that the tiny metal plates would not get hooked or snagged on the material. Luckily they all fell back into place. Then I allowed the trousers to drop to my feet and I stepped out of them.

I ran my hands carefully over my waist and hips, getting ready to face the man, and to give him permission to turn around.

I looked up, but he was already staring at me in appreciation. I should have rebuked him, but such admiration is so rare that it would have been wrong to spoil it.

'You look wonderful,' he said, and for the first time I took the compliment and believed it. 'The dress is a work of art. It's as though it was made for you.'

'Thank you,' I said, looking down at my feet in what I hoped was a demure fashion. Not that the dress made me look demure. I had no idea what other people might think I looked like, but I felt very special.

He walked over slowly and when close enough he put his hand out towards the centre of my chest as though about to scrutinise the way the dress had been made. At the last second, though, his hand hovered but did not touch it.

'How does it feel?' he asked. 'I mean, it's metal.'

'Surprisingly good.'

'You're not wearing. . . .' He had started to ask if I had anything on underneath the dress, but he stopped himself.

As he made no further move I took his hand and carefully put his palm flat against my waist. The thrill of it went right through me so that I believed that I might almost faint. I couldn't breathe. I couldn't say anything. All that I could do was appreciate the sheer physical pleasure of his hand on me.

And that was when the first of the tiny metal plates came free, tumbling gently down onto the carpet like a delicate, shiny petal. It almost seemed to float, not fall, and then it lay there, still, and I stared at it without understanding the implication of what had happened. And then this tiny fragment of the dress was joined by another piece, and, inevitably, by yet another. It was as though the lightest breeze had started to persuade the petals to fall from a flower in a late summer garden. I looked to see where they were coming from.

The dress was very slowly, almost unnoticeably, falling apart under his hand. He was moving around to my side and when his other hand cupped my breast the pleasure was almost unendurable. I had a decision to make. The dress was disintegrating at his soft touch, compliantly, of its own volition.

With absolute clarity I knew that I should either tear myself away that instant and escape, or stay and watch the dress come to pieces.

A Woman of the Party

Birgit made the mistake of sitting down and closing her eyes for a few moments. She knew she shouldn't have done it because when she opened them again and tried to stand the room reeled around her. She had to make a grab for the doorframe to steady herself but nobody seemed to have noticed; those in the kitchen were talking loudly over the thudding music to which everyone in the darkened living room was dancing. The party was a success, and a few moments later somebody again shouted in her ear, asking why it had taken her over a year to arrange a housewarming?

She gave the answer that she had honed during the evening, about the paperwork and permissions, about the renovation and the redesign of the large nineteenth-century house. Not for the first time she was complimented on her luck, her vision and her good taste.

Once again she saw the large red wine stain on her expensive imported carpet and the rip in the curtains. But the damage did not upset her as it would normally have done; her guests were happy and so was she. She looked around for her husband, Manfred, but could not immediately see him.

'He's out in the garden,' shouted Yelena, as though divining her thoughts. 'He was talking about the Party with my husband the last time that I saw him. By the way, that punch is strong!'

Birgit agreed, thanked Yelena, and pushed her way through to the back door. She used the press of bodies to keep herself upright, leaning on shoulders and smiling her apologies. Through the door the blast of cold air was a shock but failed to sober her up. It stung her face and bare arms but it felt superficial, even when she breathed in and it invaded her lungs. She had known that the punch was potent because Manfred had made it with two bottles of vodka. She had later seen Gunter empty a whole bottle of *Goldkrone* into it, and God knows who else had thought it amusing to increase the alcohol content. She had drunk nothing for the first two hours, but once she succumbed she lost count of the glasses she had consumed. Too many, that was all she was sure of.

The sky was clear but intensely dark. She could not make out any stars because of the light pouring from the windows. Birgit noticed that her sister was inside with a man the hostess did not know; he had her pressed up against the glass in the full-length doors, obviously unaware that they could be seen from outside. Birgit tactfully looked away and peered around at the handful of people talking out on the patio. She identified Yelena's husband, Willy, but not Manfred.

'Gone back inside,' Willy said. 'Excellent party!'

And so she returned to the house. The kitchen immediately seemed too hot and airless.

'Shut the door!' she heard somebody shout as she stood half in, half out. She did as she had been asked and plunged through her guests into the living room. It took a few moments, but now she saw him, dancing with Silke. Dancing! He must have been drinking heavily, Birgit decided, for he never usually danced. At least he wasn't with Christa.

She wondered, would it have been right to make a scene if he was? Would she have had the nerve, in front of their friends? Perhaps the drink would have given her the courage to scream at him and Christa. After all, somebody has to have a row, she thought, at any respectable party. And it would make it all the more memorable if it was the hostess who instigated it.

She followed the wall around to the far door, steadying herself, feeling worse than ever after being outside in the cold air. Looking into the hall she saw Yelena talking to Tina. It had been Yelena who had alerted Birgit to the apparent intimacy between Manfred and Christa. Birgit had been looking out for the obvious signs that they were having an affair but she had discovered nothing herself. How would he have had the opportunity, she asked herself? He was always so busy with Party work. What had made Yelena so suspicious?

The record came to an end and there were shouted requests. She looked back over her shoulder and watched Manfred take control of the stereo. He put on a new record but placed the needle on it so that it was already several seconds into the song. And she noticed that he had not put the last record back in its sleeve. These things would normally have bothered her, but somebody had taken her by the waist to dance and she didn't have time to think. It was Jurgen, and, really, she was very happy to dance with him. Did that make her a hypocrite? She thought that perhaps it did; she rather liked Jurgen and his hands on her hips would have excited her more if her senses hadn't been so clouded.

'I'm sorry Jurgen,' she shouted into his ear as the volume built around them. 'I've drunk too much and I'm in danger of falling over.'

'I'll hold on to you,' he shouted back.

They danced, and as she turned and saw Manfred he grinned at her and waved.

'Just about everybody's here,' Jurgen said into her ear. 'It's a good turn out.'

'I'm really pleased,' she admitted, enjoying how close he was. 'I don't think any of our friends are missing.'

'Apart from Yevgeniy and Fabiana.'

'Well, they can be excused, seeing as they're down in Zittau at the moment.'

'Oh, and Christa hasn't turned up.'

'Really?' she said, genuinely surprised. Christa was the one woman she was meant to be keeping an eye open for; she wanted to make sure that the slut kept away from Manfred. Well, she was happy that the woman wasn't there.

'It might've been a little awkward for her,' she said.

'Why's that?'

'Well, I think that just about all of us here tonight are couples. And her being on her own. . . .'

'It might be she's feeling a little fragile, what with being pregnant.'

Birgit stopped dancing, which wrong-footed her partner and he nearly fell over.

'Who's the father?' she asked.

'I've no idea,' he said, regaining his composure. 'I don't know if Renate even knows. You could ask your sister.'

They resumed dancing, and Birgit stared over at Manfred as he had a shouted conversation with Wolfgang, into which Silke was trying to interject. Wolfgang was getting a little boisterous but Manfred was taking it with good humour.

'You're going to have to renovate the house for a second time after this party,' Jurgen suggested.

'What?' she asked, not having listened to him.

'You're going to have a hell of a job cleaning up tomorrow morning!'

'I know, and I don't think I'll be in much of a mood for it,' she forced a smile. She suddenly wanted to kiss him, there and then, and to hell with it, but she told herself to be sensible. She always was bloody sensible, she thought angrily. Why shouldn't she do as she pleased? But good sense prevailed. Everyone would have been angry with her; not just Manfred. Jurgen would have pushed her away, she knew, and then she'd have to explain to his wife, Renate, and all the others.

'Oh God,' she said out loud and pulled away from Jurgen.

'Feeling unwell?' he shouted, and she nodded. She used him for support as she walked past him and through another couple to get to the door.

Yelena and Tina were still talking in the hall and she walked over to them.

'Did you hear that Christa's pregnant?' she asked.

'Tina was just telling me,' Yelena admitted.

'She's keeping the father a secret,' the other woman said. 'Any guesses?'

'No,' said Birgit promptly and pushed through them. She started to climb the stairs, pulling herself up by the banisters as her legs didn't feel too strong. 'I need the bathroom,' she excused herself. She had seen the look that Yelena had given her. 'Oh, say it isn't so,' Birgit said, knowing that nobody would hear her over the noise.

On the landing she took a deep breath and walked to the bathroom door which, when she tried it, she found to be locked. It wasn't really a problem as she didn't want to use the room as anything other than a refuge. She turned and walked into the darkened bedroom adjacent to it where the single bed was piled high with coats.

'The guest bedroom,' she said to herself, laughing a little at the thought that she was talking to herself. She repeated the words, accenting 'guest' to suggest to her audience that the word was not quite the correct one. Since Manfred had first shown her around the house, telling her that it could be theirs, she had thought of it as the nursery.

She stood there unmoving, looking down at the pile of coats, while the floor thumped underneath her with the bass notes of the music. Laughter and shouted conversation came up to her from different parts of her house. She thought again of Manfred and Christa, and her certainty that the woman was pregnant with his child reared up at her like an all too probable monster. She looked around the room and despaired that it would ever be a nursery where she would look after her own baby. Everyone had said what vision she had in renovating the house, but none had seen this room as she envisaged it. The bright, pastel colours were those she thought that a child might like, and where there was the bed she hoped there might soon be a cradle. In her anger she threw herself down on the pile of coats, sobbing.

After perhaps a minute she controlled herself. The noise continued as before, but then she heard somebody calling her name. It was Manfred, shouting for her up the stairs. She didn't want to see him, and as there was nowhere obvious to hide in the room she slipped down onto the floor and then burrowed in between the coats and the bed, forcing her way under the weight of them all.

And then she felt very stupid. If he were to discover her there how would she explain herself? She looked out from under the far edge of the coats, towards the wall and in the darkness something in front of her moved; something close. Her eyes were slowly adjusting to the dim light that came in through the door, up from the hall and over the pile of coats.

She flinched; there was someone there. In the space between the bed and the wall she saw a face a few inches from hers. It was the face of a child.

Birgit immediately backed out from under the coats and stood up, straightening her clothes. The child was still there, looking interested in what Birgit was doing. The little girl had to be about five, the woman decided.

'Hello,' she said carefully, wondering what the child was doing there. 'What's your name?'

'Katia,' the girl replied. 'And you are Birgit.'

'That's right,' she said, smiling reassuringly, wondering who she was trying to comfort, herself or the child. 'Have we met before?'

The little girl frowned, and then looked behind Birgit, who turned. It was not Manfred at the bedroom door but Christa.

'Katia,' the newcomer admonished the child. 'What are you doing up here?'

'Talking to Birgit.'

'Birgit who, sweetie?' Christa asked, and the child pointed.

'Christa?' asked Birgit, but Christa blatantly ignored her. 'Christa!' she almost shouted as the woman walked forward, took the child's hand and led her from the room. Finally she shouted but was ignored.

What the hell was Christa doing bringing a child to the party? Whose child was it?

Birgit strode out of the room and immediately bumped into Jurgen. She apologised and tried to go around him but he had a hold of her shoulder.

'I will come and see you tomorrow,' he said. 'I will bring a man who can get that stain out of your new carpet.'

'Thank you,' she said. 'Please forgive me; I'll be back in a minute. I need to speak to Christa.'

She reached the head of the stairs and could see Christa and the little girl, Katia, going down hand in hand. Manfred was at the bottom, calling up to her. Birgit attempted to follow them, expecting to take the stairs two at a time but as soon as she had started she knew that it was a mistake. She had misjudged her very first step and the next didn't seem to happen as everything wheeled around her. She tried to grab the banister but missed it and she flailed around with her arms for a moment without being able to hold on to anything. Then she felt a blow to the side of her head and there was what seemed to be an intense flash of light.

'Are you sure you are all right?' asked Jurgen.

Birgit closed her eyes tight and shook her head to clear it. She was sitting on one of the hard chairs in the kitchen with a cup of coffee in her hand. She released it in horror, wondering how she had got there. It was daylight and the house was empty of guests. The cup smashed and the brown liquid was released over the linoleum.

'You're not all right, are you,' he answered himself, getting up and walking towards her.

'No. I think I've lost my memory.'

'I told Willy you weren't all right last night. I said you should go to a hospital, but *he's* the doctor.'

'I fell down the stairs.'

'That's right. You knocked yourself out.'

'I'd drunk too much.'

'We all had. But you seemed all right afterwards. You said first thing this morning that it had cleared your head, but you'd forgotten I said I'd be bringing Carl with me.'

'Who's Carl?'

'Now I am worried about you. Carl's my friend who's cleaning your horribly expensive carpet.'

'The wine stain?'

'That's right.'

'That's who I can hear in the living room?'

Jurgen nodded, stopped, and then shook his head: 'You really are not right, are you? I came to talk about some important matters, but perhaps I should wait until you are well.'

'Do you mind?' she asked, and got up from her chair, walking around the coffee on the floor. She went to the door and saw that there was a small man in her living room with a device like a very complicated vacuum cleaner. He looked up at her arrival:

'As good as new,' he beamed. 'In fact, almost too good.'

'Thank you,' she said.

'Can I take you to a doctor?' Jurgen asked. He was now standing at her shoulder. She put her hand up to her temple and felt a very tender spot.

'No, I don't think so. I feel okay now.'

'But I'm worried about you. Look, take it easy, go to bed. Tell that husband of yours to keep an eye on you.'

She agreed that she would, and eventually she was able to show Jurgen and his colleague out of the house. When she had closed the door after them and looked back around her she realised that she couldn't possibly go to bed; not yet. The place was in a terrible state after the party. It would take all day to get it straight, but at least the wine stain was gone. The first thing she had to do was tidy up the cup of coffee she had just dropped.

A week later Jurgen appeared at her door just after Manfred had left for work. He offered to drive her to the park where he said that he wanted to talk with her. When she suggested he come inside instead he declined and said that he would explain all, if only she would go with him. Birgit insisted that she had too much housework to do but Jurgen was firm; there were reasons for going to the park. Annoyed, she took off her housecoat, put on a mackintosh and allowed herself to follow him down the path to the big black car.

As they walked up to it and he opened the door for her she noted that Jurgen had a driver just as Manfred did, even though he was a great deal less important than her husband. As soon as they pulled away from the pavement she asked what he wanted to talk about but he told her to wait until they arrived. He did, however, ask with some concern about the bump on her head and how her memory was. She assured him she was quite well.

She was regretting getting into the car, worried about where they were going, but Jurgen was true to his word and they got out at the Park and started to walk. He began by talking about the

Party, and the importance of its image. At the entrance to the park was a large fountain with an improbable statue of a horse and as they walked past it Birgit saw a small child with its mother. She was instantly reminded, for the first time since it had happened, of Christa taking the hand of the little girl at her party. She remembered how she had led the girl out of the bedroom just before Birgit had fallen down the stairs. She wondered who the little girl had been; she couldn't remember her name. Christa's presence at the party was understandable, but why was there a little girl at the house at some time past midnight? And what was her relationship to Christa? She thought with horror that the child might be Manfred's, but it seemed impossible.

The questions she was asking herself meant that she had not been listening to Jurgen properly. He had moved on to pointing out her husband's importance and position within the Party. He seemed to be concerned about Manfred. She tried to give Jurgen her full attention but her thoughts kept returning to the child.

'So you would have no hesitation to help me?' he was asking her.

'Of course not.'

'I know what you're thinking, but it isn't anything like informing on him.'

'I'm sorry, what isn't like informing?'

He stopped and frowned at her.

'Are you sure you're fully recovered?'

'Yes, sorry, I was just distracted. I was remembering seeing Christa at the party, and a little girl. . . . But what were you saying about informing?'

He was patient with her and started again:

'Your husband now holds a very important position in the Party. He's a very visible and vital part of it. The last thing that any of us wants is for him to make a silly mistake, or slip up. We want you to tell us if he does or says anything that he shouldn't; anything that would reflect badly on the Party or on himself.'

'You want me to inform on my own husband?' she was incredulous now she realised what was being asked of her

'As I said, it's not informing. It's protecting him. And it's a case of protecting yourself.'

'Even if he was doing something he shouldn't, a wife would never do that to her husband. There's a trust between us . . .'

Jurgen put his hand up to stop her.

'I understand,' he said.

'My husband and I trust each other,' she dismissed his request. 'I wouldn't do anything to undermine that.'

Jurgen considered his next move, and then made it with deliberation.

'Your husband is having an affair with Christa Smisek.'

'I don't believe you,' Birgit replied with as much composure as she could muster. To have her fears realised made her feel weak, and she was unable to order her thoughts.

'You are in an awkward situation,' he said simply. 'The beautiful house you have, your social position, your friends . . . they are all as a result of your husband's position. You lose your husband and you lose everything else.'

'Am I going to lose him?' she asked quietly.

'I hope not. We do not want any kind of scandal. As far as everyone knows you are happily married. We want your husband to keep his position in the Party, his nice house, his friends, his wife . . . But he is weak and needs to be helped, by us and by you. But, surely he has forfeited his right to trust?'

In her thoughts she agreed, although she would not give Jurgen the satisfaction of hearing her articulate this.

'What do you want me to do?' she asked.

'Very little. Perhaps we can meet once a week and you can tell me if he is saying or doing anything against the Party. I promise you that he won't be punished, but we will make sure that the temptation to do anything wrong is removed. As I say, he is weak, but we need him to appear to be strong.'

'What about Christa? She's a temptation.'

'In return for your help you have my word that we will remove that particular temptation.'

And so Birgit heard, a few days later, that Christa had moved away. A new position of some importance had been given to her somewhere down south. There was no mention of any child, born or pending. Birgit wasn't sure what she thought about any of this but when she met Jurgen the following week he explained that the Party only wanted harmony and it was better to persuade a person to act sensibly than to force them.

'We only want what's best for everyone,' he smiled, in a fatherly fashion. 'I know what people say about the Party, and the rumours and the gossip. There are times when people need to be punished, and punishments can be severe. But usually we can modify any wrongdoing, any unbecoming behaviour. We can use persuasion, subtlety, understanding even.'

'Manfred has been in a bad mood since he heard that Christa had left,' Birgit told him. 'But this morning he seemed genuinely caring towards me; loving even.'

'Did we do the right thing?' Jurgen asked, apparently eager for her approval. 'Have we handled it well?'

'Yes, I think it might work out.'

'Good. And now you can get back on with your life with Manfred. And he doesn't need to know about our little talks. You just need to keep an eye on him so that he doesn't do anything silly again. If he does, or if you're worried that he might, then let me know and we will quietly put things right.'

'I'm not sure I'll feel the same way about him again.'

'It was simply a minor infidelity, a slip.'

'Surely it's more than that,' she said, and screwed together the courage to ask: 'Is it his baby she's carrying?'

'We're not sure. We don't know. Perhaps.'

'Manfred has betrayed me.'

'You don't know that for sure. All that we know is that he was weak. He needs a strong woman, like you, Birgit.'

She had resolved to also ask about the little girl but the conversation took an unexpected turn.

'Perhaps you should consider trying for a baby again yourselves?' he suggested. 'Now Christa has been removed perhaps Manfred will be a little more attentive and sensitive to your needs. Think of it as an opportunity to start again.'

'Attentive' and 'sensitive', he had said. It was like a blow that winded her. 'Attentive' and 'sensitive'; the words recalled a painful memory from immediately after the party; with the last guest seen out of the house Birgit had asked Manfred to hold her. She didn't say that she required reassurance because of Christa, but she had needed help and he had said that he was too tired.

'Do you love me?' she had asked, and he replied with a mechanical 'Of course.'

It wasn't enough, she said, and he had asked why not? He stated, obviously bored, 'Birgit, I love you. There, now let's go to bed.'

'I don't believe you do love me,' she replied. 'If you did you'd be, well . . .'

'Well what?'

And then she had said it: 'If you loved me you'd be more attentive and sensitive to my needs.'

They weren't words she remembered ever using before. She had immediately thought them too melodramatic and clichéd. She was embarrassed by them.

And they were exactly the words that Jurgen had used.

She considered the possibility that Manfred had told someone else what she had said, but it seemed unlikely. He was not that kind of man. He would not have repeated her accusation of inattention and insensitivity; the suggestion that he was not fulfilling her 'needs'.

She had certainly told nobody. It was as though Jurgen had been there at the time and had heard her say it. She couldn't get over the thought that he had been listening. She had a mental picture of Jurgen standing in the corner of the room, observing them, making notes. It was stupid, of course, because everyone knew that wasn't how the authorities worked. No, they concealed cameras and microphones if they wanted to know what was going on.

Cameras and microphones; they were what the authorities used if they wanted to listen in to the conversations of people they distrusted.

Why had she not realised before? They were obviously interested in Manfred's private life. And any of those friendly tradesmen in their nice new house could have put in surveillance equipment. Everyone knew that's the kind of thing they did, but it had never once crossed her mind that she and Manfred might be important enough. Of course *she* wasn't, but *he* had certainly become so. Why else was she there in the park with Jurgen, driven there in the back of his car? Why else was she being asked to act as an informant?

'Do you just have microphones in my house?' she asked him directly. 'Or are there cameras as well?'

'We don't do that kind of thing!' he laughed.

'If I go home and tear down all the light fittings, pull out all the sockets, I'll find nothing?'

'You would do a lot of needless damage.'

'Those nice plaster mouldings on the ceilings could be smashed up. I'll rip off the wallpaper and tear up the carpets and pull up the floorboards.'

'You're letting your imagination run away with you.'

She imagined someone in an adjacent building listening in to her conversations with Manfred on headphones. Worse still, he would be watching a low-quality picture on a television monitor. Would they have cameras in every room? Please, not the bedroom! Would they have surveillance equipment in the bathroom, just in case?

Jurgen was talking, trying to reassure her, when she remembered the night of the party and hiding under the coats. She remembered the little girl. Now she even remembered her name.

'Who's Katia?' she asked.

'I don't know,' he replied, apparently genuine.

'She was the little girl in the house, with Christa, on the night of the party.'

'Christa wasn't at the party.'

'Your people would've been watching, listening, noting who was there, listening to the conversations. You'll have it all in a file somewhere. I thought you were there as a friend!'

'I was there as a friend. I wasn't there in an official capacity.'

'But somebody will have been there "officially". You've been keeping an eye on my husband; spying on him. You'll have known Christa was there, with the little girl.'

He considered this and then said, seriously:

'I wasn't aware that Christa was at the party. But I will find out for you.'

She supposed that he might not have noticed her, or the girl, but it seemed unlikely. No doubt they had left in the confusion when Birgit had fallen down the stairs?

'I'll look into it,' he reassured her. 'We are on the same side, aren't we?'

'I don't know.'

'We are both making sure that you and Manfred lead a happy life together in your new home. We want him to retain his position. We want you to stay together.'

'I suppose so.'

'Then we're on the same side,' he smiled broadly, as though it was all decided. 'We will work together. I'll help you and you'll help me.'

She grudgingly agreed, and he drove her back home.

It was hard to go back into her house knowing that she was being listened to, and probably watched. Birgit went immediately to the bedroom and lay down on the bed. From that position she was able to naturally look around the room and examined it for the possible hiding-places of cameras. She knew that they could be small and she decided that there were a number of places in which they could be hidden. Feeling increasingly uncomfortable she retreated to the bathroom and sat on the toilet. There, she was sure after looking around her, there was no camera, although there might well be a microphone. She ran the water in the bath and carefully inspected every surface, every nook and cranny. But then she began to doubt herself. And would she ever really be able to tell whether she was watched anyway? Hadn't technology developed to such a degree that almost anything was possible?

On that afternoon she resolved that she could not live in that house. Even making dinner for Manfred she moved around the kitchen as though she had an audience. There was probably only some dull, bored operative simply noting down her movements, but she felt so exposed that she might just as well have been on a stage in an auditorium, in front of thousands.

She did everything with the thought that she was observed, minding every action, and when Manfred returned home that evening she chose her every word with care. When it was time to go to bed she changed into her nightgown in the bathroom. It was not a part of her normal routine but Manfred did not seem to notice. She went through to the bedroom terrified lest he would want to make love and was relieved when he turned the light off on his side of the bed and left her alone. She would normally have read by her own bedside light but she was grateful to turn it off and lie in the darkness.

The following morning she got dressed in the bathroom and went down and made breakfast. Manfred's driver called for him at 8:30 precisely and she was alone again, with her hidden audience. She tidied the house and did the washing. She found herself imagining the notes that would be taken and how dull they would be. In her head she started to narrate her movements and slowly found the whole idea of being observed quite ludicrous, if not almost amusing. Was somebody really noting down in a file that she was dusting her living room and then vacuuming it? Would they write that she poured the remains of her coffee down the sink, rinsed it away and then decided to add a small dash of bleach?

When Birgit made the dinner that evening she imagined that she was the star of a cookery show that she often watched on the television. She was nervous, and broke the eggs badly into the bowl but, on balance, she felt that she performed well. Perhaps she had missed her vocation? She fantasised that she would ask Jurgen how she might get on to the television. He seemed to know how things worked, and Manfred was powerful enough and could exert his influence, surely?

When Manfred came home that evening she listened to him talk about his day as they ate, initially worried lest he should say something questionable. However, he behaved impeccably and she was proud of him.

The next day she visited Yelena and was bursting to tell her what had been happening, but could not bring herself to do so. If she herself was being observed what was to say that there were not also cameras in Yelena's house? Maybe she had her own little faceless, grey man acting as an audience? She laughed at the idea; the line had to be drawn somewhere; if half of the population was observed then it had to be by the remaining half, and who would observe the observers? It was all too ludicrous, she tried to tell herself.

She and Manfred ate out at a restaurant that evening, and the following day was Saturday. Manfred was at home but had resolved to work in the garden so Birgit promised that she would make him a favourite dish. It was one that required a great deal of preparation, and immediately she had washed up and tidied away breakfast she got to work. She took a glass dish from out of the cupboard and as she walked across the kitchen the sunlight caught it. For a fraction of a second there was a reflection from something in the far corner of the room, where the two walls met the ceiling in a simple plaster moulding. She had been right! There was the camera lens!

She turned to it: 'First we marinade the meat,' she said to it quite naturally. She walked around the table so that she could be observed fully. 'But make sure you have the best possible meat. Don't let the butcher give you any old cut that he wants to be rid of. . . .'

Jurgen arrived in his car as usual on the Monday morning immediately Manfred had left for work. She went down the path and met him as he was getting out. He looked annoyed and she was worried. As the driver pulled away from the kerb he demanded of her: 'What do you think you're doing? Talking to the cameras?'

'I'm sorry,' she apologised, embarrassed.

'You have to play the game!' he told her.

'I promise I will. I don't like being watched. It's how I cope, I think.'

'You haven't told Manfred about the surveillance?'

'No. He's acting naturally, isn't he?'

'Yes. And I've told the operator to ignore your behaviour; I've explained that you're under pressure. I've made sure there's no reference to it in the files.'

'Thank you. I'm sorry. I was very silly.'

'Well, yes, you were,' he agreed, and then laughed for a half-second. 'But the operator said that he liked your recipe for pot roast pork.'

Birgit laughed naturally, and he resumed. She wondered if any of this was really important? He had called it a game, and perhaps he was right? But why should she play? She reasoned that she would probably go along with it because she hadn't the courage to argue. Isn't that what everyone did? Was it even possible not to play?

At the park they got out of the car and walked together down the dusty paths. Not once did Jurgen ask about Manfred. For some reason she did not understand he started to talk about his childhood. He reminisced about growing up in the countryside on a collective farm. He said how idyllic it had been, how good his teachers were and how well they lived generally. He was sure their standard of living was much better.

'I'm not at ease in the city,' he said. 'But in the countryside I feel alive. It's the air, the closeness of nature. . .'

His words faded away, as though the volume had been turned down. When she was sure he had stopped Birgit tentatively explained that she had been brought up in Berlin, where her parents still lived. She wondered if her story was already known to him? There would be files on her, she assumed, files that he would have had access to. Jurgen seemed genuinely interested in what she had to say, though, and even asked friendly questions about her parents and sisters. He was an only child, he explained, although he had been close enough to other children that they might as well have been related. He asked her what it had been like growing up in a city with all of its temptations. He said that he never felt cool coming from the countryside.

They leant over a wall and looked down at geese on an ornamental lake. They were close enough that they almost touched each other. Stretching out her hand directly in front of her he did the same and the backs of their hands almost came together. She could feel the fine hair on the back of his hand tickling her and it was a moment of intense intimacy such as she felt she had never shared with Manfred.

Birgit decided that it was the moment to ask about the girl she had seen with Christa.

Jurgen very slowly moved his hand away, and when he answered he didn't look at her:

'I don't know who she might be.' He looked out over the lake into the distance. 'I think one of our operatives must have been over-tired the night of the party. There was more than one because we knew there would be several people to observe. The file says that you went to the spare bedroom and got under the coats?'

'Yes, I was hiding. I was a little tired and drunk.'

She was unhappy that he had moved his hand away. He said:

'The file states that a woman then came to the door and took out a child.'

'Christa and . . .' Once again she struggled for the name. Then she found it: 'Katia.'

'I am telling you too much,' Jurgen shook his head slowly and then looked at her for the first time. 'But the other operative only saw you leave the room. You talked to me. There was no mention of a woman or child leaving before you.'

'That's strange.'

'No, not really. The files are not always accurate.'

'I suppose not.'

'But I didn't see Christa or the girl,' he said.

'Your memory might not be accurate either?'

'It is usually.'

Birgit's affair with Jurgen started several weeks later. Each Monday they would meet and their discussions seemed to her to be quite unimportant, although she enjoyed them and quickly came to look forward to them. They did not discuss what was happening, and there were times when she doubted that anything ever happened. But on the day that it happened properly he drove her out of the city to the countryside where he had been as a boy. They left the car parked in the road with the driver, and in a wood he remembered fondly they had kissed, and walked back hand in hand, releasing each other only as they came in sight of the car. The following week it was raining and they took shelter in a barn. She was sure that he enjoyed the danger of it, but with him she felt safe; as though there could be no possible threat from the world. They had made love slowly and tenderly, and afterwards she fell asleep with her head on his chest, looking up at him. He was alert to the sound of anyone coming upon them and she trusted him. When she awoke he was still in the same position, looking around, but not too nervous. He was very careful.

The week after that they must have walked a couple of miles from the car over fields where the boundaries seemed to be lost over the distant horizons. The field was vast and she told Jurgen that she felt able to comprehend the curvature of the earth. Out there in the open they made love; he said that they would see anybody coming long before they were observed themselves.

He took her to several different places, but on the tenth week of the affair the car was driven into the centre of the city rather than out of it. Jurgen would not talk to her properly in the car, she understood that, but she ventured to ask where they were going. His unwillingness to reply scared her, and when they turned off the busy roads into a quiet side street her worst fears seemed to be realised. They were allowed through a barrier into the courtyard of a large and impersonal concrete building. There were very few windows in the forbidding walls, and no sunlight seemed able to penetrate down to where the car stopped.

They got out of the car and Birgit obediently followed Jurgen to the entrance. He showed an identity card and they went inside and down a long beige corridor. Birgit did not know what was happening but assumed the worst; she assumed that this was the end of everything. She did not know what she had done wrong or what her punishment would be, but she was convinced that her old life was finished.

Birgit and Jurgen waited on hard chairs outside a nondescript door and she did not have the nerve to ask Jurgen why he had brought her there. He now seemed as nervous as she was, if not more so; she felt somehow horribly resigned to anything that might occur.

They waited without speaking for a quarter of an hour before the door opened. A woman appeared and beckoned Birgit inside on her own. It appeared to be a doctor's consulting room although the old man who looked up at her from behind the desk was not wearing a white coat. He did, however, produce a stethoscope, asked her to remove her coat and listened to her chest through her blouse. He took her pulse and her blood pressure and all the time asked indifferently after her general health. Once he had made a few notes he took a little blood and finally she was sent behind a screen to provide a sample of urine. When she had finished the doctor dismissed her and out in the corridor she found Jurgen still waiting for her.

He took her down another corridor, down some stairs and they doglegged back, along a similar corridor a floor underground. Half way down they were met by another man who asked them to sit down on hard chairs. This time they did not have long to wait before being asked inside a dark room by a tall, fat man whose clothes did not seem to fit him properly.

He walked over to a curtained window and Birgit followed. She suddenly realised that the door was closed behind them and that Jurgen had not followed them in. For the first time she felt really afraid and started to shiver nervously.

'You are Birgit Haker?' asked the man.

She agreed that was her name.

'Look through this window please.'

He pulled open the curtain. In the brightly lit room beyond was the little girl she had seen at the party.

'Do you know who this is?' Birgit was asked.

'I think her name's Katia,' she said.

The man seemed pleased. He then asked: 'Is she your daughter?'

'No, why do you ask?'

'Is she your husband's daughter?'

'Not that I know of.'

The man closed the curtain and said: 'You may go out.'

Birgit stayed where she was.

'Can I ask . . . ?' she started to say.

'No,' said the man unemotionally and so she turned, walked over to the door and fumbled to open it in the gloom. She was assisted from outside by Jurgen who showed her immediately across the corridor to another room. This time she discovered that Manfred and Christa were inside. It was a small room with four chairs against the back wall.

Her husband stood up as Birgit entered and she walked tentatively towards him. She wasn't sure how he would react but he put his arms around her and hugged her. While in his embrace she stole a glance at Christa, who was staring at the floor.

'Do you know why are we here?' Manfred asked Birgit.

'No. But I was asked if I knew Katia.'

At the mention of the little girl's name Christa looked up.

'What do you know about her?' she demanded.

'Nothing, other than that she was with you at our party.'

'At the party?' asked Manfred. 'And who's Katia?'

Jurgen shut the door behind them from the inside, but almost immediately it was opened again and the man from the room opposite came in.

'Would you all sit down please?' he asked. 'Can I ask you not to do or say anything?'

He waited until Manfred, Birgit and Jurgen were seated and then went back out of the door. Birgit was surprised to see Jurgen was sitting, waiting, like the rest of them.

The door then reopened, and in came Katia, with an expressionless woman of indeterminate age walking behind her, her hands on the little girl's shoulders.

'Now, Katia,' the woman addressed her, stooping down to her. The little girl looked up at the tall man and Birgit wondered just how tall he must seem to her.

'See these people here,' she said to Katia, directing her to look at those in the room who were seated. 'Do you recognise any of them as your parents?'

The little girl looked shyly at each in turn and lingered longest on Christa. Birgit noticed the subtle changes that had happened to the woman; the swelling belly and breasts; the healthiness of her skin. She wondered if Manfred had done that to her.

The little girl eventually looked at Jurgen.

'Is it him?' she asked in a small voice.

'No,' laughed the woman.

'Is it you?' the little girl asked, looking up at her. It was obvious that she just wanted to please the woman; to get the right answer.

'No, it's not me, poppet,' she said. 'Let's go back out.'

They left and the tall man followed. When the door was closed they all looked around at each other. Manfred spoke first:

'They can do a test, surely?' he asked.

'They are,' said Jurgen.

Manfred then looked at Christa: 'Is she yours?'

At this Christa suddenly started to cry. She stood up, looked about her and then fled the room.

'Can we leave as well?' asked Manfred.

'I think so,' said Jurgen uncertainly. He got up and went to the door, took a breath before opening it, and peered out into the corridor. He looked back at them conspiratorially: 'Yes, I think we can go.'

They followed him down the corridors and up the stairs. His car was still waiting outside and he told them he would take them back home. None of them spoke on the journey through the traffic, out to the suburbs. Birgit was cautiously optimistic that somehow a disaster had been missed, or averted but did not want to discuss it for fear of her luck turning. She did not even want to think about what had happened but as she walked back in through her own front door she realised that it would be impossible just to carry on as before. She knew that it was far from over. She simply sat down in her living room and waited for the next chapter to begin. She looked into the top corners of the room, trying to locate the camera. She wanted to communicate to them that they might as well begin then and there.

'What are you doing?' Manfred asked.

'You don't know?'

'No. I'm not sure I understand anything.'

'We are being observed.'

'Don't be so stupid.'

'This is just another scene in a film that has not ended.'

'What?'

'Me, you, Christa, Jurgen . . . we are all actors in a drama.'

'What drama? What's this all about?'

'I don't know.' She felt that perhaps she had not been concentrating properly. She looked to Manfred, wondering if her lines were to be spoken next, or his.

'You're having a nervous breakdown,' he decided. 'I almost think you *want* to have one. I'm going to call a doctor.'

She let him make the call and then, together, they waited. When the car pulled up outside he seemed baffled when it was one of his colleagues and when he asked Manfred, not her, to go away with them. He argued, but she paid little attention. A short while later another car arrived for her and she didn't demur. She didn't question anything. She didn't once look back.

The following days passed quietly and happily for Birgit. They eventually explained that she was to stay in the all-female community until the last month of her pregnancy. Nobody told her directly that she was pregnant, but she knew immediately when she saw the state of the other women around her. Then she felt the changes to her body; it felt almost a response to her environment. They were very kind to her and gave her light work to do which she quite enjoyed. She felt more stimulated than she had done before and didn't miss Manfred particularly. When she thought she might do she considered her relationship with Jurgen and decided that she missed that more. She was, after all, pregnant with his baby.

She began, slowly, to think more and more about the new life growing inside her. What was initially something of a surprise was discussed by the nurses, when talked about at all, as something almost conceptual. In her mind it started out like that, but as the weeks passed she recognised the new life within her as a nascent person. There would be a child; a little girl or boy. It was odd that nobody wanted to discuss her future beyond the fact that for the last month of her confinement she would be taken to another hospital. She was told that it would be down south, and was very well-appointed and comfortable, and they were right.

Birgit's labour, when it finally arrived (she was two weeks late and they were considering inducing her) was a long and painful one. She hardly knew what was happening afterwards and was encouraged to sleep. They gave her pills which she was happy to accept.

Although she was sore and they gave her more medication, the next few days were more emotionally painful. She was not allowed to see her baby and she realised that the pills they were giving her were meant to stop her from worrying about this. She existed in a mental fog until she was moved again to another all-female community and the medication suddenly ceased. The work there was harder and as days passed, then weeks and finally months, her emotions seemed to resolve themselves. She knew intellectually that the child had never been hers. She liked to imagine it with a foster family in a house like the one she had once lived in with Manfred. The little girl was actually somebody else's daughter. If there was a strange feeling inside her, an ache, then it was one that she knew she would have to come to terms with.

They checked on her health every week to start with, then once a month, and then they seemed to stop entirely. When she was told many months later to report to the doctor for a check-up it was a shock to realise that it was exactly twelve months since she had given birth. They were simply checking on her health and well-being but she could not stop thinking that it was the birthday of her child.

In a room eerily like that in which she had seen the grey-haired doctor, a woman doctor now checked her blood pressure and then took a sample of blood and urine.

Birgit decided to risk asking:

'Is my baby doing well?'

The doctor smiled at her: 'Do you think of her often?'

'No, not often,' she said, noting the use of the word 'her'. So, she had a daughter. 'I just hope she's healthy, and happy?'

'I'm sure she is.'

'There's nothing about her in my notes?'

'No,' the doctor looked down at the file. 'She's entirely separate. Apart from a name and a date of birth, we have no information.'

'What is her name?'

The doctor looked worried for the first time. Birgit sensed this and tried to look disinterested.

'I was just wondering.' She added, disingenuously, 'I suppose it's a bit sentimental saying "my baby".'

There was a silence while the doctor deliberated. Finally she said:

'Your child is called Katia.'

Mathilde

Bernard heard the news one busy evening in my bar on the rue des Abbesses. He heard it from Jules, who had been told by Lulu. I wasn't sure that either of these were the most reliable sources of information, but why would they make up such a story? Why would they tell Bernard if it wasn't true?

Come to think of it, why would they tell him at all? Why didn't they just keep quiet and hope that Mathilde would be in Paris for perhaps a few weeks and then leave again before Bernard became aware of her presence? I assume it was because their meeting was somehow inevitable, and they wanted to warn him. Somebody would have told him that she had arrived. Perhaps she would have sought him out if he had not gone to her?

'But you know what happened before,' said Jules with barely concealed impatience. 'You remember what she did to you?'

'Keep away from her,' pleaded Hortense, Jules's wife.

'I don't know if I can,' replied Bernard slowly. He was sipping his Pernod while they stood at the counter, and I'm certain that he was already considering how soon he could leave us and go to Mathilde. He wasn't normally a man of action or impulse, but I could see that he was excited. He was in his later middle-age, unshaven, stooped and slightly unkempt, but he was visibly drawing himself up to an unaccustomed height. He was putting his shoulders back; he was defiantly meeting the eyes of those who would tell him how to act. With quiet determination he added: 'I don't know if I want to keep away from her.'

'But when she came into your life before she broke up your marriage,' Jules reminded him. 'And lost you your job.'

'I know, I know.'

'She played with you before, and if you let her she'll do the same again,' Hortense told him. 'She makes promises she never intends to keep. While she's around you're a slave to her every whim.'

'It's not quite like that.'

'She's not worth all of the unhappiness; the upheaval and destruction. You know she's not. For a few hours of pleasure, for a few days, a few weeks if you're lucky, you're content to throw away everything. I know that if she asked you to give up all of your friends, your money, your apartment then you would, for her, wouldn't you? She'd take everything from you again if she could.'

'I know,' Bernard repeated slowly. 'I know. I realise how much I've given up for Mathilde. And I know what I've lost, but what you don't seem to realise is that I think she's worth it.' He looked from Jules to Hortense and then back again. 'If you want to put a value on these things then yes I'd happily give everything for an evening with Mathilde. For one full night with her I'd lay down my own life.'

'You are utterly hopeless!' his friend shook his head. 'What have you ever received from her except pain? You used to work in finance; can't you see that all your time, money and heartache was a very poor investment?'

From my side of the counter I had heard about Bernard and Mathilde from some of the other regulars, but I knew none of the details. I carefully asked Bernard, 'She must be a rather wonderful woman, for you to feel as you do?'

'She's a witch,' said Jules decisively.

'And it's not even as though she's anything to look at.'

'Not to you, maybe,' conceded Bernard. 'But to me she's beautiful. Her smile, and her voice. . . .'

'She's got to be in her forties, and she's got a good figure for her age,' admitted Hortense, 'but she's ugly.'

'Have you really sacrificed everything for her?' I asked.

He held up his hands and shrugged: 'I've given everything willingly.'

'And how does she feel about you?'

'Less than nothing,' said Hortense.

'Is she married?'

'Oh yes, happily married, apparently,' Hortense explained. 'When she and Bernard had their great affair they holed-up in that apartment on rue Véron, but everybody got to know about it, whether they wanted to or not. Bernard's wife, not unreasonably, kicked him out. But when Mathilde had taken everything from Bernard she simply went back home and apologised to her husband. And he forgave her! I expect she does it all the time. There are probably Bernards all over the city . . . all over France.'

'Bernard lavished such gifts on her,' Jules added. 'He rented that apartment he still has and they stayed inside for a couple of weeks; he didn't even bother to go into work. He lost his wife, but what did he care? He had the wonderful Mathilde! He lost his job, but so what? He still had Mathilde! But then she got tired of him and left him on his own. He had lost everything. He had a breakdown and only survived because his friends supported him.'

'Mathilde's husband is a politician,' Hortense pointed out. 'He shut up his town house and took his wife back to the countryside where there'd be no scandal. She forgot all about poor Bernard back here in Paris. He was only just kept out of hospital because of friends like us. We kept the roof above his head. We helped him with his debts. And we did all that because we felt sorry for him.

He'd been an utter fool, but after all, everyone is allowed to make a mistake once in a while.'

'Which is why we can't believe he's even thinking about seeing her again,' explained Jules. He shook his head, finished his drink and put his glass down loudly on the marble counter.

'Bernard. As your friend I am telling you to keep away from her. If you don't then I'm not sure that any of us will be willing to pick up the pieces again.'

He got up and his wife did the same.

'Please do as he says,' said Hortense, and the couple left the bar.

I picked up their empty glasses and wiped down the counter.

'She does seem to be trouble, this Mathilde?'

'Oh yes, she is,' Bernard conceded. 'But, to me, she's worth it.'

'Now she's back, are you going to see her again?'

He looked over to the door to make sure that his friends had gone, looked back at me, and nodded.

I have to admit that I was intrigued. When Bernard left a short while later I was convinced that he was not going home but was off to find this woman. I really can't claim any special powers of intuition; there was a fatalism in the way in which he had been staring unseeing into the middle distance, contemplating what he was about to do. He ordered one more drink and swallowed it with determination, readying himself for the inevitable.

When he got up from the counter I wished him good night and watched him leave. He turned right, once through the door, rather than cross the street to go home. There were only a couple of other customers left so I asked Gerard to look after the bar. I snatched up my hat, gloves and scarf and followed Bernard out into the night.

Although I couldn't see him, I had heard that the infamous Mathilde lived on the rue St Vincent. He had to have turned right up rue Ravignan, and when I did the same I was pleased to see him only fifty yards ahead of me.

I kept back, worried that he might notice he was being followed, but I needn't have bothered. He was oblivious to his surroundings; so much so that when he crossed the rue des Trois Frères he stepped out in front of a car and was nearly run over. The driver swore at him, quite reasonably, but Bernard walked on, apparently not registering the incident.

I followed him with my hands deep in my pockets, wondering why I was at all interested in walking through the cold wet streets after a man I really did not know at all well. It wasn't as though he was a particularly good customer. Apart from his attachment to this woman, Mathilde, he did not seem to be that interesting. He had apparently worked in a bank for many years and was now employed part-time in an art gallery at the far end of the rue des Abbesses, where it met the rue Tholozé.

We continued up towards the Place Jean-Baptiste Clément where a few late-night revellers and tourists still hung around. He passed Le Consulat on his right and continued on down the rue Des Saules. There could be no doubting his destination.

I followed him down the narrow lane, Bernard striding along the roadway while I kept to the high stone wall to the left, the buttresses offering me the opportunity to hide if he had turned around. But he was thinking only of her. When he reached the junction he turned right along rue St Vincent, his pace still purposeful. When he stopped I did so too.

He was standing opposite the gates of a large townhouse of brick and stone. All of the first and second floor windows blazed with light. He looked to be in a kind of rapture as he stood there, and I looked too but I could not see what held his attention so. There were no figures at the windows, nobody came and went through the main door into the little gated yard at the side. He looked foolish, his mouth slightly open, his whole air one of expectancy.

But if Bernard looked foolish I knew that I must do so too. I certainly felt an idiot, and turned away and went back to the bar. I finally admitted to myself why I had followed him: I wanted to catch a glimpse of Mathilde; a woman who was able to bewitch and ruin a man.

Bernard spent a great deal of the following week in the bar, staring out of the plate glass windows into the street. He had tidied himself up; he wore well-pressed clothes and was always clean-shaven. A couple of times I noticed that he left the bar suddenly, leaving behind him a smell of aftershave and his drink half-finished. I could guess what might be happening. Eventually I found the courage to ask him:

'Have you seen Mathilde yet?'

'Yes, twice, but don't tell Jules. I know I shouldn't have, but . . .'

'How did the meetings go?'

'The first time we walked over to Montmatre Cemetery. We kept at least a foot apart as we wandered around, pretending to examine the graves. We talked about how we shouldn't be seeing each other; how we should never see each other again. We didn't even touch.'

'But you did meet again?'

'Yes, in the hotel on rue Houdon.'

'Aha! I guessed as much.'

I suddenly realised how intrusive my interest sounded, but he didn't appear to mind. He smiled and said: 'Whatever you think happened, you're wrong.'

He took his time before continuing:

'I cannot describe the room that we hired for an hour. I do not recall the colour of the carpet, the walls, not even the bedspread on which we lay. We simply talked, turned to each other. We laughed at the folly of the situation and of how it would appear to an outsider looking in, expecting the action that usually attends such an assignation.'

'You mean . . . ?'

'Yes, we were being chaste, behaving ourselves, discussing the dark blue dress that she had worn for our meeting . . . a dress that she wore as a test . . . a dress that I had bought her five years before and which she had put on to find out if I remembered.'

I raised my eyebrows questioningly.

'Of course I did! And I recognised the earrings that I had given her along with other little things like the bracelet that she played with nervously. And I recalled the smell of her perfume; a scent I've occasionally discovered on other women and which always reminded me of her . . . she whom I feared I would never see again. But it had happened, and there we were, together, lying side by side in a hotel bedroom, both of us talking quietly, almost whispering, knowing that our meeting should not be happening.'

'Will you be seeing her again?'

'I hope so,' he said, looking around him as if emerging unexpectedly from a dream. 'Her husband is very wary of her being back in Paris. He is very suspicious and has engineered engagements for her; people to constantly visit and be visited by. She will come to me when she's able to. And I'm ready . . . I've been ready every day for the last five years. . . . And I've tidied and cleaned my apartment. I bring in new flowers every day. I've had all my clothes at the laundry, I've changed the sheets on the bed.'

'You are hoping to do more than just talk next time?'

'I don't know,' he said nervously. 'You see, our affair before was too intense for it to possibly continue. I know why she left me then. There's an inevitability about it all this time, which is why I can afford to take my time. If she can get away she'll come past the bar, here, and I'll follow her. If we go to the cemetery then that is fine, or perhaps a café, even a hotel again . . . But if we go to my apartment then that is it. Our love will take its preordained course and can only end in . . .'

'End in what?'

'Triumph? Disaster? Exaltation? Complete and utter degradation?'

'I don't really know what your problem is.'

'The danger is that if Mathilde comes to my place then she might not leave. I don't know how she managed to last time.'

'As I say, what's the problem? If you love her and she loves you?'

He shook his head. 'It's not as simple as that.'

'She won't leave her husband?'

'I've never asked her to.'

'Are there children?'

'No, there aren't any complications. . . .'

'So, if she loves you?'

'It's not a question of *her* love. It's mine that's in doubt. Do I really love her enough?'

'Surely you've demonstrated your devotion?'

'Have I?'

Bernard continued to sit by the window. I was busy with other customers but kept an eye out for him the whole time and he did not move from his seat. Over the next few days he spent more and more time at his table, making coffees last until they were stone cold, lingering over Pernod that must have evaporated before he drank any of it. He was embarrassed that I knew why he was there. I knew who he was waiting for, but I did my best to be discreet and said nothing more.

And then, one morning a week later I looked up from whatever I was doing behind the counter and saw a well-dressed woman outside. Although it was an overcast day she was wearing sunglasses and had to take them off to peer in at the window. She was quite small and dark, and at this point I feel that I must claim a degree of intuition. I imagined that perhaps she was Bernard's Mathilde, and so she turned out to be.

I went up to the door and opened it

'Pardon, Mathilde?' I asked, and she started.

'Yes. Do we know each other?'

'No. I'm Charles,' I said. 'A friend of Bernard's.'

She looked even more suspicious.

'I'm a friend who's not critical of him as some others are,' I explained.

Mathilde still backed away a little, worried.

'This is my bar. If you would like to come inside and wait for Bernard you are welcome to a coffee.'

'No, thank you. I can't stay.'

'If Bernard comes along in the next five minutes and I say you were here, but I didn't detain you, well, he'll be very annoyed with me.'

'You're expecting him here soon?'

'He's here most days, waiting for you. He could arrive at any moment.'

She agreed, reluctantly, to come in, and walked up to the counter with me.

'Have you known Bernard long?' she asked quietly. 'You say you're a friend, but I don't remember him mentioning your name before.'

'Customers, friends . . . the distinctions are blurred, but we certainly have good friends in common. I've seen quite a lot of him recently and he told me something of your, ah, relationship.'

The woman appeared uneasy once more. She looked down at the marble counter and ran a small finger over a part of the pattern in it. Looking at her closely I decided that Hortense was wrong to call her ugly; Mathilde had an odd, but not unattractive face. Her mouth was small, her chin wide, and her nose was hooked. But the overall effect was not displeasing; far from it. Her eyes were large and dark and quite heavily made-up to hide the unfortunate bags under them.

'You say you are not critical?' she asked. 'Perhaps you should be, a little.'

Bernard was right to say that she had a pretty voice. I was able to notice these things while I prepared her coffee. She had turned her attention to those passing outside in the street.

'His friends think that you lead him on,' I said as I worked. 'But I don't feel able to judge.'

She frowned: 'That I lead him on?'

'Yes. That he's given up too much for you, but you don't appear to want to sacrifice anything for him.'

'Is that how Bernard represents our relationship?'

'No, that's how his friends tell the story.'

'I love him,' she said simply, quietly, but added nothing else as another customer came in and asked for cigarettes. She stood there, sipping her coffee, looking out of the window. When the customer had been served she continued:

'I've offered to leave my husband for Bernard, but he refuses to let me do it. I love him so passionately, but I'm not worthy of his love.'

'He's obviously devoted to you.'

'I know.'

And then she smiled, for the first time, and it was such an odd smile. It had something in it of pleasure, of embarrassment, regret even; certainly disbelief. The smile didn't simply lift the corners of her mouth, but raised her cheeks and changed the shape of her eyes in such a way that I was astonished. It was an original and quite lovely smile, and for the first time I understood what it was that Bernard saw in this woman.

'I love him so much, but it's not enough.'

'His friends say that you've already ruined him, twice; in his heart and in his bank account.'

'I only ever asked for his heart, not all of those gifts. I didn't realise he couldn't afford them.'

She put her hand out on to the counter, letting her wrist and lower arm emerge shyly from the sleeve of her coat as she stretched out her little fingers. A pretty diamond bracelet fell to her wrist. I wasn't sure that she was reaching out towards me, her hand was not extended that far in my direction, but I think she was asking for help.

'I am afraid of our love,' she said. 'There is a danger to it.'

Bernard did not arrive during the quarter of an hour that Mathilde dutifully and nervously waited for him. When she went out of the door she put her unnecessary sunglasses back on and looked around her as if worried she was being followed. Perhaps it was only in a final hope of seeing Bernard appear in the distance.

My curiosity was somewhat appeased, but it seemed strange that Bernard did not come by the bar after that time. All of the other regular customers appeared, but it wasn't for several days that I saw Jules and Hortense either. They said how busy they had both been and passed on inconsequential news and gossip. Because Bernard wasn't mentioned I had to ask if there were any reports of him.

'None at all,' Hortense replied. 'And anyway, we'd rather not know. If he's with that woman then he's only himself to blame.'

' "That woman"?' I quoted back at her with a laugh. 'She really has annoyed you, hasn't she?'

'If you'd seen the state that she left Bernard in then you'd understand.' Her patronising tone annoyed me.

'Have you ever met her?' I asked. 'I mean, have you ever talked to her?'

'Yes, I've seen her. But I haven't talked to her. I wouldn't, not unless it was to tell her what I think of her.'

'Maybe there's another side to the story? Perhaps she's not quite the monster you assume she is?'

'You've not known Bernard for as long as we have. He's an old friend and we care about him.'

She was right, of course, but I was annoyed by the remark. Looking back on our exchange I know that I was quite unsure of myself at the time. I was uncertain of the new friendships I had formed in a city I had only moved to six months previously. To be reminded of the strength and importance of their relationships made me feel how recent and fragile my own were.

'I think that there may be more to Bernard and Mathilde than you understand,' I said without considering how I would reply to her obvious retort:

'And what's that? What have you understood that we haven't?'

'Go easy on poor Charles,' Jules defended me, for which I was grateful. 'He might be right. Who knows what really goes on in other people's relationships?'

Hortense gave me one of those horribly penetrating stares that she is capable of, puckering up her lips and concentrating hard. Then she released the expression, but her eyes stayed fixed upon me:

'What do you think you know? You've met the bloody woman, haven't you?'

'Yes,' I said as simply and as unemotionally as I could. There was competition in her whole demeanour, and if I was acting in the same way then I tried not to let her see it.

'And?' she demanded. 'What is it; did you fall under her spell too?'

'No, I just couldn't quite believe her to be the fiend you've described to me in the past. She seemed to be a really quite ordinary woman, capable of love and confusion and doubt, the same as the rest of us.'

'Rubbish! She's got her claws into you too! Which means that you're going to be of no help to Bernard.'

'Just be wary of her,' warned Jules, who was looking down at Hortense.

'Wary?' she asked, looking up at him, incredulous.

'I'll be very careful,' I promised, hopefully with just enough condescension to annoy Hortense.

I went to visit Bernard the following afternoon. I called Lulu and she was able to give me his exact address on the rue Véron.

Bernard sounded pleased that I had come when he answered the intercom and opened up the door on the street. I climbed up to the sixth floor and he was waiting at the open door to his apartment when I finally reached it. He asked me inside, offering me a drink, laughing that the roles were reversed.

I accepted coffee and he showed me through to his living room before going off to the kitchen. I had expected the Spartan accommodation of a single, middle-aged man like my own apartment above the bar, but it was tastefully appointed with comfortable, perhaps antique furniture. There was no television, games console, or collection of cds and dvds. The only item of a mechanical nature was an old stereo record player and a collection of vinyl records. There was a bookcase which was given over almost entirely to poetry in both French and English.

'You met Mathilde, then?' he asked me when he came back in. 'Sit down, please. Tell me, what do you think of her?'

'She seems very sweet.'

He nodded, pleased. I added:

'And not quite the man-eater that Jules and Hortense have made her out to be.'

'No, they've got her all wrong.'

'Hortense really doesn't seem to like Mathilde.'

'I don't see how she could have an opinion either way; she's never met her.'

'You do realise that her opinions are partly the result of how you've portrayed Mathilde to them?'

'I hadn't thought of it like that.'

'She's prejudiced against Mathilde because of what happened to you when she left last time.'

'I've done everything I can to persuade her and Jules that they're wrong. I've told them how wonderful Mathilde is, what she means to me. . . .'

'It might be that you just haven't explained very well.'

'That must be the reason.'

'Or . . . that you've misrepresented the situation a little, perhaps?'

'In what way?'

'Mathilde told me that she's offered to leave her husband for you, but you refused to let her?'

'She told you that? Well, it's true enough. I'd feel awful if she gave up her life so as to be with me. Our love is my greatest desire, to be with her my only wish, but I know it would be a complete disaster.'

'I don't understand.'

'No, and I don't believe anyone else ever can.'

'She said there's danger in it?'

'And she's right,' he agreed, and returned to the kitchen. He called back: 'This time, though, I think it will all come to a conclusion whether we want it to or not. Our relationship seems to be moving inevitably forward.'

When he returned with my coffee he sat down opposite me and explained:

'I missed her that day you talked to her in the bar because I had to work; we were installing a new exhibition at the gallery. I was going to the bar the next day but it was raining and I doubted that she'd come out in such weather. By the time I got to your place the rain was heavier still and I decided to carry on and risk going towards her house. Of course, I didn't know which route she'd have taken. Luckily, though, I remembered that the last time she said she'd come down the steps at the end of the rue de Calvaire. So I carried on towards the Place and there she was coming down the rue de Vieuville.

'We met at the end of the street and took shelter in the entrance to an old taxi business whose garage doors were open. We were both drenched, and the rain was drumming off the roof and hissing back up off the pavement and the road outside. But inside the dark and dusty garage it seemed like an oasis of quiet and calm. No cars or pedestrians passed. We talked, but it was so cold and we were both shivering. . . . We held each other, for warmth.'

'For warmth?'

'I couldn't stop myself. I took her cold, wet face in my hands and kissed her icy lips. Her eyes became very wide. Surprise? Resistance? I don't know. Whatever it was she took a time before her lips answered mine.'

'The relationship is still moving forward then? Slowly though!'

'I shouldn't have told you,' he said angrily, standing up. 'You're laughing at me.'

'No, not at all,' I lied. 'It's just that, in some ways, it all seems a little anachronistic.'

'In what ways?' he asked, annoyed.

'You know; anyone else would have leapt into bed with her, if they'd met their true love again after five years of separation.'

'You don't understand. . . Life is meaningless, but still we live it. Death is meaningless, too. I live only for her love, but love turns to *la petite mort*, then perhaps *le grand morte*.'

'No, I don't understand.' I stood up as well. 'And I know it's really none of my business . . .'

'You're right, Charles, it really isn't,' he agreed, and with his hand he motioned that I should perhaps leave. 'And it's no business of Hortense and Jules, or anyone else.'

'We're all concerned for you,' I tried to tell him. I walked reluctantly to the door, Bernard close behind me.

'So what if I'm making a fool of myself?' he asked. 'Maybe I'm a permanent adolescent as Lulu once said. But Mathilde makes me exquisitely happy. I'm not sure that Hortense and Jules will have ever experienced a fraction of that happiness in the whole of their conventional time together.'

'Perhaps you're right,' I agreed, turning to him. 'But as Jules said to Hortense just the other day, who knows what really goes on in other people's lives?'

'I've no interest in their relationship.'

'But what happens next in yours?'

'Mathilde and I have to make a decision. If she comes back here then it all begins again.'

I couldn't help but look through the half-opened door into the bedroom. It was tastefully furnished, and had a large double bed with a heavy damask cover over it.

'But the beginning is also the end,' he said matter-of-factly.

A week or so later Jules came in to the bar and asked if I had seen Bernard, which I hadn't. He was concerned because his friend didn't appear to be at his apartment and had not been in to work for several days.

'It's all happening again,' he said grimly.

'Mathilde?'

'Exactly. I hate to think what Hortense will say when she finds out.'

'She seems to take Bernard's private life very personally.'

Jules looked me straight in the eye:

'She and Bernard were a couple before she met me . . . and before he ever met his ex-wife. Since then Hortense has always looked out for him.'

'Oh,' I said, and decided to leave it at that.

Jules's wife was quite vocal when she came into the bar with him later that evening and questioned me about Bernard and his movements.

'It's that bloody woman!' she insisted. 'He'll come back in less than a month, in a complete state, sorrier than he's ever been. He'll have emptied out his bank account and his silly little heart. He's destined to make the same mistake for the rest of his stupid life.'

Jules and I both tried to calm Hortense down, but as Bernard was not there she took her anger out on us. She also drank heavily, which I had seen her do before, but normally she could handle it.

'You know what I'm going to do,' she decided at about ten that evening. 'I'm going over to that house on rue St Vincent and I'm going to see if her husband knows what's going on.'

'Don't do that,' I said, and in return she told me how little she valued my opinion. Jules said that I was right and he too was told in what low esteem she held him. She picked up her glass, saw that it was already empty, and pulled a face.

'I'll see you later,' she said to Jules, and we both watched her leave the bar.

'Perhaps you should go after her?' I asked.

'Would you? When she's in that temper?'

I had to wait a few more days before I heard what happened when Hortense reached the house on rue St Vincent. She had insisted on seeing Mathilde's husband; she had barged right into the house. When she explained herself to the poor man he was in tears apparently. It appeared that Mathilde had left him a note several days before saying that she was leaving, but not saying where she was going or why. The authorities were already looking for her, and after her husband made another phone call to the police then they were looking for Bernard too.

But neither Bernard nor Mathilde were discovered. The police suspected foul play at first. It was reported that the bedroom of his apartment appeared to have been the scene of a fight, but this was later denied. I was interviewed on three different occasions but I am sure that I was unable to be of any help. Back at the bar I was also interviewed by my customers, but they had less interest in finding out the truth than they had in gossip. The disappearance of Bernard and Mathilde was a mystery, and one that was avidly discussed by my regulars. The most fanciful and the most mundane solutions were frequently suggested, but, without any proof, who was to say what had happened? Hortense and Jules claimed that Bernard and Mathilde were still somewhere in Paris, perhaps living in the suburbs under aliases. Lulu was convinced that they were both at the bottom of the Seine, bound together by a heavy chain that stopped them from floating to the surface. I didn't offer an opinion; I just served the drinks, listened to the theories of my customers, and hoped that wherever Bernard and Mathilde found themselves they were together.

The story died away, and after a couple of months so did my customers. I don't know why, but my takings slowly declined over the following year and I finally had to admit that I was losing money. A new bar, *The Umbrella*, started up two doors down from me and was suddenly the place for people to go to. I was forced to give up the lease on my premises, and I took a job running the bar in a nightclub near the Champs-Élysées. That was a hard time for me. I worked all the hours possible so as to pay off my debts and the club where I was now employed was rough. Fights were common most nights, and if the customers weren't in trouble with the police then the owners often were. I developed something of an alcohol problem and had a succession of sordid relationships. I was not proud of myself.

When the nightclub closed down I was looking for work again. At that very time, by coincidence I saw an advert for a job working in the very bar I had once run on the rue des Abbesses. It struck me as particularly cruel, but I needed a job and I had some fondness for the old place. I telephoned and went around that afternoon for an interview.

I took the Metro to Abbesses. It was raining hard and it was dark when I emerged into the Place from under the Guimard canopy. It was strange to walk past shops I had once known and into a bar that was so little changed since I used to run it. The patron was a business-like older woman who was amused when I told her my history, but she was not particularly impressed. I suspect that she was worried I would be just as unsuccessful in her establishment if given a second chance there. She told me that she would get back to me after she had interviewed another couple of candidates.

As I passed by I looked into *The Umbrella*; my old competitor for customers. It looked a little tatty and down-at-heel after just three years, and this gave me some comfort. Then I saw somebody inside whom I recognised.

I went in and walked up to where she was sitting alone at a table.

'Can I buy you another coffee?' I asked Lulu.

She looked confused, and then there was a slight flicker of recognition, but that was all. I could tell she wasn't going to be able to remember why she might recognise my face. I introduced myself quickly.

She accepted a glass of wine. After we had caught up with our news our conversation inevitably turned to Bernard and Mathilde.

'Neither of them have ever been in touch with friends or family since their disappearance,' she said.

'I remember you were convinced they were at the bottom of the Seine.'

'They've never reappeared to prove me wrong. The authorities say that their separate bank accounts have never been accessed. There's been talk recently of them being declared officially dead *in absentia*, but it may have to be a few more years before they can do that. Besides, another lead was uncovered recently.'

'Really?'

'Haven't you been living in Paris? Apparently a man fitting the description of Bernard attempted to sell a bracelet in Aubervilliers and for some reason the jeweller became suspicious. The man ran off and the bracelet was handed in to the police. It's thought to've once belonged to Mathilde.'

'Can they prove it?'

'They're not sure, because it wasn't something that her husband had ever bought for her and properly documented for insurance.'

'She had a little diamond bracelet, I remember.'

'That Bernard bought for her?'

'I think so. I saw it, once . . .' I said, but suddenly she didn't want to talk about them. Soon she had an excuse to leave and I finished her wine for her. I ordered another for myself and sat there on my own thinking of Bernard and Mathilde and the story they had left behind them. I decided that people would still be talking about them for years to come, whereas I was nothing; nobody. Feeling rather sorry for myself I walked out into the failing light of that autumn afternoon, into an enveloping rain, and looked both up and down the rue des Abbesses. And then, in the distance, down by the Place, I could see a couple arm-in-arm. My mind was primed to think of Bernard and Mathilde, I know, and I couldn't quite believe what I thought I had seen. I stood there arguing with myself until I realised that running after them was the only way to resolve the matter.

When I got to the Place they were not there. They did not appear to have continued down the road, and neither were they walking away up the rue Yvonne le Tac or rue de la Vieuville. I rushed down into the Metro but nobody was there who looked even remotely like them. Nevertheless, I was sure it had been Bernard and Mathilde. I wandered around the Place, hoping that they might reappear from within a shop or a café but I was disappointed. After a quarter of an hour, as I was considering going home, a gendarme appeared. I told him whom I thought I had seen.

I know that he did not take me seriously. I looked a little wild; I was wet-through and I'd been drinking. I could see that he did not consider me to be a reliable witness, and when he asked me where I worked and I said I was unemployed he closed his notebook. He said I should go home and I reluctantly did as he suggested.

I returned to Abbesses the next day, and the next. It was to no avail, but I was pleasantly surprised to go home one evening to a message saying that I could have a job, after all, in my old bar.

I was pleased to be back, but I became a little obsessed by thoughts of Bernard and Mathilde, I admit. Every few weeks I would rush from the bar having thought I'd seen them, separately or together. Sometimes I would mistake other people for them, locals and tourists, but occasionally my quarry would disappear into the crowd. When I was not working I would often wander around the area, an eye on the faces in the streets and in the other bars. I would walk over to the rue St Vincent and back again, taking the various different routes that linked Bernard's old apartment to where Mathilde had once lived.

After a while I tried to restrain myself, only following those people that seemed the most likely to be Bernard or Mathilde, not just those who vaguely resembled them from a distance. And then, one evening the following winter, I was locking up the bar after a busy night. I was physically tired, it was dark and raining ferociously. The water was running down the granite sets in the street. I hurried towards the Metro at Abbesses, but for some reason my eyes were drawn across the Place. I saw, obliquely, the dark entrance to the garage at the bottom of the rue de Vieuville. I thought, momentarily, that I glimpsed somebody inside and I could not stop myself from investigating. I continued across the Place and entered the dark, cold garage.

I could see nobody within, and turned to look back out at the rain which was now hitting the street so hard that it ricocheted back up into the air. It was reverberating on the roof, but I still heard a quiet sound behind me. When I turned a small, dark woman stepped out of the shadows further back inside the garage. I recognised her odd but not unattractive face; her hooked nose, small mouth and wide chin. Her eyes were wide and dark.

'Mathilde,' I said, and she smiled, the corners of her mouth rising, her cheeks lifting and the shape of her eyes changing in that astonishing fashion.

'Yes,' she said walking over to me very slowly. 'I know you. You were a friend of Bernard's.'

Her voice was so quiet I could barely hear her.

'What happened to you both?'

'La vie . . . la mort . . .' she said simply. 'It is all the same. *La petite vie, la petite mort, la grande vie, la grande mort. . . .*'

'I don't understand.'

'No, nobody else can.'

'But I'd like to try?'

She took two further steps toward me and drew my face down to hers. I don't know what made me think she might kiss me on the lips, but I had completely misread and misjudged the situation. Her cold lips barely touched my cheek before she pulled away.

'You must stop looking for us,' she said quietly.

I must have looked confused, disappointed even, but she did not seem to notice, or was too polite to show it. She stepped back and her expression was inscrutable. I hoped that she might at least smile again, but she did not. She slipped back into the shadows.

I was dumfounded. I put my hands to my cheek, wondering if she had really kissed me or not. There had been something so insubstantial about her. And then I realised that she had gone.

I walked tentatively forward, into the shadows at the rear of the garage, but could find nobody there. The one door I came across was locked, and when I went back out into the street I could see no lights elsewhere in the building. I knocked sharply on the entrance door to the taxi business but there was no answer. I could not see Mathilde's slight, retreating form walking away up the rue de Vieuville, or in the Place. I went back to the rue des Abbesses but she was not there either. In the distance there was a gendarme and I considered going to him for help, but I decided otherwise. It was probably the same man I had reported to before and I knew he wouldn't be sympathetic.

And anyway, Mathilde had told me to stop looking for her and Bernard. I walked reluctantly to the shelter of that Guimard canopy to the Metro and continued on down the steps. I decided that the following day I had to start looking for another job. I didn't care what it was, or where, just as long as it was not near the rue des Abbesses.

A False Impression

I had to go outside. The air in the room had grown almost unbreathable from the cloying smoke; a mixture of hashish and incense. Normally I revelled in such an atmosphere, in the artificial light and warmth. Living up there on the edge of the moors I had a house with solid stone walls at least three feet thick to keep out the elements. The windows were few and small, shuttered and curtained. In that place where I worked I was cut off from the outside world; space and time were reduced down to one room measuring ten feet by ten. Normally that suited me just fine; I could work undisturbed whenever the mood took me, and for as long as I felt the need to continue.

But on that particular night, in the hour before dawn, I felt a sudden and overwhelming requirement to quit the room, to leave my house and go outside. I can't claim that I had a presentiment of what would happen. I don't think that it was anything but the merest chance that sent me out on to the moor that night, at that exact moment.

It was bitterly cold, but still and clear. The air was like a knife in my throat and my lungs felt as though they froze with the indrawing of every breath. I had been drinking wine but any feeling of intoxication immediately departed. The hoary scene before me was dominated by the full moon that hung low and close, every detail of its surface brilliantly and clearly etched. It was so bright that it hurt my eyes.

I was idly attempting to examine the lunar maria, the plains once thought to be seas, when I felt a sudden and fundamental jolt in the earth. I found myself lying on my back on the hard ground with no memory of having fallen. But I had no interest in how I had come to be in that position for I was concentrating on the profound, aching, rusty reverberation that I could still hear and feel. The jolt itself had lasted only for a moment, but the dull ringing aftermath, a sound almost too low for the human ear, seemed to be so horribly revealing. Like some vast echo-location device, it measured out significant dimensions, surfaces and materials. It implied depths, heights and volumes. It all seemed to offer a sudden insight into the universe around me.

I was convinced it was that momentary, revelatory understanding that somehow allowed me the brief glimpse beyond the curtain of darkness, into and beyond the night sky I knew and had taken for granted. It was as though the great and complex mechanism that held everything in its place was briefly, if dimly, illuminated.

I saw, or sensed, the way in which our planet, and all the others, were slowly grinding their way around the universe, each heavenly body impossibly heavy, badly lit by distant suns. I knew for certain that ancient rails kept them to their course. I could not understand why nobody else had ever realised this, but I had always been told that in space there is meant to be no sound so we cannot hear the eternal din, the monstrous shrieking, of machinery that is not properly maintained. The jolt I had experienced was some small fault in this colossal mechanism as the earth made its way around it.

I immediately thought of the orrery that once had pride of place in my late uncle's study; the curious device in various metals that illustrated the relative positions and motions of the planets and moons. But this was nothing like his heliocentric model with the heavenly bodies at the ends of brass arms. What I had seen was infinitely more complex, more like a great three-dimensional astrolabe. I had been vouchsafed a vision of the universe as it really was; a monstrously clever and elaborate, if perhaps over-designed and out-of-date, feat of engineering. How far it reached into space I could not tell. I was sure that those reverberations were continuing to return as echoes from unimaginable distances, just too muted now for me to able to hear them.

Lying upon the frosty ground, looking up into the darkness, I hoped in vain to catch another glimpse of what I had seen. By pressing myself flat to the surface of our planet I hoped to feel any further jolts, but nothing so violent came again. After a while, however, I could almost sense an infinitesimally low vibration that seemed to confirm that our planet was indeed a giant sphere rolling around on gargantuan tracks.

As my mind assimilated this revelation my senses lurched and it was as though I was suddenly clinging to the underside of the earth, looking down and ever down into the black space below me. It seemed impossible to believe that physical gravity was keeping me in place; I was mortally afraid of falling off the world.

Eventually, however, the cold of the ground started to seep into me. Flesh and bone began to ache and I knew that I had to move or risk perishing out there on the moor. It took a great mental effort to trust to the concept of gravity, the illusion of 'up' and 'down', and to work with it by rolling over onto my front and pushing myself back up and on to my feet. I retreated shakily and unsteadily into the house, my eyes always on the heavens. Only the extreme cold finally forced me to pull myself away, to go inside and close the door.

When I awoke the following day my first thoughts were of what I had seen in that hour before dawn. The experience was imprinted clearly on my mind but I reasoned that it had to have been a dream.

I had slept through the morning and it was now early afternoon. The sky was clear, an almost translucent blue that seemed so close to disclosing what had been fleetingly visible to me in the night. I stood out under the vast expanse of sky staring into it in vain.

I could not quite shake off the memory of what I thought I had seen, but after a while my thoughts turned to food. I had not eaten in over thirty-six hours and was ravenously hungry. I had intended to go down to the village for provisions the previous day but my work had swept aside all such considerations.

Grudgingly, but with little real thought for my errand, I left the house and took the accustomed track down off the moor. The views that had been so important in bringing me to this place of isolation did not properly register. I didn't even look at the unmade track where my feet must have found a sure path without me consciously realising that they did so; my attention remained resolutely on the vault of the heavens.

I prided myself on being a rational man, and I knew that long hours of work sustained only by hashish and a little wine must have clouded my perception and judgement. I knew that the combined effects of hunger, drugs and alcohol must have been responsible for the hallucination. But I was not able to simply dismiss the idea of the universe being such a ramshackle and Heath Robinson affair.

I continued walking down off the moor and was coming into the wooded valley. I would normally have followed the beck that ran down into the village, but at the small footbridge, for some reason, I looked up into an old mountain ash. I was distracted by a story I had once heard about William Blake seeing a vision of angels in a tree.

My thoughts were disordered. It was hard to distinguish between hallucinations and visions, I told myself, and like religious beliefs, were often given credence by otherwise sensible people. I would have called them delusions. I would certainly have put into that category the story of what I thought I had witnessed if anyone else had reported it to me.

I thought of Blake's angels, and God, and wondered where any divinity could possibly have been in the universe I thought I had seen? It wasn't a question I would normally have asked myself. I am an atheist, but as a purely academic consideration, I wondered where God would have been in that cosmos of colossal spheres rolling around on convoluted and rusty tracks? Hadn't I looked on it all and described it to myself as 'unmaintained'? My initial thought was that there was nowhere in the vast mechanism for any deity to hide away. But there still remained the question of who, or what, would have created it all, and why?

These distracting and troubling thoughts may have been the reason I continued on down the overgrown path rather than over the footbridge and along the rather wider track that I would normally have taken. My distracted mind was not on my immediate, physical surroundings, but after a while these did intrude. It had become so muddy underfoot that I nearly slipped and fell, and I found myself having to push through ancient, vigorous and half-dead brambles if I was to continue on to the village, which I did. I had to look about me and consider where I was, and seeing the shape of the hills I decided that I would simply reach the village from an unaccustomed direction.

And this is exactly what happened, but the aspect that the village finally presented to me was wholly unexpected.

I thought at first that the buildings I came across were simply derelict. This would have been surprising as this part of Northumberland is relatively wealthy. The normally picturesque village is a desirable and sought-after location; the buildings are well maintained. I was walking along a path that led me to the bottom of the village green, where the houses were large and comfortable, but they appeared to be façades held up by a framework of buttressing timbers. I passed between them to emerge into the centre of the village I knew, and looking back the houses then presented an entirely comfortable and lived-in aspect. All around me everything was as I would have expected it; a man was walking past the war memorial with his dog, there were a few cars, and the post office and general stores were a couple of hundred yards ahead of me.

I turned and went back down the path, doubting myself, but no, the buildings immediately around me were, as I thought, just façades. The matter distracted me from my previous thoughts, and as I walked up to the village shop I finally had to put my mind to what I was going to buy. I felt in my pocket for the assurance of money; there was enough for my immediate needs.

A neighbour was leaving the shop as I entered it and we acknowledged one another. Inside I collected together bread, tea and biscuits, taking them to the half-deaf old woman who habitually sat at the till. I paid for and bagged-up my goods and went out having exchanged only the mechanical pleasantries that were required to effect the sale.

On the pavement again I looked down at those houses and saw how they still appeared as substantial as all the others from that angle. I had never taken that path between them before so I would not have known about the illusion they presented. In fact, I had never taken any path to the village in the past other than my habitual one down the track over the footbridge. I couldn't help but wonder what else I hadn't noticed about the place.

I didn't really want to acknowledge any suspicions to myself, but I decided to follow the road back down towards the garage and I turned up another small alley between it and a building that purported to be the local office of the Farmers' Union. The garage seemed to be substantial enough, but its neighbour had only two walls between which, normally out of sight, was simply a patch of waste ground.

Retracing my steps and going across the green I intended to investigate a driveway that appeared to lead up to a builder's yard; that too was an illusion. When I walked back up to the shop I could see how everything had been constructed to look entirely realistic only from those angles at which I would normally have seen the village.

I strode up to the shop and threw open the door. There was the old woman behind the till as usual.

'What is going on here?' I demanded of her and she smiled back vacantly: 'It is a clear day, isn't it? But very cold.'

'Never mind the weather. What's happened to the village?'

'Snow? Oh, I shouldn't think so.'

Understanding, of a sort, seemed to be offering itself. I walked through the shop and pulled opened the door that should have led to the private part of the building. Rather than some parlour, or even a storeroom, there was simply a rough, overgrown and rubble-strewn patch of land. I stepped out and looked back at the building which only existed insofar as it provided the illusion of a shop.

Back inside I was going to question the woman but decided on the futility of it. As I went out of the door a car drew up and a man I recognised got out with his red setter. Now, I had exchanged words with him in the past because my mother had been fond of setters and I had learnt that he bred them. It was always an easy topic of conversation. We would inevitably discuss the weather first, and then his dogs.

'This village is all a series of façades,' I said to him without any preamble. 'The whole place is like some film set. What's going on?'

The man nodded gravely and looked around him: 'I think snow unlikely.'

'I didn't mention snow. I want an explanation for this sham village.'

'My oldest bitch gave us a nice litter last week, but I think it'll have to be her last,' he said.

This angered me. He had left his keys in the ignition of his car, as was the local custom, crime being unheard of locally, so I told him I was taking it. He made some further comment about his blasted dogs as though sticking to a pre-rehearsed script. He didn't stop me getting into his car and starting it up. He simply walked over to the shop as I familiarised myself with the gears. I turned the car around and drove out towards the Hexham road. In the mirror I saw him go into the shop without looking in my direction.

After a couple of hundred yards I noticed a single-track road that ought to lead me in the direction of somewhere called Cross Keys. I had never had any reason to take it before; I only ever took the route towards Alnwick and the main road. I was struck by my predictability, my habit of only ever moving in accustomed grooves and tracks through life, and for once struck off in a wholly new direction.

I drove the car up past a large stand of fir trees to a small summit that I recognised as forming a part of the view from my own house only a few miles away. From this alternative angle it looked different, but the outcrop of rocks along the ridge were a local landmark. The road took me around them, and then to a crest that would give me a view that I didn't recall ever having previously seen.

But there was nothing there. The road stopped and everything beyond was a bleak, barren plain of dun-coloured rock.

I don't know how long I spent staring at the desolate scene. Eventually, without thinking, I was able to reverse the car down the track to where it could be turned around. I drove back to the village and left the vehicle by the green where I had previously abandoned my bag of shopping. I picked up my groceries and strode off towards my house on the moors in a state of shock; it was remarkably easy not to think about what I had seen; not to consider the implications.

Standing up at the kitchen table I ate some of the food mechanically, tasting nothing. I fetched in fuel and relit the fire in my study. Already it was getting dark and I shut the doors, shuttered the windows and lit my incense. When I felt warm and secure again I opened another bottle of wine and crumbled hashish into my pipe.

I had seen the artificiality of the universe the previous night and had refused to believe it. Now, however, I knew the truth and it caused me to re-evaluate the whole of creation. If that had been all then it might have been a task that I was equal to. And asking where God might be found in such an unimaginably vast mechanism would have simply been an interesting academic or theological question.

I really think that it would have been possible to come to terms with the revelation, but then I had tried to drive along that unfamiliar road. I was still considering myself to be one of millions inhabiting the surface of the globe with our creator, whoever or whatever it was open to question. If there were no God, as I suspected, myself and the whole of humanity would have come to terms with the idea, I was sure. If, in fact, the existence of God was somehow proven by what I had seen in the heavens then perhaps I might have even found some comfort in it. I had honestly felt able to confront either possibility.

But this was an altogether different prospect; the universe did not seem to have been created for mankind in general. It appeared to have been constructed purely for my own benefit!

I could not now afford to think of the Creator as some academic argument. Now that I knew the universe had been fashioned with me specifically in mind my relationship to the Creator was of spectacular importance! How should I begin to address the idea? How would I begin to address my God?

But then the other possibility struck me with an almost physical blow. If there was no God, if whoever had constructed the universe around me was now absent, then I was alone; truly and profoundly abandoned!

In my almost hermetically sealed room, stone-built, ten foot by ten, I had to consider my situation. I could not leave that sanctuary until I had come to a definitive conclusion. Then, when I next walked out under that artificial sky I might know how to act. Either I would be ready to address my Creator, or the universe would belong solely to me and I would have dominion over it.

Gala Gladkov's Exquisite Process

When I heard the knock at the door on that Friday afternoon in early December I was in my workshop at the back of the house. I was carving some panels that were to form the backs of a set of chairs and the last thing I wanted was an interruption. Still, I thought, the caller might be for Anna rather than for me, and I decided to ignore the summons. After putting off the job for several weeks I had finally got down to the work and I was hoping to finish at least one panel before I gave up for the weekend. It was a surprisingly bright afternoon and I was enjoying not working by artificial light.

A slight change in pressure in the workshop told me that my wife had opened the front door at the other end of the house. There was almost immediately a distant exclamation of surprise and I could hear her inviting the visitor inside. She was talking excitedly to somebody as she brought them through the house, inevitably heading for my workshop. I looked up with annoyance, but when I saw that the caller was Nikolai Bednyi I put down my tools and told him how genuinely pleased I was to see him.

'I know I should've written to tell you I was coming . . .' he said.

I walked over and I gave him a hug that seemed to make him feel uncomfortable. It wasn't the kind of thing we had ever done back when we had known each other so well at University.

'Is Maya not with you?' I asked him.

'He wouldn't explain,' said Anna, concerned.

Nikolai looked from me to my wife and then took hold of her hand.

'I thought I should tell you together. Maya's dead,' he announced.

It would have been an awkward reunion even without Nikolai's tragic news. Somehow we had remained distantly in contact with him and Maya since University at Petersburg some thirty years earlier, but it was inevitable that the intimate friendship of the past had been neglected. When we had all acted together in the Theatre Group in the early 1900s we had been very close. We had witnessed the troops firing on the striking workers in 1905 and had believed that we would never see anything so horrific again. But then came the war, just as we were settling to marriage and jobs. Somehow I and Nikolai both survived when so many didn't, and I settled in Toksovo with Anna, while he came back for Maya and returned to his family farm somewhere outside of Strelna. Perhaps we should have made the effort to see each other, there were opportunities, but the upheavals and uncertainties brought about by political terrors and years of shortages meant that we all had little concern for anything but ourselves and our own survival. This was the first time, for instance, that Nikolai had ever visited us in Toksovo, and yet we had been living there for fifteen years.

In addition to the sad news we also had to come to terms with the fact that Maya had died six months earlier and Nikolai had not told us before.

'I was so upset,' he said. 'Her family had to arrange the funeral. I forgot to let them know about old friends like you two. I should've written.'

'Don't worry,' I told him. 'It'd been a long time.'

We did understand and besides, we weren't going to add to his distress.

'Would you mind if I stayed for a few days?' he asked.

'Of course we don't.' My wife and I had replied almost in unison.

'We'd love to have you here,' added Anna. 'How are you coping?'

'Not well, actually. There's something I want to talk to you about,' he said to me. 'But not now, not just yet.'

'Shall I leave you two?' asked Anna.

'I'm sorry,' he said, obviously realising that he sounded rude. 'I have to do some thinking first.'

'Take as long as you like,' I assured him. 'The room at the front of the house is all yours. We'll make you up a bed there.'

'I think, perhaps, that I'd like to do some walking. I can get out into the forests easily enough from here?'

'Yes, just continue on up the road and there they are . . . Not that you'll have many hours of daylight for walking, not at this time of year.'

'Thank you, thank you both,' he said, slightly pathetically.

Anna showed Nikolai to his room while I tidied my workshop and then cleaned myself up. When my wife came back I could hear her putting the kettle on the stove in the kitchen before coming out to talk to me.

'We've lost so many friends over the years,' she said. 'And Maya was a friend so long ago, but time doesn't mean anything. If she'd arrived with Nikolai it wouldn't have mattered that we'd not talked in years.'

'I know,' I said, and we held each other tight. 'I'm really upset, but I'm not sure if I have a right to be, not after all this time, not after everything we have all been through. But we'll do what we can for Nikolai.'

'I'll go and talk to him,' I said, and Anna unwillingly let me go.

'We will,' she said.

I kissed her forehead and went into the house, where I found Nikolai in the front room, staring out of the window.

'Six months isn't long enough to come to terms with it,' I said.

'I still find it hard to believe she's gone. The stupid thing is that every now and again I forget she's dead. I'll turn around to tell her something and be surprised that she's not there.'

'I'm sorry. If there's anything we can do . . . ?'

'Thank you.'

'And please treat this place as your own.'

He lowered himself into one of our shabby armchairs. 'As I said, there's something I want to talk to you about, but I need some time to get it all sorted out up here,' he tapped his forehead with his index finger.

'Of course,' I said, resolving that I would be patient with him.

It took Nikolai several days before he would say anything. He did go out for walks, but he seemed singularly indifferent to the scenery or the weather. When we were able to observe him indoors he seemed very preoccupied and at first we tried not to leave him to his own thoughts. He had told us that he wanted time to think, but it seemed natural to try and stop him from dwelling on matters that obviously upset him. When he decided to talk to me he chose an awkward time, but perhaps he realised that if he didn't say something at that particular moment then perhaps he would not say anything at all.

I was in my workshop still trying to carve the stylised foliage into one of the panels. The party official who had commissioned them was very embarrassed when he said what he wanted, but I was pleased that they weren't going to be entirely utilitarian. To make the panel match the preceding example took a lot of concentration, but Nikolai suddenly asked if I remembered us acting in a play by Ostrovsky.

'I do,' I said, looking up. 'And we weren't very good! It only ran for one week, to poor audiences? And on the last night the whole cast got exceedingly drunk in some awful bar.'

'Something happened that very night,' he said.

'Like what?'

'I don't know how to explain it. But something did, or so I'm told.'

I laid down my tools, not realising that this apparently random recollection was the matter that he had come over from Strelna to talk about.

'Are you telling me that our bad performance was what persuaded you to take up your career in farming, and mine in carpentry?'

He was lost in thought, not registering my lame attempt at a joke. Then, as though this preamble was totally unrelated, he said: 'Two months ago, one Saturday evening, I was at home. It was almost midnight and I was ready to go to bed when there was a loud knocking at my door. It was completely unexpected. The fire had burnt down in the grate and my eyelids were heavy. I think I'd been determined to finish the book I was reading, but I was about to admit defeat and turn in for the night.'

Nikolai was staring out of the window at the view out towards the forests, but I don't believe that he saw anything.

'It was an appalling night,' he continued. 'The rain was lashing at the front of the house and I did wonder whether I hadn't imagined it. But no, three distinct knocks came again.

'Now, you may think you're pretty isolated up here in Toksovo, but a visitor to our house at any time of day is a rarity because we're so isolated, even though we're only a few miles from Strelna.'

Then he shook his head and said 'I keep saying "we" . . .'

'It's alright. Carry on,' I assured him. I swept away the shavings and sat on my bench.

'A caller so late on a winter's night was almost unimaginable. I got up warily, sensing trouble, or bad news, and went into the hall. When I opened the door I did so cautiously. I found on the step a man I didn't recognise who was probably a little older than me. He was wearing a large waxed coat that didn't appear to be very effective in the driving rain, and he was very apologetic. He asked if I knew a blacksmith or a wheelwright because his carriage was damaged and needed repair.

'I explained that it was some miles to Strelna and he was quite upset. He asked if there was any accommodation locally, and I said no. I was loath to ask him in, he was a complete stranger, but then he said that his wife was still sheltering in the stricken carriage. He said she was unwell and I had no choice but to offer them a bed for the night. I asked if I could help him bring his wife up to the house.

' "Oh no," he thanked me. "She can walk."

'I felt a little strange letting him back out into the wild night, and it was some time before the knock came again at the door. By then I'd stoked-up the fire and in the kitchen I'd put on the kettle.

'I found my visitors standing on the doorstep looking forlorn and miserable. I insisted they both immediately go through to the front room while I found some towels.

'When I got back the woman said to me, almost inaudibly, "We are very, very grateful." She looked much older than her husband, and moved slowly, but no slower than any other elderly woman might do. They took the towels and agreed to let me make them coffee. I offered them vodka but they said they didn't drink alcohol.

'When I returned ten minutes later with hot drinks he was drying the woman's hair for her and put the towel down to take both of the cups. "I know these roads a little, by daylight," he was saying, "but on a night like this . . ."

'I told him that there was a blacksmith I could recommend just three miles away. It wasn't really that far to walk normally, but on a night like that . . . .'

Nikolai seemed to register my presence suddenly. 'You've not visited us out near Strelna, have you?'

I shook my head and he admonished himself again for saying 'us'.

'You should come over,' he said absently, and then resumed. 'And then I noticed the woman. She said something very quietly like "We don't want to impose," and she was staring at me intently in a manner that I found very disconcerting.

'The man said that they didn't want to cause any trouble; they would stay in the front room until morning. I told them I had a second bedroom and I only needed to get out some clean sheets. He didn't seem to know whether to be pleased or disapprove, but the weather outside had turned more violent.

'He insisted on helping his wife to sit down in a chair, and he draped the towel around her shoulders. Then he moved her cup of coffee on to the table beside her.

' "My wife suffers from an obscure form of premature aging," he said.

'I tried to sympathise, saying something about my mother and her aches and pains, but he was having none of it:

' "My wife's symptoms are quite extreme," he said, effectively putting an end to my bland attempt at sympathy. He said that she was only forty-nine, the same age as me! This left me flailing around for an appropriate reply. She looked at least thirty years older.

' "I'm sorry," I replied, as simply and as levelly as I could, and all he could say was "Yes, well. . . ." His tone was confrontational and made me feel uncomfortable.

' "Do you live here alone?" he asked.

'I said that I did, and was about to explain that I was recently widowed when he said "It seems like a very large house for one person."

'I told him about Maya, wondering why I had to explain this to a complete stranger. "My wife and I used to have a large farm and farmhouse," I explained, "but we had to move here."

' "Much more equitable," he said, and, really, I know I shouldn't complain, but to be lectured by him when I was offering him my hospitality!

' "You were married?" asked the woman with such a tone of surprise that I was rather taken aback. Her husband changed the subject. "You have some expensive-looking paintings and ornaments."

'I explained that our nicest pieces were there in the front room, to show them off.

' "It isn't in keeping with the new, modern Russia," said the man. "You're clinging to a past that is no longer relevant." '

'It's something one hears all too often,' I told Nikolai, remembering the family pieces that Anna and I had been forced to part with.

'I decided that we should start again,' said Nikolai. 'I said that we hadn't introduced ourselves properly and that my name was Nikolai Bednyi.

' "Vasili Gladkov," he replied, and walked over and gave me a curiously formal handshake. "And my wife is called Gala."

'I said something about it being good to meet the both of them, in spite of the unfortunate circumstances. It was really very awkward because Gala Gladkov was still staring at me, as though desperate to catch my eye or communicate with me. I noticed that she was not drinking her coffee and I explained that it wasn't the real thing, of course, but I hoped that it was to her taste.

' "It'll be fine," Mr Gladkov answered for her. "Gala can't very well pick it up, and certainly shouldn't try to when it's hot."

'I apologised and he insisted that it wasn't a problem. But he'd dismissed my thoughtlessness rather too quickly, and an awkward silence followed. To alleviate it I asked:

' "Were you travelling far tonight?"

' "Back to Leningrad, from visiting friends in Petrodvorets," he replied. "We were horribly delayed."

' "I used to know the city when it was Saint Petersburg," I said, attempting to be friendly. I made a joke about it having been a completely different city in between, Petrograd, but he didn't share my sense of humour.

'And then she said something like, "It's such a shame." She said it so quietly that I wasn't sure I'd heard her correctly, and I certainly didn't know what she was referring to.

' "Calling the great city after Lenin is fitting! It is just!" said the man, and I would've been inclined to tell him to go and wait in his carriage if I hadn't felt so sorry for his rather strange wife. But, really, she was making me feel very uncomfortable as well. She'd returned her absorbed gaze to me.

' "You don't approve of the glorious Revolution?" her husband persisted, annoying me further.

'I think I told him that our country was a better place for it, but the discomfort of the situation increased. He walked over to his wife and proceeded to help her drink the coffee. He lifted the cup to her lips, with a handkerchief at her chin to catch any drips, and none of us spoke. I didn't feel inclined to make any more small-talk, and anyway, I wasn't sure that it would've been appropriate while he was carefully helping her.

'I went and prepared their bed. It was easily done and when I returned I told them that I was tired and that they were welcome to retire for the night whenever they wanted to. To my great relief they agreed to do just that. I showed him the room and explained the other arrangements, and he went back to help his wife out of her chair.

'Later, before we all retired, I passed her on her own in the hall and said goodnight. In reply she quietly said: "You really don't know who I am, do you?"

'I wasn't sure that I'd heard her correctly because of the sound of the rain and wind, and I didn't have the chance to reply because her husband appeared and wished me good night.'

'Did she get the chance to explain her comment?' I prompted Nikolai, and he nodded.

'Eventually, yes. The following morning Vassily Gladkov set off to find the blacksmith and left me with the company of his wife. I asked her if she thought she knew me and at first she was so tearful she was almost incoherent. She asked if I remembered all kinds of things and when I denied all knowledge of them she became upset. She said we'd first met in Petersburg. She said that she was staying there with other students who had come up from Moscow. While she was there she'd seen an amateur performance of a play by Ostrovsky . . .'

'Not our production?'

'Apparently, yes.'

'What a coincidence.'

'I didn't know what to think about it. Apart from anything else, I was certain that the poor old woman was mixing me up with another person entirely. All the details, except those of the play, seemed to be sheer fabrication.'

'She'd have been our age?'

'Having seen her in my house thirty years later it was hard to believe, but yes.'

'And this is the business that's been troubling you?'

'Yes. It's related to Maya, though not in any way you can possibly imagine.'

At this point in his narrative we heard the front door open and Anna coming into the house.

We didn't resume the conversation until later that evening. I told Anna that Nikolai had started to talk to me about what was troubling him and she decided to go up to bed strategically early. Nikolai and I were alone in the front room and we had started on a bottle of vodka that he had brought with him.

'The prematurely aging woman?' I prompted him.

'Ah yes. And that play . . .'

'Didn't you have some romantic intrigue with a girl that last night of the play?'

'I did, and that was Gala Gladkov.'

'Then, apart from the coincidence, what an amazing memory the woman had. Imagine her recognising you all these years later.'

'I said to her that it had been a long time ago,' Nikolai continued. 'And she replied that it had been twice as long for her as it'd been for me. When I said that I didn't understand she managed to compose herself, and started to explain.

' "I don't know if it is really much of a coincidence coming across you?" she said. "I've spent the last thirty years looking at every face in every crowd, hoping to see you again. I moved to Petersburg in the hope of finding you, hoping you were still there. I knew it was probably a forlorn hope. In all these years so many people have died, or moved . . . But I've never really given up looking, and then, last night, you let us into your house. But you didn't recognise me."

'At which she started to cry.

' "You don't remember how we met?" she asked. "No, why would you remember? As far as you were concerned we talked for a half hour, kissed briefly on the Bank Bridge . . ."

' "The one with the griffins?"

' "That's right, over the Catherine Canal, although we now have to call it the Griboedov Canal. We kissed, and then I stormed off into the night with my friend Tonya."

'She looked into a bag she was clutching and pulled out a photograph unmistakably of herself when younger.

' "That was me at about the time we met." And it was a bit of a shock looking at it, you know? It was then that I suddenly remembered that I *had* kissed a girl on that bridge with the griffins on the abutments, and that she *had* run off into the night after acting very strangely. I had a feeling like vertigo. But after all this time, dredging the event up from where it had lain undisturbed for so many years in my memory, I couldn't recall any of the details. . . . I admitted this and she became upset once more.

' "I was Gala Krylov back then," she said.

' "I'm really sorry," I told her, as carefully as I could. "We obviously did meet, but I've a poor memory."

'Eventually she calmed down, but then she started claiming that she'd never called me Nikolai, and there were tears in her eyes. "It's silly," she said, "but your friends called you Bednyi and I stupidly thought it was your first name. I always called you Bednyi after that."

'I asked her if this was on the night we'd met.

' "Yes, and *afterwards*," she said, and paused. "I know that you have a long scar on your left arm, from an accident on your family's farm as a child." '

'She's got one hell of a memory,' I suggested to Nikolai. I had seen the scar.

' "You used to love the music of Tchaikovsky," she told me. "You prefer to sleep on the right hand side of a bed, no matter whether you are at home or staying somewhere different. When you were about thirty-two your wisdom teeth gave you so much pain they had to be removed."

'She asked if I was right and I said she was. I asked how she knew all this.

'Her answer was "Because, my darling, after that night on the bridge with the four griffins in Petersburg we went to Moscow and lived together for nearly thirty years." '

I shook my head: 'It's alright Nikolai. You aren't going mad. I can attest to the fact that for thirty years you were with Maya, not this other woman.'

'Thank you,' he smiled weakly. 'But she then told me that I'd probably still have my late father's cufflinks. They're not real gold but I do wear them on special occasions. And she knew other things.'

'Presumably she had some way of finding all of this out?' I asked.

'I don't know how. She told me that I collected cigarette packets.'

'Well, you used to.'

'I did, but Maya was never particularly impressed, so I collected stamps instead. But this woman, Gala, claimed, "I was always very happy for you to collect cigarette packets. In fact, I encouraged you to. . . ."'

'I remember,' I said to Nikolai. 'After the play we were drinking and you went outside with this girl. You said you'd kissed her, but then she'd started accusing you of all kinds of strange things. She was really very angry with you, but she seemed to've mixed you up with somebody else. Back in the bar we made fun of you for trying to kiss a madwoman.'

'But thirty years later, in my house near Strelna, this woman said that after we kissed she'd smuggled me back to the hostel where she was staying with her friends!'

'She was fantasising.'

'Perhaps, but then she said some more things that worried me. She said that I'd been writing light operatic pieces.'

'Well, you used to in those days.'

'She said there was a song about a woman called Nadezhda.'

'I remember it.'

'And another that was a kind of sea-shanty.'

'It was called "Breaking Point".'

'And another very beautiful song, apparently, called "The Saddest Eyes".'

'I don't remember that one.'

'No, nor do I! But she insisted it was written afterwards, in a life that we'd lived together.'

'She's clearly very confused.'

'Is she?'

'You don't mean that you gave credence to her story?'

'I met her again last week. Gala says that when we first met we fell passionately in love and our relationship lasted for thirty years. . . . Don't shake your head like that until you've heard me out . . .

'Gala said that in the last year or so of us being together there were misunderstandings and arguments. In a fury one day she insisted that she wished she'd never met me all those years ago. She said that she knew a way of turning back time and she was so angry with me that she did just that. She found herself nineteen again, back on Bank Bridge in Saint Petersburg, and instead of inviting me back to her hostel she shouted at me and ran off into the night. She remembered what had happened before, but as far as the rest of the world was concerned those thirty years with me had never occurred. In the confusion of suddenly being back in Saint Petersburg, and being nineteen again, she went back to Moscow where she met Vasili Gladkov. By the time she'd really understood all of the implications of what had happened, she'd also realised her mistake in leaving me behind on that bridge. But it was too late to track me down.'

'And you'd gone on to meet Maya . . .'

'Exactly.'

'And you believe all this?' I asked him.

'I don't know, but she does. She says that she was pleased to be young again, but she found herself aging at twice the normal rate. At thirty she looked forty, at forty she looked sixty, and so on. It's taken its toll; it seems that you can't turn back time with impunity.'

'If she'd lived with you for thirty years and knew you as well as she says she did, then of course she'd have been able to track you down. She'd know where you lived, where your parents and friends came from.'

'Gala says that at that moment on the bridge my two alternative lives diverged markedly. The first time around, the life she experienced with me that I wouldn't remember, I had success with my songwriting and acting. We moved down to Moscow together and I really made a name for myself. We were successful and busy and didn't see anything of old friends or relatives, and then the war came and we got through it comfortably. We did well under Stalin, and managed even to be favoured by Lenin.

'So, do you really believe that you might have had another life with this woman?'

'It's theoretically possible.'

'But practically it's impossible.'

'She's told me how it might be done. In theory I could go back to that time on Bank Bridge. I could run after her and beg her to stay. I could see what that life might have been like, with her, with success.'

'And what about your life with Maya?'

'Or I could go back to that bridge and live my whole life again, with Maya. I've been agonising over what choice I would make.'

'But why put yourself through the agony? You can't go back so there's no reason to worry about choices.'

'Gala entrusted me with the secret before she died.'

'She's dead?' I asked.

He nodded. 'Once she had explained her process she insisted on going out of the house. It was still raining and I wasn't inclined to follow her. I watched her from the window as she walked across the back yard towards the well. I had no idea what she intended to do. She sat on the side of the well and allowed herself to fall backwards into it.'

'How horrible!'

'She did it just as her husband returned with the carriage repaired. We got her out with trouble, but it was too late.'

'But if she really knew how to turn back time why didn't she do it again? And then a few years later do it again, and again?'

'She said that after you've done it the first time you realise that it's only available to you the once. She said that if I ever tried the process then I'd understand.'

'You're not seriously thinking about trying it?'

'Why not? What've I got to lose?'

'Everything that you have here!'

'But there's nothing here for me without Maya.'

'Well, I'm not sure how I'd feel about you wiping out my life for a start! I assume that nobody else gets to go back with you? What happens to this thread of history if you return to Bank Bridge thirty years ago? What makes you think you won't start a whole new third thread in which you end up without either Maya or Gala?'

'I'd take that risk. At the moment I have neither of them.'

'But I'm quite comfortable here with Anna and my carpentry. And you're happy to destroy that through snapping your fingers?'

'If I do manage to go back and make my choice, then you'll inevitably be back there in Petersburg with me, only you won't remember any of this.'

'But will you remember? Would you be able to make an informed choice?'

'Gala says that I'd know. And as for you, you'll still meet Anna and become a carpenter and come to live here. The only thing I've got to decide is whether I want to go back and watch Gala run off into the night, or follow her.'

I didn't know how to react to Nikolai's story. I was about to laugh at it all when I realised that he was completely in earnest. I did gently suggest that he ought to talk to a doctor, but he was upset at the suggestion that he was ill and needed help. We did discuss the matter further, going around in circles because, as he said, there was a very simple method of ascertaining the truth. All he had to do was start the process that Gala Gladkov had explained to him. If it failed then he said that he would know himself to have been a fool. But if it worked . . .

I went to bed that night annoyed with my old friend, but also interested by the theoretical questions posed by his story. I wanted to discuss it all with Anna but she was already asleep.

Waking up the next morning I still had his story going around my head and walking past his room I saw that the door was open. The curtains had not been drawn and the bed did not appear to have been slept in. I had an awful presentiment of what might have happened.

Nikolai had obviously walked out of the house at some time during the night, and he never returned. His bag was still in his room with his clothes, his papers and some money. We informed the authorities and there was an extensive search, but nothing was ever found of him. A dog tracked him into the forest but then the scent suddenly stopped.

I had to explain what his state of mind was to a detective who quite rightly dismissed Nikolai's preoccupations with the stories of Gala Gladkov. Some time later, though they did confirm that the woman had recently died in an accident at Nikolai's place in Toksovo.

I don't know if Nikolai Bednyi ever reappeared or was officially pronounced dead. It wouldn't matter to him, Anna grimly joked one day; presumably the thread of time we inhabit was no longer of any interest to him.

I do not believe his story, but I do not know what happened to him. I do think, though, that he was convinced that Gala's process, whatever it was, would work. And I'm intrigued to know what decision he would have made: to live his life quietly again with Maya, who he obviously loved, or to take a chance with Gala and follow a potentially successful career. I didn't really know him well enough, not in recent years, to be able to suggest which thread he would have chosen to follow.

Reunion

Shaffer returned home at five, just as it was getting dark. He had to put down his bags to unlock the front door, and picked them up again feeling annoyed that he had set so much homework for his pupils; after all, he was going to have to mark it all.

As he started climbing the stairs to his rooms he noticed that the sound of his landlady's television set was louder than usual; the door to her basement flat had to be open. He tried not to think about it but by the time he had reached the first floor landing he realised that something wasn't right. He deposited his bags outside his own door and grudgingly went down the two flights to investigate.

He reluctantly peered around Miss Simpson's doorframe and could see his landlady lying unmoving on the floor just inside. His heart raced. Although he could tell that she was unconscious he still called out to her, asking if she was all right. When she didn't reply he carefully opened the door as far as he could, with her in the way, and sidled inside.

The old woman was lying on her back, her mouth open, and she didn't immediately appear to be alive. Shaffer took a moment to compose himself, then looked around for the telephone. It was a bright-red old-fashioned one, and it seemed to take forever for the dial to turn so that he could ask for an ambulance.

He had to reach over and switch off the insistent television. He gave the operator Miss Simpson's name and address, and then his own. When asked, he said that he didn't know what was wrong with her. The person on the other end of the line enquired whether the woman was still breathing and he squatted down on his haunches and looked across the room at her. Miss Simpson's bulk was considerable, but he could see, measured against the paisley material of an armchair behind, that her chest was slowly rising and falling. He was then asked if there was anything obstructing her airway. When he said he didn't know he was told to look.

It seemed to take forever for the ambulance to arrive. He was kept talking on the phone; he was asked questions and given things to do such as see whether there was any obvious medication lying around. He also had to go out and leave the front door open for the paramedics. He kept checking on Miss Simpson's breathing, certain that she was about to expire. The aspect of the front room seemed to change, to become gloomier and shabbier than ever. He had been inside his landlady's flat on the first of every month for many years, paying his rent, and he reasoned that it was her personality that had previously made it seem quite friendly and welcoming. She was a large woman and was usually animated by a considerable, if mindless, *joie de vivre*. Now her unmoving bulk seemed almost menacing and tainted everything around it. He thought of her whole house as dark and precarious. He felt as though it was in danger of collapse if she was no longer there to act as its foundation.

When the paramedics arrived they too had to sidle around the door. The first inside the room remarked that Shaffer was sitting in the dark and switched on the lights. With calm efficiency they took her pulse, looked into her eyes, listened to her chest with a stethoscope and took her blood pressure. They asked what her name was.

'Miss Simpson.'

'Does she have a first name?'

'Kathy,' he replied without thinking, and then wondered how he had known that. He supposed she must have told him at some time.

'You don't know if she's on any medication? Any history of illness you're aware of? No fainting or falling in the past?'

Shaffer shook his head and watched as the other paramedic looked around the flat, presumably to see if there were any bottles of pills she might have taken. His attention was then given to the first paramedic who gave Miss Simpson an injection, although he didn't say what it was. He tried talking to her in a loud and demanding voice, calling her 'Kathy' which seemed too familiar and almost rude. His partner had obviously looked elsewhere in the flat and returned to the living room only to go back out of the main door. When he came back it was with a stretcher.

'She's a big girl,' he remarked as they moved her on to it.

'Do you mind locking up after us?' Shaffer was asked. 'You can come in the ambulance, if you want to.'

'I'm not sure where the keys are. I'll see if I can find them and come along later,' he excused himself.

'Right-ho,' the man replied amiably. 'We'll look after her.' When they had strapped her on to the stretcher they had to concentrate on negotiating the angles to get her out of the door and up to the ground floor.

Shaffer followed them outside and watched the ambulance leave. He felt uneasy returning to the basement flat; Miss Simpson's cat had come cautiously into the front room, but darted back out into the kitchen when she saw him. It didn't seem right being there on his own, he decided. But if he couldn't find her keys and simply left, letting the dead lock close after him, then nobody would be able to get back inside without breaking in.

As the keys were nowhere obvious in the room he put his head around the kitchen door. The arrangement of her flat was the same as his and probably identical to the one above that under the roof. It was only on the ground floor that the arrangement was different; there was a small, un-let shop with its own access onto the street.

Like Miss Simpson, Shaffer had a living room and a bedroom at the front of the building, but unlike her he was able to look out over the road and the park beyond. All she had was the view of a small space above which a metal grille let through both light and litter. His flat and hers had the same arrangement of kitchen and a bathroom at the back of the building, although she did, at least, have access to a paved yard where she hung out her washing.

Shaffer was spooked by a sudden, strange sound, but then realised that it was the cat going outside through the flap in the back door. Then he spotted Miss Simpson's handbag on a chair and decided that he ought to take it into the hospital for her. It was open and peering into it he was relieved to see that her keys were inside. Back in the front room he turned off her little gas fire and unplugged the television at the wall. Then he switched off the lights and left.

As Shaffer exited the flat and walked up to the ground floor the lights were turned off on the timer, but then came back on before he could reach out for the switch. He could hear footsteps up on the top floor landing and for a moment it seemed quite natural that somebody was starting to come down the stairs. Then he remembered that the other tenant, Mr Miles, had recently moved out.

He immediately wondered if Miss Simpson hadn't been attacked by an intruder? Whoever it might have been could still be in the building. The footsteps in what should be an empty house caused him to run up to the ground floor and open the front door so that he could make a quick exit.

Standing on the threshold, Shaffer watched nervously for someone to arrive at the first floor landing and start to come down towards him. The man who appeared did not inspire confidence; he was unshaven, his face ravaged by wrinkles and he had wild, unruly hair. He had to be in his sixties and was wiry, with an oddly weasel-like face. He continued to descend, looking relaxed, and Shaffer stayed in the open door, not sure what to do. His heart-rate increased for the second time that evening.

'Hello,' the man said, noticing Shaffer only as he was half way down the final flight. He slowed, but continued. He seemed to take a great deal of thought before he said, 'You must be the teacher?'

'Yes,' came the automatic, if uncertain reply. 'Philip Shaffer.'

'I'm called Terrance Cope,' the man said, coming across the hall and putting out his hand. Shaffer automatically moved forward and shook his hand. He had to let go of the door, allowing it to close. The older man noticed that Shaffer was clutching a handbag and he grinned.

'It's Miss Simpson's,' Shaffer explained hastily, still worried. 'She's had a fall and's gone off to hospital. I said I'd take it in to her.'

'The poor old girl!' he considered. And then, as if he had only just realised it, he said, 'I was only talking to her a couple of hours ago.'

'Really?'

'I'm the new tenant. I've taken the top flat.'

'Oh, okay.'

'Will she be alright?'

'I hope so.'

'So do I. If she dies I might get thrown out, and that would be bad luck.'

'Hopefully it won't come to that. When are you moving in?'

'I settled it all this morning. I've already moved my stuff up there.'

'That was quick.'

'Yeah, well, I don't have much. I've spent my whole life moving around, looking for the right place. I've a funny feeling that this is it, you know?'

'Well, the rent on that flat's reasonable because it gets hot and stuffy up there in the summer,' Shaffer said, calmer now. 'The man who was there before you, Mr Miles, he used to complain about that. And the fact that it gets so cold in winter.'

'Miss Simpson warned me. She's a funny old girl, isn't she?'

'In what way?'

'I don't know. It's a bit like she's not quite in the room with you.'

'She can be a bit vague,' Shaffer admitted, thinking that this man, Cope, was probably worse than their landlady. If Miss Simpson could seem a little vacuous at times, then Cope appeared to be a little simple. The children at school would have said that he 'wasn't all there'.

'Well, give her my best wishes,' he said.

Shaffer stood aside and let the man go out the front door. Then he went up and saw that his bags of schoolbooks were still on the landing. He put them inside his flat and found a carrier bag for the handbag. He didn't want to be seen wandering around the city with it.

It was an hour later that Shaffer arrived and was told to wait in the relatives' room. A doctor appeared after ten minutes and told him that Kathy Simpson was conscious and would be fine. They weren't sure what had caused her collapse, apparently, and she would be staying in for observation.

A nurse then appeared and asked if he had 'Kathy's' keys. He produced the handbag.

'They're inside,' he explained. Again, the use of his landlady's first name by somebody who didn't know her seemed disrespectful.

'I'll take the bag to her, but you'd better keep the keys yourself,' the nurse said. She opened it up and took them out. The doctor took the opportunity to leave.

'She'll need some things brought in, if you don't mind,' explained the nurse. 'Can you get her washing things? You know, toothbrush, flannel, hairbrush etc? And her nightdress. She'll also need a change of clothes for when she's up and about again, and probably her make-up.'

'I'm sorry, but I'm not sure I can. I mean, it's awkward.'

'Why?'

'Well, I'm just a tenant in one of her flats. I happened to find her earlier this evening.'

'Oh, I assumed you were a relative. That's what the paramedics said when they explained you were coming along with her keys.'

'Really?'

'They thought you were her son? You're not? Oh well. Do you know if she has any family we can get in touch with?'

'I'm sorry, I don't.'

'Well, the Friends of the hospital can probably find her most of the things she'll need, but I'm sure she'd prefer her own. Let me go and talk to her.'

Shaffer was left alone again. The nurse's tone made him feel as though he was a disappointment to her, inadequate even. He knew he was making too much of it; probably she was simply disappointed that he was making more work for them. When she returned she was friendlier.

'Kathy asks if you wouldn't mind taking her keys after all. You'll need to feed her cat. And she says she'd be grateful if you were able to bring in her dressing gown from the back of her bedroom door. And there should also be a pink cardigan in her bedroom.'

'I'll see what I can do,' he promised.

Shaffer let himself into Miss Simpson's flat the following morning. He had risen earlier than usual so that he could collect what she needed and take it into the hospital before he carried on to school.

The cat leapt off the old woman's chair when he entered her front room and ran to the kitchen. By the time he had followed it in there the animal was once again out of the cat flap. He looked in a couple of the cupboards near the empty bowl on the floor and found some food for it.

Shaffer went back out and crossed the living room to the bedroom door. If he had felt awkward walking around her flat before, his discomfort increased immeasurably when he entered the woman's bedroom. He felt that he had no right to be in there and he was annoyed that he was under the obligation.

His landlady's room was very feminine, but not in a chintzy way, which surprised him. It was also a little less shabby than her front room. Somehow it seemed to have been frozen in time, in the 1960s, he decided. It was a reflection of the date when the photographs of the young woman on the walls and on the chest of drawers had been taken. The studio portraits that were on display all over the room were of the same model dressed in the high fashion of the time. She wore mini-dresses and was stick-thin, with huge hair and incredibly heavily made-up eyes. In several pictures her mouth was open as if in surprise, as though she had just been told something shocking. Shaffer wondered if they were meant to have been slightly risqué at the time; she was showing a lot of flesh. She also looked oddly androgynous. He couldn't quite understand why the photos were there; the model was so utterly unlike big old Miss Simpson.

And then Shaffer remembered why he was in the room. The dressing gown was on a hanger on the back of the door and he stuffed it into the carrier bag he had brought with him. Behind it was a voluminous green dress with a dainty lace trim at the neck. He wasn't sure if he had seen Miss Simpson wearing it in the past, but it looked very familiar. Then he realised that it was similar to the dress worn by the model in the photograph on the chest of drawers. It was at that moment he understood the significance of the photos.

Shaffer walked over and picked up the photograph. Then he took the time to look more closely at the others on the walls. If they hadn't been in Miss Simpson's bedroom then he would never have thought there was any similarity between the younger and older women. He returned again to the photo on the chest of drawers and it struck him as strange that Miss Simpson would now own a dress that was a gross parody of the model's stylish mini-dress; the one from the sixties would have been made with significantly less material.

'Hello?'

Shaffer jumped as though he was a thief who had been caught in the act.

'Hello?' enquired the voice again. It came from the living room and Shaffer went to the door warily. In the middle of the room was the tenant from the attic rooms.

'What you doing in here?' he interrogated Shaffer good-naturedly.

'Miss Simpson asked me to collect a few things for her. She'll be in hospital for a few days yet.'

'Oh?' the older man said nonchalantly, looking around the room. 'Do they know what happened to her yet? Pooh, it stinks in here; old lady, cheap perfume and something else.'

'Cat?'

'Yeah, that's it.'

Terrance Cope had walked to the window and picked up a book.

'They don't know why she collapsed,' said Shaffer. 'How would you know it's cheap perfume?' he asked, annoyed by the man's assurance. As soon as he had asked the question he recognised its irrelevance.

'I wouldn't know, but it's been sprayed around liberally and you wouldn't do that with the expensive stuff.'

'I suppose not.'

Having read the spine of the book Cope tossed it onto a chair and picked up an ornament which he put back down immediately and with an almost equal disdain.

'I'm paying £250 a month,' he said. 'What does she charge you for your rooms?'

'A little more,' Shaffer replied non-committally, annoyed at the man's attitude. 'I don't have the low ceilings you've got up there under the roof.'

'No, I suppose not. Or the seasonal temperature fluctuations.'

'Quite.'

The man had crossed the room and tried to walk past Shaffer into Miss Simpson's bedroom.

'I was about to leave and lock up.'

'Really? Give me a chance to have a quick nose around, would you. I'd like to see what kind of person my landlady is. For some reason I find her quite fascinating.'

'That's hardly fair.'

'No, but she's not here to know,' he said, and then, once he had disappeared from Shaffer's view he said, 'Blimey.'

Annoyed, Shaffer went back into the bedroom and found the man staring at one of the photos.

'What a looker.'

'I assume it's Miss Simpson when she was younger.'

'That old whale?'

'She's let herself go a bit.'

'I should say. But blimey, she was amazing in her day.'

'Look, I've got to go. Come on out, will you, so I can lock up?'

'Hold on, there're more photos. They're from my era, you know. I don't recognise her, but then, if you remember the sixties, they say, you couldn't've been there.'

The man had moved on to the next photo and was equally appreciative.

'Please, I want to lock up,' Shaffer repeated.

'So, what are you taking her?' he asked. Shaffer knew the question was a ploy so that he could continue to examine the photographs.

'Her dressing gown,' he replied. 'Oh, and a cardigan.'

He saw it draped over the arm of a chair and stuffed it into the bag.

'What else? She hasn't got you taking in her underwear for her?'

'No!'

The man put down the photo and looked around the room. He walked to the chest of drawers.

'Look, I'm going to have to ask you to leave,' Shaffer insisted, but the man ignored him. He opened up the top drawer.

'Either you leave now . . .' Shaffer threatened, but the new tenant laughed, closed the drawer and raised his eyebrows. He waited to see what the threat might be but then, almost instantly, he laughed again and started to walk out.

'I was only interested,' he said, 'just like you.'

The episode upset Shaffer. He was angry at the casual way that the man had behaved in Miss Simpson's flat, and especially in her bedroom. It had been rude and intrusive. Shaffer was also irritated by the suggestion that he was just as interested in looking around as the man had been.

Shaffer told himself that he was annoyed because he was in a position of trust and should not have allowed the new tenant inside the flat. On the other hand, he argued, the man should not have behaved as he had done. It was because he didn't want to have to mention the episode to Miss Simpson that he decided not to go into the hospital that morning. He left the visit until the afternoon, after school. He was able to walk the short distance, and hoped that perhaps he could just drop the clothes off without seeing Miss Simpson.

The hospital corridors were labyrinthine, but he found the women's ward. Going up to the desk he couldn't see any nurses, but Miss Simpson had already noticed him arriving from her bed at the far end. She beckoned him over, but he decided that he had to talk to a member of staff first. When the nurse appeared, looking suspicious, he explained who he was and why he was there. She took the bag from him and walked ahead, over to where Miss Simpson was sitting up in her bed.

'Thank you Mr Shaffer,' his landlady said at once. 'They told me that you found me, and called the ambulance. I don't know what I'd have done without you. And thank you for feeding my cat and collecting my things for me.'

They both watched the nurse disdainfully pull the cardigan out of the bag and smooth out the creases before folding it properly. She then shook out the crumpled dressing gown, shaking her head.

'I've really got nobody else,' Miss Simpson said quietly, making Shaffer's stomach fall in an unpleasant way that he didn't want to analyse.

'Are you going to be all right?' he asked.

'I don't know. You see, the doctors can't say why I collapsed. Modern medicine is all very clever . . .'

'But if they don't know what it is they're treating?'

'They'll get to the bottom of it,' said the nurse abruptly.

'Of course,' said Miss Simpson carefully. She turned to Shaffer but her attention was on the nurse. 'It is a little presumptuous of me to ask you do these things.'

'It's no trouble at all,' he repeated.

'The staff here were concerned when I said you could go into my flat. I assured them that I've known you for twenty years and you're completely trustworthy.'

'Have I been your tenant that long?'

She assured him that he had, and that Mr Miles had been there for longer before his recent departure. Shaffer was aware that they were waiting for the nurse to finish at the bedside cupboard. When she had left Miss Simpson lowered her voice and said:

'Something did happen in my flat, just before I passed out. I mentioned it to the doctors but they said that I was probably going in and out of consciousness; hallucinating. I got the impression it was best not to mention it to them again.'

Shaffer was about to ask if it was something to do with the new tenant, but she surprised him by asking, 'Do you know what it means to see your doppelgänger, Mr Shaffer?'

'No. Why?'

'I read somewhere that it portends death.'

'I wouldn't know. Why do you ask?'

She looked around theatrically and said in a whisper that was as loud as her usual speaking voice, 'Because I think I saw mine just before I passed out. My doppelgänger was there, in my house, just as though I was looking in a mirror.'

'Goodness.'

'So you don't believe me either?'

'I didn't say that.'

To Shaffer's relief another nurse came over and said that she had to take a blood sample. She explained to Shaffer that he was welcome to stay and wait, but he was pleased to use her as an excuse to leave. He assured Miss Simpson that he would check on her cat daily, and hastily retreated. He was relieved to retrace his path through the maze of corridors and told himself that at least Miss Simpson's strange delusion meant that they had kept away from the subject of the new tenant.

Miss Simpson was discharged from hospital on the Saturday afternoon, after three days. It was as his clock chimed two that Shaffer heard the car draw up and looked down from his window to see it parked outside on the double yellow lines. He could see his landlady get out, clutching her handbag. She waited while the driver went to the boot and brought out another small bag for her.

Shaffer had replaced the bottle of milk in Miss Simpson's fridge that morning before taking the keys back to her in the hospital. Ever since his return home he was meant to have been preparing lessons for the following week, but he was feeling restless. He decided to give Miss Simpson a couple of hours to settle in and then would go down and make sure she didn't need anything else.

He listened out for any movement upstairs. For a couple of days he had heard nothing and he wasn't sure if anybody was up there at all. In the past Shaffer had been able to hear Mr Miles moving about in his flat, going from room to room. He was always fairly quiet and Shaffer had found the little sounds vaguely reassuring. He had been listening out for the new tenant, ready to be irritated by the slightest sound, but none had come. As he sat marking homework he strained to hear the slightest sound and was still annoyed that nothing was forthcoming. He found himself being unforgiving of the mistakes that he found in the exercise books before him. After twenty years of teaching it suddenly seemed to him a personal affront that his pupils were still making the same stupid errors; he was unable to see them as a progression of young people who were learning, albeit slowly. He pictured them as an unmoving, dull mass that, if not wilfully ignorant, was at least intent on being that way just to annoy him personally.

Eventually Shaffer got up from his work. He couldn't shake the idea that Terrance Cope was so quiet upstairs because he was waiting for something. Shaffer imagined that he might have been waiting for the return of Miss Simpson and he suddenly felt worried about her. He also felt strangely proprietorial; he didn't want the other tenant to get any credit for being the first to check on her.

He decided that he couldn't rush downstairs in a contest that existed only in his own mind. He would hold his nerve and go down to check on Miss Simpson at four o'clock.

With the self-imposed time-limit he was surprised to find that he did manage to get his work done. He even completed some administrative paperwork that he hadn't intended to tackle for another week. While he sat at his desk he had never once heard a sound from above, or on the stairs, and it was with some satisfaction that he left his flat exactly at four.

'Oh, do come in Mr Shaffer,' said Miss Simpson, opening the door wide for him. 'I've only just got back from the hospital.'

'I thought I'd give you time to get settled before seeing if there was anything I could do for you.'

'That's very thoughtful,' she said. 'Please, sit down.'

Miss Simpson returned to her usual armchair and the cat came in cautiously from the kitchen. She leapt up onto her mistress's lap, all the time staring at Shaffer.

'And thank you for the bottle of milk,' the woman said.

'If you need anything else?'

'I think I should be up to a little shopping tomorrow. But tell me, Mr Shaffer, while I was in hospital you went into my bedroom to get my dressing gown for me?'

'Yes, I did.'

'And did you see the photographs in there?'

'Yes, I did. They're all of you, I assume?'

'I usually keep them out of sight of visitors. It's hard to believe they're of me when you look at what I've become.'

'I don't know . . .' Shaffer said, not wanting to insult her but unable to say anything complimentary.

'I was one of the faces of the 'sixties,' she said with a sad smile. 'I had perfectly proportioned features; symmetrical and unblemished. I still have good skin, you know.'

She was right about that, he had to admit. She was now in her mid-sixties but she didn't have any wrinkles. He wondered if they would necessarily show up on somebody that plump.

'Photographers and designers loved me because I was pretty without being distinctive. They said I was "malleable". The sixties were good to me; I had a wonderful agent and made enough money to buy this house.'

'Did you get to meet anyone famous?'

'Oh yes. Perhaps I'll tell you all about some of them one day. . . .'

He didn't really want to encourage the reminiscences but couldn't help suggesting: 'Don't they say that if you remember the sixties then you weren't really there?' Then he remembered who had recently said that to him.

'Well, there is something in that. . . .'

Shaffer laughed, dutifully, but then saw that she was in earnest:

'At the height of my career I met a man and I fell in love. He was rich, I was successful, and we did a lot of stupid things. We drank a lot, and took too many drugs. And then something happened in about '67 or '68. I can only think that we were taking too much LSD. I lost a whole year of my life. I have no memories of what happened. I simply woke up one morning and I was an addict. I was a mess; my looks and my figure were gone, and they were all I'd really had to offer. My boyfriend and all my other friends had disappeared. I had no career, and no money, but I did have this house, thanks to my agent. I woke up feeling as though

I'm only half in this world; my life has been one great big hangover.'

'I'm sorry. But at least you've some great memories.'

'Not many, but those I have are so desperately important to me . . . and this was what I was getting around to say; one of my photographs appears to be missing.'

'Really?'

'And nobody else has been in my rooms?'

'Well . . .'

Shaffer didn't immediately know how to reply. To mention that Terrance Cope had been in the room would require some explanation, but not to mention it would throw suspicion on himself.

'I don't know what to say,' he stuttered. 'Is there anything else missing?'

'Not that I can see. That photo faced me as I walked into my room. It was a reminder of happy times, though it always reproached me for what I've become.'

'It may be that in the confusion, after I discovered you'd fallen . . .'

'Yes?'

'Well, I did go out with you to the ambulance and probably left the door open,' he offered, wondering why he was making excuses. Why was he not sharing his suspicions?

'Perhaps,' he said, leaping to a possibility. 'I never checked to see if the back door was locked!'

'It certainly was when I returned earlier, and I don't think I'd opened it that morning. Mind you, I don't remember much about it.'

'The morning you collapsed?'

'All I remember is what I told you about in hospital.'

'The doppelgänger?'

'Yes, but I'm not sure what happened, or where I was.'

'You can't remember any other visitors that morning?'

'Not that I can think of.'

Shaffer could see his way forward.

'You'd have talked to the new tenant.'

'What new tenant?'

'Terrance Cope. He's taken the top flat.'

She frowned: 'I don't remember letting it to anyone. As far as I know it's still empty.'

'Apparently not.'

'Is he up there now?'

'I'm not sure.'

She shook her head and he seized the opportunity.

'When I came into your flat to collect your dressing gown he followed me inside, without me knowing. I didn't realise until he was actually in your bedroom.'

For a full half minute she said nothing. Then she decided: 'I think I need to have a talk with this man. Will you go and see if he's up there, and bring him down?'

'I'll go up now.'

'Thank you so much, but please make sure you come too. I'm a little worried. I don't know who he is.'

Shaffer didn't have any expectation that the door would be answered when he knocked upon it. However, he immediately heard footsteps and it opened.

'Mr Cope,' Shaffer began, quite forcefully, and then found that under the man's gaze he was less sure of himself. 'A delicate matter, I'm afraid, but I was talking to Miss Simpson earlier. . . .'

'Is the old girl back?'

'Yes, and she'd like to have a word with you.'

'Oh, okay. When? Now?'

'Ideally. And I said I'd go down with you.'

'What is it? A meeting about house rules?'

'No. You see, she doesn't remember letting the flat to you.'

He frowned, considering Shaffer's words. 'Is she going a bit senile?'

'It might be something to do with the fall. She doesn't remember much about that morning when you arrived.'

'Okay, well, I suppose we ought to go down now and get this sorted.' He seemed entirely relaxed. 'I hope she's not lost the money I gave her,' he laughed as he started down the stairs. 'I paid her two months rent in advance.'

They exchanged no further words, and once outside Miss Simpson's door Terrance Cope rapped on it ineffectually. She called to them to come in.

'Miss Simpson,' Shaffer said from behind the new tenant, 'This is Mr Cope. Do you remember him?'

The woman started to slowly get out of her chair, but then sat back down as her mouth opened in apparent shock. She was unable to speak.

'Hello Miss Simpson,' said Cope. 'You remember me, don't you?'

'I remember you,' she replied.

'The money I paid you should be in that little pot on your mantelpiece.'

She looked past him to Shaffer.

'You see,' she said, pointing. 'My doppelgänger!'

Shaffer laughed. He couldn't help himself. There was the big, fat woman claiming that this skinny, wrinkled man was her double.

'You. . . .' said Cope, troubled. He turned around to Shaffer, frowning: 'Look, I think you'd better leave us, teacher. I think that me and Miss Simpson have things to discuss.'

'Only Miss Simpson can ask me to leave,' Shaffer declared pompously.

'Mr Shaffer,' she said carefully. 'Would you mind leaving us alone?'

'Are you sure?'
'Quite sure.'

He was reluctant to leave. He was angry. He wondered what she had really meant to say when she had called Cope her doppelgänger? He should have realised that she was uneducated. The phrase that the children used, and which he had applied to the new tenant, came back to him; 'not all there'.

When he reached his own door Shaffer opened it but did not go inside. He remained on the landing looking up the next flight of stairs. He had only caught a glimpse of the inside of Cope's rooms and hadn't thought anything about what he had seen at the time. Something had been wrong, though, and he wondered if he would be able to work out what it was if he just put his head inside the door.

Listening out for Cope he could hear something down below, voices perhaps, but they weren't raised. Could he hear crying? He considered listening out and running back down if he was required, but the sounds were not of a quarrel. He was certain that whatever was happening down below, the way was clear for him to go upstairs. On the landing up there the door was slightly ajar. Beyond it he could see that the front room was empty except for a bare bulb that would illuminate only a bare expanse of old, marked carpet.

Shaffer cautiously entered the flat. Through the open door to the kitchen he could see that there was nothing in there either, apart from the basic fittings. There was no more furniture and absolutely nothing that looked personal.

The bedroom door, though, was closed. He stood still and listened. There were no footsteps on the stairs and he reasoned that he could go over to the bedroom door and open it, take a glance inside and be out of the flat before Cope could return. He was unwilling to do so, though. He told himself that good manners and respect for the privacy of another were the reason for not investigating, but he knew that he was afraid of what he would find. His fear was growing, but it was unaccountable. He sensed that there was something inside that room.

The house was not quite silent. There was something going on down below and he wondered if it was, perhaps, of a sexual nature. Whatever it was it was distant and nothing to do with him. He wondered, though, whether the answer might be found beyond the closed door in Cope's flat. Without any hesitation he walked over and opened the bedroom door.

It was empty except for an old sleeping bag on the floor and the framed photograph of Miss Simpson beside it. And then he realised that the sound from down in the depths of the house was rising and could not be ignored. He ran out of the flat and took the stairs three at a time. He got to the very bottom of the building in moments and without knocking he tore open the door. There was Miss Simpson, alone, lying back in her chair, looking weak and somehow smaller. Everything was suddenly silent. She was wrapping her dressing gown around her and she looked like she had been beaten up. Her face was swollen and red and there was blood from her nose and mouth.

'Where is the bastard?' Shaffer demanded, but she would only shake her head.

He strode to the bedroom and pushed open the door but he was not there. Neither was he in the kitchen or bathroom. Miss Simpson was inarticulately trying to ask him to stop.

Shaffer ignored her and went to the phone and immediately started to dial. He heard Miss Simpson say 'No' with greater strength and she waved her hand dismissively. Her voice was rough and tired.

'I have to call the police. And for an ambulance. Look what he's done to you!'

'No,' she repeated, with surprising sternness. 'It's over. And it's for the very best, for both of us.'

'What is?' he demanded, realising that she was not just beaten and swollen, but she looked quite different. It seemed impossible to believe, but her looking smaller was not an illusion; she seemed to be half the size she had once been. And despite the redness and swelling, her skin was different; it was more lined than before.

A voice was distantly demanding from the telephone but he held it away and listened to Miss Simpson as she said: 'He *was* my doppelgänger.'

'You don't mean "doppelganger",' Shaffer was exasperated. 'A doppelgänger is meant to be your double.'

'No, I *do* mean doppelgänger. He was my exact double. Couldn't you see it? At some time in those confused years of drink and drugs I lost a half of myself. He was that other half.'

'That's preposterous!'

'Is it? Take a look at me Mr Shaffer. Sit down and just look.'

He replaced the receiver of the phone and did as he was asked. She then weakly stood up and with some trouble pulled her dressing gown tight around herself. As she did so he suddenly saw Terrance Cope in her features. For a few moments he saw the man, and then the woman, like the illusion of the drawing of a vase between the candlesticks, or the faces of the old and young woman in the same picture. He could see either her, or him, but not both at once. And then it was impossible to see either of them. The woman before him looked as though she had suffered a severe beating, but her features finally had definition; he could see that she was actually quite a handsome woman.

'I am a whole person once more,' she said, smiling. He nodded and she sat carefully back down again.

'What happened to Terrance Cope?'

'I thought you understood? He's here, and so am I. We are one and the same. When I have my strength back I can resume a life that stopped so many years ago.'

The Beautiful Room

Maria said to him, 'I'd be tempted to rent the house for just this one room.'

'It is lovely, yes.'

'The way the light comes in from that window, through the curtains on to the plain walls . . .'

'What is that material?'

'Muslin,' she replied. 'It's not very practical. It would be too bright in here in the mornings but who cares? Look at that view down over the town. I wouldn't mind being woken up early just to stare at that.'

'I suppose it *is* magnificent.'

'You can trace the pattern of the old streets in the shapes made by the rooftops. I could sit here at this windowsill for hours on end, just looking out, contemplating this view, losing myself in it. . . And if I had to return to the real world, I wouldn't mind because I'd be coming back to this beautiful room.'

He frowned, and looked around him, suspicious: 'This house may be a couple of hundred years old, but they've done exactly what they do in brand-new show-homes; it appears big and airy because there's only this bed in the middle. There're no cupboards, no chest of drawers . . . Once you've hung a few pictures, maybe put up some shelves or added a bookcase . . .'

'But we couldn't do that. It would ruin the room. The other bedroom would have to become a dressing room.'

'And what about guests?'

'They'd have to sleep downstairs.'

'We have to be practical, Maria. When we get a new place sorted out I'd be expected to do quite a lot of entertaining. We'd need at least one decent-sized guest bedroom.'

'But the walls are so good in here, so bare and white. The light coming in through those crooked window panes, through the curtains moving in the breeze . . . It's so cool in here although it's baking outside.'

'But what about the winter? Then it'll be bloody cold.'

'Why can't you be positive for once?'

'What do you mean?'

'Well, we've looked at a dozen apartments and houses in the last few days and they've all had their good and bad points. And there've been things about each that we've disagreed on, but for once we've both decided that this is a beautiful room.'

'But we've got to be realistic. It would be cold up here in the winter.'

'There's a fireplace.'

'That small grate wouldn't give out enough heat! And even if we stoked it up in the winter it would mean carrying fuel up two flights of stairs. And every morning it would have to be cleaned out and the ashes taken back down. I can see you starting to complain about that pretty quick.'

'It'd be a small price to pay . . .'

'So you say right now. But when the January winds are blowing and the few hours of daylight only give us a view of driving rain over wet rooftops . . .'

'So which one of the properties that we've looked at so far do you actually like?'

'The ones in the city. They were all far more practical.'

'But I don't want to live in the city.'

'There'd be so much more for you to do there, while I'm out at work.'

'Look, John, I don't know this country and I don't know its language. I'm willing to follow you here, and learn. It's a lot less daunting in a small town like this, and it's so picturesque. It's no further from the vineyards than if we were in the middle of the city. In fact, I think you'd get to work quicker from here.'

'But you agreed to come abroad to support *me* in *my* job. I need to get us somewhere to live and I won't have much time to go looking once I've started work on Monday. I've indulged you. I've shown you these ramshackle old places out in the middle of nowhere and you still won't understand how impractical they are. Let's just go back to the city, rent that apartment with the three bedrooms that I liked with the view towards the airport.'

'You've *indulged* me?'

'Yes. I've shown you the pretty little properties in the countryside that you wanted to see.'

'Just to keep me quiet?'

'I'm the one earning the money and paying for our new life, so I think I should have the casting vote.'

'But I've given up my job to follow you here, to support you.'

'Yes, so support me now . . . We'll go back to the city and sign the contract on the flat that I liked.'

She sat down on the bed. At that moment there came an odd noise from behind her.

'What was that?' he asked.

'It sounded like a bird, in the wall.'

'These'll be solid stone walls. They won't have a cavity.'

She got up from the bed and walked over, putting her hand on to the wall gently, carefully. As she did so there came a scuffling, almost a fluttering, that did remind her of a trapped bird.

'We've got to get it out of there,' she said.

'And how do we do that?'

'I don't know.'

She backed away from the wall, glad that for a few moments they were not talking about where to live. She had known John like this before. She knew that he was worried about his new position with the company and she could see the old behaviour returning. She had hoped that moving to a new country would be a fresh start, but was now considering that she might have made a mistake.

'I'll bang on the wall,' he said. 'If I make a noise just behind where the bird is, it'll drive it back along to wherever it came in.'

'But we don't know *where* it got in,' she replied cautiously.

He walked to the window, opened it wide and hung out. However, he could see only a couple of metres of the stone wall before it turned the corner, out of sight. He came back inside the room.

'It'll probably have come in through the eaves,' he suggested. 'We'd best just leave it.'

'No, not if the poor thing is trapped.'

'It's just a bird.'

'But it might die in there.'

'So what? It's not as though we're taking this house. If it dies and rots it's somebody else's problem.'

'That's not good enough. We must get it out.'

She saw the old anger for a moment, but he controlled himself: 'If we bang on the wall under it, maybe that'll frighten it back up and out.'

With the flat of his hand he slapped the wall low down, under the spot where he thought they had heard the noise. There was a frantic scrabbling around and the sound of debris falling. He repeated the action twice more.

'Stop!' she shouted. 'You're frightening it.'

'That's the idea, isn't it?'

When he did it again there was yet more frenetic activity from within the wall, but it appeared to have divided into two distinct sources either side of him.

She put her hands over her ears: 'I don't like it. I hate to think of it being so scared.'

'*Them* being scared,' he said. 'There's more than one.'

'I'm scared.'

'But they're just birds. They're not mice or rats.'

'I'm not scared *of* them, I'm scared *for* them. I wouldn't care about rats. Maybe there was a nest in there and the babies have fallen out and down into the wall?'

The sound continued, although intermittently.

'No, they're making far too much noise for babies. Now I come to think of it . . . of course . . . this wall is lined. They're in between the lining and the stone wall.'

He slapped it again in confirmation and the sounds resumed, louder than ever and startling him so much that he took a hasty step back.

'I think it's best to leave them,' he decided. 'We'll let them find their own way out. We're just making things worse.'

'I'm sure they seemed higher in the wall that time.'

'I don't know . . .'

He walked forward decisively and slapped the wall hard. Maria felt that the whole room had shifted slightly out of alignment at that moment. The noise suddenly intensified and appeared to be coming from all of the walls all around them.

'Stop it!' she shouted over the din. 'You're upsetting them.'

'Me?' he shouted, and this time the sound did not seem to want to die down. 'Whose idea was it to try and help?'

Now the scuffling, scratching, beating racket seemed not only to be in all the walls, but under the floor and in the ceiling. It was even more insistent, faster, almost enraged. It was as though all the furious activity was actually in the room with them, although there was nothing to be seen.

'We'll leave,' he decided, surprising her by taking her hand and trying to pull her to the door.

She resisted and so he repeated his words, shouting. When she shook her head he threw his hands up and went to the door. It was closed and when he tried to turn the handle it would not move.

'Just go,' she insisted, afraid more of his rising anger than of the birds.

'I can't,' he shouted back over his shoulder, furious with her. 'The bloody thing's stuck.'

'Why won't it open? Is it locked?'

'It's wedged in the frame.'

And all the time the sound seemed to become yet louder. He left the door and strode back to the open window. He looked out over the bright, idyllic view and decided that although there was no way down for them (they were four storeys up), he could at least call for help. He had only to wait for somebody to pass in the street down below. It was marginally quieter with his head out of the window but his anger would not subside. He couldn't see anyone immediately but he shouted for help anyway.

A few moments later Maria tapped him on the shoulder and made him jump.

'What?' he demanded.

'You try the door again; you're stronger. I'll shout for help.'

He was reluctant to turn back to the room but did so. The noise within the walls seemed to be worse still, the ceaseless scuffling and scrabbling of wings and claws. As he walked to the door his mood shifted finally into its old, familiar deep groove. When he turned the handle and pulled at it roughly he found that the door still would not move, so he pulled at it again with all his strength. He had hurt the muscles in his arm and so kicked at the door, which stayed firm.

He looked around and could see Maria hanging out of the window and could hear her shouting, although her actual words were lost to him. He shouted as well, sudden profanities, but they did not make him feel any better. He couldn't believe that anyone else in the building hadn't heard the noise as well.

Maria left the window and came over to him warily. 'There's nobody out there to help,' she shouted, her eyes darting from wall to wall, putting her hands over her ears. 'We've got to do something.'

He looked around and then walked over to where he thought the noise was possibly the most extreme. He kicked the wall with his shoe and decided that the lath-and-plaster really would be quite old and fragile. He turned, and with determination he kicked back at the wall with his heel and felt it give way.

She watched as he kicked again, and twice more, creating a gaping hole. When he bent down and started tugging at the plaster whole sections came away with rotten strips of wood and billows of dust. And then that part of the wall suddenly seemed to explode.

Birds fell and flew out, taking to the air all around them. Large, ungainly, filthy things flapping and churning the dust from rotten wood and plaster in the confined space of the room. Frightened creatures with desperate wings surrounded him. He tried to grab hold of Maria, but she had moved away from his grasp. It was suddenly hot and hard to see or breathe with all the buffeting birds, the feathers and particles of plaster. He instinctively fell to the floor to escape the pandemonium.

He put his hands over his face, head down, trying to filter the air that he strove to breathe calmly and deeply. With his eyes closed against the detritus he relied on hearing and was relieved that almost immediately the sound was reducing. There was still an uproar in one part of the room and he opened his eyes nervously and looked up. He stood carefully, watching as the last few birds were throwing themselves towards the window. In just a few more seconds there was only one left trying to escape. It was almost white, covered in the dust from the debris. It crashed against the frame, recovered in a confusion of wings and falling feathers and then somehow made it out.

It wasn't quite quiet in the room; at least three birds were thrashing about on the floor, exhausted and broken, unable to follow the others to freedom. Around him, the fragments of birds and decades of fine litter thinned out and settled over the room.

He wheeled around in a full circle, wondering what was missing, confused. He remembered the need to escape that had so recently preoccupied him and he tried the door again. It was still stuck fast so he directed all of his force into a kick. A panel split but did not immediately give way. It took several more kicks before he had made a gap wide enough to get through. He was about to leave when he remembered the open window.

He did not know why but he felt compelled to go and look at the view one more time. He peered out, uncertain, and it was unchanged. The street immediately below was empty, and the roofs of the town spread out before him haphazardly. Up in the sky there was a flock of birds that were just distant shapes becoming smaller and smaller. All that he could do was watch, alone in the silent room, as they became so distant that they disappeared into the deep blue sky.